Juliet
Immortal

Juliet Immortal

A NOVEL BY STACEY JAY

EMBER

Text copyright © 2011 by Stacey Jay
Cover photograph copyright © 2011 by Yolande de Kort/Trevillion Images
Title lettering by Dia Calhoun

All rights reserved. Published in the United States by Ember, an imprint
of Random House Children's Books, a division of Random House, Inc.,
New York. Originally published in hardcover in the United States by
Delacorte Press, an imprint of Random House Children's Books,
New York, in 2011.

Ember and the E colophon are registered trademarks of Random House, Inc.

Visit us on the Web! randomhouse.com/teens

Educators and librarians, for a variety of teaching tools,
visit us at randomhouse.com/teachers

The Library of Congress has cataloged the hardcover edition of this work
as follows:
Jay, Stacey.
Juliet immortal / Stacey Jay. — 1st ed.
p. cm.
Summary: For seven hundred years, the souls of Romeo and Juliet have
repeatedly inhabited the bodies of newly deceased people to battle to the
death as sworn enemies, until they meet for the last time as two Southern
California high school students.
ISBN 978-0-385-74016-6 (alk. paper) — ISBN 978-0-375-89893-8 (ebook)
ISBN 978-0-385-90826-9 (glb : alk. paper)
[1. Characters in literature—Fiction. 2. Love—Fiction. 3. Good and evil—Fiction.
4. Revenge—Fiction. 5. Supernatural—Fiction. 6. California, Southern—Fiction.]
I. Title.
PZ7.J344Ju 2011
[Fic]—dc22
2010049563

RL: 6.0

ISBN 978-0-385-74017-3 (trade pbk.)

Printed in the United States of America

10 9 8 7 6 5 4 3 2 1

First Ember Edition 2012

Random House Children's Books supports the First Amendment
and celebrates the right to read.

For Julie Linker,

who always believed in Juliet

SHE WILL FIGHT FOR LIGHT, AND HE FOR DARK,

BATTLING THROUGH THE AGES FOR LOVE'S SWEET SPARK.

WHEREVER TWO SOULS ADORE TRULY, YOU WILL FIND THEM, LO,

THE BRAVE JULIET AND THE WICKED ROMEO.

—MEDIEVAL ITALIAN BALLAD, AUTHOR UNKNOWN

Juliet Immortal

ONE

Tonight, he could have come through the door—the castello is quiet, even the servants asleep in their beds, and Nurse would have let him in—but he chooses the window, climbing through the tangle of night flowers, carrying petals in on his clothes.

He stumbles on a loose stone and falls to the floor, grinning as I rush to meet him.

He is a romantic, a dreamer, and never afraid to play the fool. He is fearless and reckless and brave and I love him for it. *Desperately.* Love for him steals my breath away, makes me feel I am dying and being reborn every time I look into his eyes or run trembling fingers through his brown curls.

I love him for the way he sprawls on the freshly scrubbed

stones, strong legs flexing beneath his hose, as if there is no cause for worry, as if we have not broken every rule and do not face banishment from the only homes we have ever known. I love him for the way he finds my hand, presses it to his smooth cheek, inhaling as if my skin smells sweeter than the petals clinging to his coat. I love him for the way he whispers my name, "Juliet"—a prayer for deliverance, a promise of pleasure, a vow that all this sweet *everything* he is to me will be forever.

Forever and always.

Despite our parents, and our prince, and the blood spilled in the plaza. Despite the fact that we have little money and fewer friends and our once-shining futures are clouded and dim.

"Tell me that tomorrow will never come." He pulls me to the floor beside him, cradling me on his lap, hand curling over my hip in a way it has not before. Heat flares from the tips of his fingers, spreading through me, reminding me I will soon be his wife in every way. Every touch is sanctified. Everything we will do tonight is meant to be, a celebration of the vows we have made and the love that consumes us.

I drop my lips to his. Joy bleeds from his mouth to mine and I sigh the lie into the fire of him. "It will never come."

"Tell me that I will always be here in this room. Alone with you. And that you will always be the most beautiful girl in the world." His hands are at the ties on the back of my dress, slow and patient, slipping each ribbon through its loop with a deliberate flick of his fingers.

No urgent, shame-filled fumbling in the dark for us. He is steady and sure, and every candle shines bright, the better to see the tenderness in his eyes, to be more certain with every passing moment that this is no youthful mistake. This is love. Real. Magnificent. Eternal.

"Always," I whisper, so full of adoration the emotion borders on worship. A part of me feels that to love so is sacrilege, but I do not care. There is nothing in the world but Romeo. For the rest of my life, he is the god at whose feet I will kneel.

His cheek presses to mine, his warm breath in my ear making mine come faster. "Juliet . . . you are . . ."

I am his goddess. I can feel it in the way he shudders as my fingers come to the buttons of his cotehardie and pluck them from their holes, one by one, revealing the thin linen of the shirt beneath.

"You are everything," he says, eyes shining. "Everything."

And I know that I am. I am his moon, and his brightly shining star. I am his life, his heart. I am all that and the answer to every unspoken question, the comfort for every hurt, the companion who will walk beside him from now until the end of our lives, reveling in the bliss of each simple chore done in his name, overflowing with beauty because I am blessed to spend my life with my love.

My love, my love, my love. I could hear the words a thousand times and never grow tired of them. Not ever.

"Forever," I whisper into the hot skin at his neck, sighing as the last tie holding my dress to my body falls away.

TWO

SOLVANG, CALIFORNIA, PRESENT DAY

Dying is easy. It's coming back that hurts like hell.

"Oh . . ." I press my hands to my forehead, where hot, tacky liquid pours from a cut above my eyebrow.

There is a lot of blood this time. Blood on my hands, smeared onto the dashboard, dripping through my fingers onto my jeans, leaving black spots I can see in the dim moonlight shining through the car's glass sunroof. It's messy, frightening, but, amazingly, the accident hasn't killed her. Killed *me*.

Me, now. Her, sometime again soon, depending on how long it takes to ensure the safety of the soul mates I've been sent to protect. Or how long it takes Romeo to convince one lover to sacrifice the other for the boon of eternal life.

It might not be long. He excels at his work.

Either way, Ariel Dragland will wear this shell again. Until then she'll wait in the realm where I've spent most of my eternity, in the mists of forgetting, that place outside of time where the gray stretches on forever.

I've been assured by my contact in the Ambassadors of Light that there are worse places, realms of torment where the boy who bartered our love for immortality will suffer someday. Nurse never uses the word *hell,* but I like to imagine that Romeo will number among hell's inhabitants. Of course, she never mentions heaven, either, or whether I might go there when my work is finished . . . *if* it is ever finished.

There are a lot of things Nurse sees fit not to mention. Including the exact workings of the magic that pulls me from the mist again and again, now more than thirty times in seven centuries. All I know is life comes suddenly. One moment I'm numb and bodiless, the next I'm slipping into another's skin, another's life—the ultimate, dreadful disguise.

I shiver as the memory of Ariel's last moments sweeps through me. I watch her snatch the wheel from the driver's hands before a deadly turn in the road and pull hard to the right, hoping the dive into the ravine will kill them both—her and the boy who hurt her. My eyes flick to the driver's seat. The boy—Dylan—slumps forward, the downward tilt of the car making his limp body curl around the wheel. He is still, not a puff of breath escaping his parted lips.

It seems one half of Ariel's wish has been granted.

I shiver again, but I can't say I'm sorry. I know what he did, can feel Ariel's shame and rage rush inside me as the rest of her life pours in to fill the empty corners in my mind.

Behind my eyes flash images from her eighteen years. I focus, sucking in every detail, taking her memories as my own.

Tiptoe, tiptoe, always on tiptoe. Up the stairs, across the kitchen, down the hall to the room where the crayons live and I can breathe. Where she isn't watching. My mother, with her sad, sad eyes.

Seven, ten, fifteen, eighteen years old and still there is nothing finer than a blank sheet of paper, the white promise that the world can be what I make it. A magical place, an adventurous place, a possible place. Erasers take away the mistakes. Another coat of paint to cover them up. Black and red and purple and blue. Always blue.

Mom sees in blue. She sees the scars she made. I was six. She sees Gemma, my one friend, as a mistake, not a lifeline. She sees my hours alone and feels more powerfully every hour she's wasted. I am the waste, the thing that's eaten her youth alive. Refused to cough up the bones.

Sometimes it seems all I have are bones, scraps, a frame with nothing to fill in the empty space. Sometimes I hate her for it, sometimes I hate myself, sometimes I hate everyone and everything and imagine the world melting the way the grease melted my skin.

Skin and bones. Mom and I are both so thin. Hugs hurt, but there aren't many. Not for years. There are surgeries and pain and bright lights and then days trapped in the house with the shades drawn on our shame. There is the darkness inside, that baleful intruder that comes just when I dare to believe I might one day be whole.

There is school and the misery of being a person unseen, the jealousy that I can't be wild and beautiful like Gemma, that I am always an audience, never a player. There is the frustration of words that won't come out of my mouth no matter how hard I try. A D in public speaking. The one step up to the podium is an impossible climb.

Everest. Higher. I hate Mr. Stark for his frustrated sighs, hate the class for their muffled laughter. I want to hurt them, to show them how it feels to have your insides twisted into knots you can't unravel.

Gemma doesn't care, tells me to get over it, stops sharing her adventures, closes the window into her vibrant world, forgets to pick me up for school at least twice a week. I'm losing everything. My only friend, my perfect GPA, my mind. How much longer can I live like this? Can I make it four more years, sleeping in that room, commuting to the nursing college in Santa Barbara, learning to live with more sickness and pain, when all I want to do is escape?

But then . . . there is him. His smile, his voice singing so strong, cutting through the curtains where I hide with my paints, curling into my ear, spinning dreams I want to come true.

They don't.

It's a joke.

We're kissing—slow, perfect kisses that make my heart race—when the text comes, asking if he's taken the Freak's virginity yet. He tries to hide the phone, but I see it. I start to cry, even though I'm not sad. I'm angry, so angry. He offers me fifty dollars—a piece of the bet—if I let him have what he's come for. I explode. I try to run from the car, but he grabs my hand, squeezing as he pulls back onto the road, telling me to "chill the hell out," promising to take me to a better place.

But there is no better place. I know that by now. There are only mirrors reflecting disappointment, shattering it in a million different directions, filling the world until there is no way out. It will always be this way. Always, even when I finally leave the house on El Camino Road.

The road, the road is . . . impossible. I won't let him drive it a second longer. I won't let him steer through the hole in the mountain down to the beach, where the cold, dark ocean waits like a nightmare creeping. I won't let him.

Not now. Not ever again.

My eyes fly open, my body humming with adrenaline, drowning in the fear and anger and hopelessness Ariel felt as the car burst through the guardrail and flew over the edge into the ravine.

They fell so fast—distance consumed by time in one awful gulp. She barely had time to scream before the car made impact and her head smashed against the passenger's window, hard enough to burst the skin at her temple and knock her unconscious, but not hard enough to kill.

Despite the damage, she will live . . . eventually. Whether she likes it or not.

"You will. You'll see," I say aloud, though I know she can't hear me.

I'll do something to improve her life before she returns to it, make it bearable, if not beautiful. The Ambassadors encourage their converts to spread love and light, but even if they didn't, I couldn't have resisted Ariel. She's just so . . . sad. I want to help her, keep her safe from the darkness, from the Mercenaries who prey on people like her.

Especially *one* Mercenary, the one who does his best to make my borrowed lives as miserable as he made the original.

Somewhere out there, in the cool spring night, *he* is finding a body too, summoned by the same energy that pulled me from the mist. In some long-forgotten cemetery, Romeo is seeking a corpse old enough not to be recognized in this small town, finding a place his soul can hide. The Mercenaries of the Apocalypse live inside the dead, restoring rotted flesh to its former glory so long as they lurk within.

For a moment, I wonder what Romeo will look like this

time, then decide it doesn't matter. Old or young, fat or thin, black, white, or green—the enemy is always the enemy.

"Unhh, awww." The groan comes from beside me, from the boy who was driving the car.

I wrinkle my nose, disappointment that he's alive leaving a bad taste in my mouth. As an Ambassador of Light I'm supposed to be above such feelings. But I am not, never have been—not when I was a living girl, and not as an immortal warrior for love.

Love. Sometimes the thought of it leaves a bad taste in my mouth too.

Still, it's for the best. It will be easier to avoid police scrutiny if we both emerge from this car alive. And though I might feel the world would be a safer place without Dylan, Ambassadors aren't allowed to kill human beings . . . or anything else. Murder feeds the cause of the Mercenaries. I am forbidden to take a life, even the one I have every justification to end.

"But it is never *right* to do *wrong*," I whisper, even as I silently wish Dylan a few broken bones or—at the very least—a generous helping of pain. I might be forbidden my revenge, but at least Ariel can have a bit of hers.

"Unh . . ." Dylan moans again, drawing my attention to his face—his full lips, dark eyelashes, and brown hair that waves softly over his forehead. The hair is matted to his skin on one side and a nasty bruise is forming on his cheekbone, but there's no denying he's beautiful. And a very bad man in the making.

There's something cruel in the set of his features—even when he's unconscious—but I can't fault Ariel for not seeing beyond the appealing facade. It doesn't seem like that long ago that I was the same way—young and naïve and ready to believe in pretty boys and love that lasts forever.

But I learned my lesson. For me, only vengeance is eternal.

The need to punish *his* betrayal keeps me fighting. I am on the side of good, working to prevent the Mercenaries of the Apocalypse from destroying what beauty and goodness remains in humankind. Of all the duties an Ambassador can have, protecting soul mates and preserving the future of romantic love is one of the most well-respected, and that's . . . nice. But ruining *his* existence, knowing he'll go back to the people who rule him without a soul to show for his work, is better. Much, much better.

It helps banish pain to the edge of my awareness as I set about finding a way out of the car. Unfortunately, it won't be an easy escape. The front end is smashed, the door on the passenger's side can't be opened, and the electric buttons that lower the windows make a sick buzzing sound when I tug them with my fingers.

Buttons. They're similar to the ones I used in my last body in . . . 1998? 1999? The years blur together, but still, the buttons and the relatively new look of the car's interior make me wonder what time I'm in. I close my eyes, pawing through Ariel's memories.

Less than fifteen years have passed since my last shift. Troubling . . .

I rarely come back to the earth more than once every *fifty* years. Despite the love songs humankind churns out like butter, true lovers don't come together every day. As the Mercenaries ply their trade—destroying hope, crushing compassion, inciting war and violence—soul-mated pairs are becoming an endangered species.

Real love has little to do with falling. It's a climb up the rocky face of a mountain, hard work, and most people are too selfish or scared to bother. Very few reach the critical point in their relationship that summons the attention of the light and the dark, that place where they will make a commitment to love no matter what obstacles—or temptations—appear in their path.

And there are others like Romeo and me, two halves of the same whole drafted to opposing sides. The others have their turns in the rotation, I suppose, though I've never met any on earth, or in the places outside of time. I'm not aware of other souls in the mist. There is only the endless gray and wisps of consciousness I can't quite hold on to.

Romeo, however, is allowed to remain on earth, dwelling in the bodies of the dead. Nurse insists the process is unpleasant, but at least he has *some* version of a life.

I am always alone, pretending to be someone else or lost in a vast emptiness. I miss life. I miss conversation and laughter and shared joy and hurt. I miss dancing and painting. I miss waking up to a day with no evil in it—at least, none that I can see. Most of all, I miss my innocence, my faith that those seeking happiness will find it. I make a decent show of being good, but in reality I'm too bitter to be an admirable Ambassador, too young to feel so hopeless.

I've seen centuries pass, but I died when I was fourteen and have spent less than twenty conscious years on earth. *He,* on the other hand, continues to live and learn, to stave off madness with open ears and long looks into human eyes. He has seven hundred years of skill and experience, and it helps him get closer to destroying me every single time.

Maybe this time. There's something . . . *off* about this shift.

It isn't just that it's come too soon. It's . . . something else . . . something that makes the white-blond hairs on my left arm stand on end.

"Unhh . . . damn . . ." Dylan's eyes flutter open.

Even in the moonlight shining through the ceiling they look dark, peculiar. There's something strange about this boy, something warped inside him. I'm not surprised that he played a cruel trick on Ariel, but I'm curious to see what he'll do next. How will he deal with the fact that she nearly killed them both?

"Ariel?" he asks, his voice slurred. "Are you okay?"

"Ye—yes, I think so." Maybe he doesn't remember how the car crashed? If so, I won't be helping him with his recall. I keep my expression carefully blank. "Are you okay?"

"I think I'm fine. I . . . think I might be . . ." His words fade as he leans closer. He's staring at me. I can feel it, though his chin is tipped down, creating hollows the light through the roof can't touch.

The roof! I look up, and a sigh of relief escapes my lips. It's made of glass! Thank goodness. Getting out of this car seems like a better idea with every passing second. If Dylan is this disturbing at eighteen, he'll be a serial killer by the time he's twenty.

"We'll be fine. We just need to get out." I lift blood-slicked fingers to pry at the latch, ignoring Dylan when he leans even closer.

The sunroof is manually operated. I see that the glass panel can pop out, but the mechanism gives me a bit of trouble. Still, I'll get it open and there will be plenty of room for us to fit through the hole. Me first, of course.

"I'm sorry, could I—" He exhales, his breath hot on my neck. I fight the urge to shudder. "Could I ask you something?"

He wants to talk. Lovely.

I sigh. "Sure." I pull on the hinges, then realize I should have been pushing and sigh again.

"Has anyone ever told you your hair looks silver in the moonlight?"

I glance in the rearview mirror. My new hair does look silver, like something from a fairy tale. And the rest of what I can see of myself is equally haunting–shocking, really.

Why does Ariel think herself so repulsive? Huge blue eyes dominate my new face, dwarfing my small nose and thin lips. The scars on my cheek and jaw are visible, but they aren't as terrible as Ariel thinks. The face looking back at me is attractive, compelling. There's something about it that makes you want to look twice.

So I do, staring a little too long, giving myself away.

Dylan laughs, his lips suddenly far too close to mine. "But soft, what light through yonder window breaks?"

No. It can't be. We've never– *He's* never–

"Did you miss me, love?" He kisses me on the cheek, a rough, playful kiss that leaves a bit of wet behind.

Dylan *has* died after all. And Romeo has found a corpse. It's my last thought before his hands are around my throat.

THREE

I gasp for air as he shoves me back against the door.

My head hits the window–hard–sending pain jabbing into
the backs of my eyes. He's on top of me in seconds, straddling
my waist, pinning me to the seat. My hands fly to my throat,
prying at his fingers, but it isn't easy, not as easy as it should be,
as it *would* be, if I'd had time to heal all the life-threatening
damage and connect with my new form.

In the first few hours after a shift, before my supernatural
strength returns, I'm often weak. But that's never worried me.
Even with his uncanny ability to hunt me down, I've never run
into Romeo until at least a day after taking up residence in a
new body. It takes that long to discover which souls I've been

sent to protect, to contact Nurse in a mirror's smooth reflection and receive my instructions from the Ambassadors.

Then it's simply a matter of waiting and staying alert. Romeo always makes an appearance. Invariably, he's summoned to the same place and time as I, to try to win the same souls over to his dark cause. He'll do his best to persuade one soul mate to sacrifice his or her true love to the powers of hate, destruction, and chaos and become an immortal Mercenary—just as *he* did the night after we consummated our wedding vows.

I still wonder what they offered him. What treat they dangled, and how long it took for him to realize their promises were lies, that he'd shoved a knife through my heart for nothing. I know he hasn't received what he was promised. I've seen the flicker of regret in his eyes.

Our new eyes meet, and for a moment, I think I see it again, just before he brings his nose to my lips and inhales. "Your breath always smells the same. So sweet."

"Get off me," I warn, willing down a wave of nausea. It's impossible to believe I once dreamt of spending my life *worshipping* this monster.

Now I dream about killing him so I never have to feel anything ever again.

"I don't think so. I'd rather stay as I am. This new body is . . . delicious." He laughs as he fights to keep his fingers around my throat, to keep choking the life out of Ariel. If he kills her, he'll kill us both, and he knows it. But he doesn't care about collateral damage. To him a two-for-one murder will be a special treat. "Seems a shame to finish you so quickly."

"You're not going to finish me."

He won't. It can't end here. I want to see him fail another

time, another hundred times. Adrenaline dumps into my bloodstream, making my heart race, giving me the strength I need to pry his fingers apart and smash the heel of my hand into his face.

"Mmph." He groans as I follow the first blow with a punch in the stomach, but I can tell he isn't hurt. At least, not badly enough. We're too close for me to put any power behind my movement, even if I were in top form.

I have to get out.

Shoving him to one side, I lunge for the handle of the roof, but he grabs my arm and twists it behind my back. "Bastard!" I scream, surprised at how much it hurts.

"Calling names. Shame. Aren't we beyond that, sweetness?" With a grunt, he shoves me into the backseat, his knee sharp against my spine. I land on my stomach with my arm still wrenched behind me. Romeo gives my arm another jerk, making me howl.

No. Not like this, not tonight. On impulse, I reach around with my free hand and grab the most sensitive bits of any man—past or present—and twist them. Hard.

Romeo growls and knocks my hand away, then snatches my other wrist and jerks it behind me as well. "I'm going to rip your arms off and eat them. While you watch!" He hauls at my limbs until my muscles and joints scream and things needed to hold my body together threaten to snap.

He's going to do it, actually *rip* my arms from my body with his bare hands.

"Is that a taste you acquired in hell?" I ask, my voice high and thin as I fight to focus through the pain, praying that my words will distract him long enough for me to catch a breath, to think of some way *out.*

"I've never been to hell. You know that, love." His grip eases the slightest bit. "I've found eternity enjoyable thus far. Why don't we go find a soul for you to steal, and you can learn about life as a Mercenary for yourself?" He leans closer, his cheek pressing tight to mine. "I know you've been dying to be together again, though it makes you feel naughty that I get under that lovely skin."

"You're mad."

"Am I?" The torture in my arms is suddenly gone, replaced by the greater torment of Romeo's lips at my neck, his hands smoothing over my hips. The part of me that recalls how his touch used to make me feel—beautiful and beloved—hums, the hint of bliss making my sick stomach even sicker.

"Get off me!"

"O, she doth teach the torches to burn bright," he whispers, helping cool the faint shimmer of need.

That *horrible* play. That contemptible, *lying* play he helped Shakespeare pen all those hundreds of years ago when he first twisted our story to fit his agenda. It worked far too well. Shakespeare's enduring tragedy did its part to further the goals of the Mercenaries—glamorizing death, making dying for love seem the most noble act of all, though nothing could be further from the truth. Taking an innocent life—in a misguided attempt to prove love or for any other reason—is a useless waste.

But what about a not-so-innocent life? Why can't I *kill* this abomination? Why is my *easily* justified vengeance forbidden by the Ambassadors? Killing me was bad enough; that Romeo made certain the world has remembered a false version of our tragedy for *hundreds* of years adds heinous insult to unforgivable injury.

But he knows that. The monster.

Time to make use of my free arms.

"It seems she hangs upon the cheek of night like a—"

Romeo's words end in a groan as I shift my legs, leveraging my feet against the seat and shoving us both backward. His spine collides with the dash with a satisfying thud. I'm getting stronger, perhaps strong enough to bypass figuring out how to work the roof's latch altogether.

I reach back, grab handfuls of Romeo's sweater as I bend double and shift my feet again, pushing against the center console, driving his skull into the rectangle of glass above our heads. The roof fractures with a crack that's muffled by the crunch of bone.

My heart lurches as I drop Romeo, leaving him sprawled across the driver's seat, and turn my attention to the broken glass. I haven't killed him—he's still conscious and moaning—but I've hurt him more than I intended. The smell of fresh blood spilling onto the upholstery makes bile rise in my throat as I punch through the roof, scattering blunt pieces of glass before pulling myself through the hole I've made. By the time I make it out onto the hood and down to the ground below, I'm trembling.

But I don't pause to look at Romeo's new face through the driver's window before turning and scrambling up the side of the ravine. Romeo can heal even greater damage than I can; it's one of the Mercenaries' greatest gifts. He brings dead tissue back to life, for god's sake. The only hope I'd have of killing him—were I allowed to do so—would be to rip his heart from his chest, and then he might *still* be able to escape to another dead body. Head trauma is nothing. By the time I reach the road above, he'll be whole, free of the car, and hot on my heels.

My already short nails break and my palms tear as I claw

my way up the side of the ravine, grabbing onto whatever my hands happen upon in the dark. The moon slips behind a cloud, and I'm climbing blind, the blackness thick and close, the heavy smell of an impending storm filling the air, making the great outdoors seem not much better than the wreck I've just escaped.

The smothering night threatens to steal what remains of my composure. I never did enjoy small, tight places. I like them even less after waking in a crypt and lying surrounded by stone for over a day before Romeo and his knife came to fetch me.

I suck in a deep breath. The sickeningly sweet smell of milkweed rushes into my lungs. It makes me cough, but the chill air is a mercy. I'm not trapped. I'm free and putting Romeo behind me with every upward lurch.

A car rushes past on the road above, close enough to vibrate in my ears. I'm nearly there! I'll wave someone down and ask for a ride back to Ariel's house. Hitchhiking has always held its dangers, but that hasn't broken me of the habit. Despite the awful things I've seen, I believe there are decent people in the world. Or people better than the boy cursing me as he crawls from the wreck below. At least most of those driving by won't want to cut off my arms and eat them. While I watch.

I push the image of Romeo's grinning mouth—flesh in his teeth, blood dripping down his chin—from my mind. No matter what body I inhabit, my vivid imagination always comes back to haunt me.

"I see you, love . . . all that silver hair." The words are soft grunts, but I can hear them. He's closing in, sending rocks skittering down the ravine in his wake.

A rusted taste floods into my mouth, and I force my thin arms and legs to move faster. Ariel could use some meat on her bones. And muscle. And food in her belly. Why didn't she eat more before she left the house? My stomach cramps and my arms shake with effort. Healing the worst of Ariel's wounds from the crash and fighting Romeo are taking their toll.

"Slow down, sweetness. Let me get my hands around your ankle and we'll see if you can fly." He laughs, but the sound is strained. He's having trouble now that he's reached the portion of the ravine that rises straight up without a slant.

I'm going to make it to the road first. Now I just have to find someone willing to stop and help. I'm a harmless-looking young girl with one side of her head covered in blood. Chances are good that I'll—

"Wait!" I scream, dragging myself up and over onto the edge of the road just as a truck zooms past. I jump to my feet and vault over the damaged guardrail, waving my arms, but the pickup doesn't slow.

Taillights fade into the distance, leaving laughter floating on the cold wind rushing through the canyon. Most likely kids from school heading to the beach party where Dylan planned to take Ariel. I could run after them, hope they come to a stop sign sooner or later or—

Something large crashes down into the ravine, but it isn't Romeo. A rock, maybe? An animal? Definitely not him. I can hear his breath coming in swift pants as he continues to labor up the side, intent on reaching me before I find help.

I spin in the opposite direction from where the truck disappeared and run. Romeo's new body is big, strong, and has longer legs than mine. I can't afford to head to the beach. According to Ariel's memories, the road in that direction is deserted. I'll be better off running toward civilization and a chance of finding someone out at ten o'clock on a school night. It's mid-March, not prime wine-tasting or tourist season, and the nearest town, the village of Los Olivos, is quiet this time of year. But surely a restaurant or something will be open.

"The world is a vampire, sent to drain . . .," Romeo is singing, bits of a song that was popular the last time we were on earth. It's a disturbing song about vampires and rats, and the way Romeo sings it makes it even more terrifying, a choir-boy confessing a murder. He always has a lovely voice, no matter what body he inhabits. Just as I always have sweet breath. Evidently.

I run faster, feet pounding along the broken asphalt, breath crystalline in the air. Romeo is out of the ravine and on the move. He continues to sing as he runs, filling the night with his haunting voice, making me feel as if he's already caught me with every note that pricks at my ears.

But he hasn't. He won't.

I see the lights of the town ahead. I'm going to make it. It's a mile, at most. I'll head for the first open business and throw myself into a crowd. Romeo won't attack me in front of witnesses. Despite his strength, bars *can* hold him, and the western lawmen of recent centuries haven't hesitated to punish men for abusing their women. Not like in the earlier days, when it was legal for a man to beat his wife, legal for him to throw her into the streets to starve, legal for him to—

"O dear mistress mine, mistress mine, your eyes like stars, your lips like wine," he sings, switching to a song from our childhood, in English instead of Italian.

We always speak in the language of the new bodies, assimilating speech as fully as memories, but I can recall the way

{21}

the words sounded in our native tongue. Back when he sang beneath my window, when the sound of his voice filled me with joy and expectation.

Now there is nothing but terror.

He's going to catch me. He's too fast. I'm tired, weak, not–

The headlights spin onto the road from a dozen feet ahead, hope in the darkness.

I race forward, screaming for help, waving my arms, willing the person inside the vehicle to hear me, see me, and *stop* before it's too late. One second passes . . . then two . . . three; the car is pulling away and taking hope with it when suddenly, the brake lights burn red.

With a sob of relief, I sprint the remaining distance to the car, throw open the passenger door, and fling myself inside without bothering to see who's behind the wheel. The identity of the driver is immaterial.

The devil himself would be preferable company.

FOUR

"What the he–"

"Hurry! Drive!" I slam the door shut behind me, cutting off the driver, a boy not much older than Ariel, from what I can see in the darkness. I quickly take in tanned skin, wavy hair to his shoulders, a thick necklace, and a faded T-shirt hugging arms too thin to belong to a grown man.

Good. Better to get help from someone younger, less likely to ask questions.

"Please drive. Anywhere. Just go!" I fumble for the locks, smash down the button on the passenger's door, then reach over to hit the boy's lock, my shoulder brushing his as I fall back into my seat. "Please!"

We have to go. Locks won't deter Romeo for long. Neither will one witness, not if he thinks he can get away with murder. I've seen him kill before—men, women, children, anyone who gets in his way. He has no moral objections, no compassion or pity.

"Where did you come from?" the boy asks, eyes narrowing as he leans closer. "Is that blood? Are you ok–"

"Please drive! Please!" I risk a glance over my shoulder, barely swallowing a scream when I see Romeo sprinting toward the car, eating up the road with powerful strides of his long legs, mad anticipation spreading across his face. He's going to kill this boy, just for fun, and it will be my fault.

And then it will be my turn to die. Unless we move. Now.

I dive for the driver's seat, straight into the boy's lap, tangling my legs with his as I seek the gas pedal with frantic feet. His arms close around me in surprise, seconds before his foot knocks mine away from the floorboard.

"You can't–"

"Drive! Hurry, we–"

My words turn to a sound of triumph as my foot finds the accelerator. The car leaps forward a few feet, only to screech to a stop when the boy pounds the brake, summoning an angry groan from the engine.

"We can't drive like this, *chica*!" His hands span my waist as he tries to shift me into the passenger's seat while pulling my foot away from the gas.

I would usually be strong enough to overpower an average person even at this early point in the shift, but not after the struggle with Romeo and the climb up the ravine. I need time to refuel. Time I won't have if this boy doesn't stop fighting me.

"You're going to kill us!" he yells.

"No, *my date's* going to kill us!" I yell just as Romeo's hands slam down on the trunk. The thump makes us jump in our shared seat, twin shouts of surprise bursting from our lips.

My eyes flick to the rearview mirror in time to catch Romeo's grin in the reflection. And then he's gone, reappearing seconds later at the driver's window, his face hovering inches from the glass. My heart surges into my throat as I slide lower in the boy's lap, pounding the floor with my feet, searching for the gas. Romeo jerks on the door hard enough to make the metal groan before he realizes it's locked. He pulls his fist back—preparing to strike—and the boy finally joins me in the search for the accelerator.

He finds it just in time.

"¡Ay mierda!" he shouts as the car zips forward and Romeo's fist collides with the rear window instead of the front. Glass shatters, sending fragments tinkling into the backseat and a cold wind whipping through the car as we gain speed down the empty road.

My hair flies into my face. I trap it with one hand, hoping the boy can see well enough to steer, my entire body buzzing from the narrowness of our escape.

"Jesus!" He sucks in a deep breath, his left hand tightening on the wheel. "What the hell was that?"

"Sorry. I'm so sorry, I–"

"You could've told me your boyfriend was *insane.*" He glares into the side mirror, where Romeo is becoming a speck in the darkness. The boy looks older with anger tightening his face, darker, almost . . . dangerous. But the arm around my waist is still gentle, careful, as if he's very aware me.

"He's not my boyfriend." I'm suddenly very aware of him,

as well, of his front warming my back, his thighs shifting beneath mine. I clear my throat, blushing for the first time in so long the strangeness of hot cheeks makes me blink.

And cough. And clear my throat again.

"You okay?" His fingers curl, digging into my waist. The warmth spreads, thickens, and something sparks inside me, a hint of longing even stranger than the blush.

I scowl. Blushing is one thing, but longing I can't afford. This is Ariel's life, not mine. Longing is futile, even if I had time to spend on pretty boys with dark eyes and gentle hands. Which I don't.

"I'm fine." I lean to the right, carefully untangling my legs as I fall into the passenger's seat, ignoring the strange clenching in my chest.

The boy keeps his gaze on the road, only glancing over when I've clicked on my seat belt. "So he's not your boyfriend."

"No."

"*Ex*-boyfriend?"

"Just a bad date."

He snorts, shoots me a vaguely amused look. "Yeah. I'd say." He shakes his head, amusement fading. "That freak is *crazy*. He probably just broke half the bones in his hand. Did he do that to your head?"

My fingers brush my temple. The wound has nearly healed, but blood still glues my hair to the side of my head and clings—sticky and damp—to my face. "No. We had a car accident, but I'll be fine."

I make a mental note to find someplace to clean up before I go home. Otherwise, Ariel's mom will certainly take me to the hospital where she works, and the last place I want to spend the night is the ER.

"How bad an accident? You need to go to the hospital?"

"No. Really. I hate hospitals."

"Then what about the cops? I know good cops, not the kind who don't listen," the boy says. "My brother works for the sheriff's department in Solvang. He's not on duty, but I can call him. I know he'd—"

"No. I'm fine. It was just a little accident, a little fight."

"A *little* accident and a *little* fight." He grunts. "Your head is covered in blood and you were running from that guy like he was carrying a chain saw. Not to call you out or anything—"

"Okay, it was a big fight. But I don't want to go to the police."

"Why not?" The boy divides his attention between the road and the passenger's seat as he takes the right turn into Los Olivos.

By the light of antique streetlamps, his features come into clearer view—brown eyes a shade paler than his skin, a strong, square jaw, and full lips that would make any woman jealous. If it weren't for the imperfection of his nose—which veers slightly to the left, as if it's been broken and reset poorly—he would be breathtaking.

Would be?

All right. He *is* breathtaking. I stare at him and can't seem to look away, but it's not because he's beautiful. It's something more, something in his eyes, a spark so familiar it's almost as if . . . as if I *know* him.

"You don't have to be scared," he says, and I shiver because I would *swear* I've heard him say the same thing before. *Swear it,* though I know it's impossible. "You hear me?"

"I hear you." I swallow, pushing the strange feeling away. He's familiar because he looks like the boys I grew up with—olive skin, sparkling eyes, and lips sculptors would swoon over. This is just a nasty case of déjà vu. Nothing more. "I'm not scared. I wasn't scared before."

"Then why were you running?"

"I told you." I lift one shoulder and let it drop. "It was a bad date."

"He smashed his hand *through a window*," the boy says. "That's not a bad date, that's—"

"Please, I'll pay for the window, I just—"

"I don't care about the window!" he says, slamming his palm on the steering wheel. "I care about you!"

"You don't even *know* me!" My voice hits a sharp note that rings in the silence that follows.

The boy's jaw clenches, making a muscle there twitch. I fight the urge to still it with a finger to his cheek, ignoring the crazy feeling that I've done the same thing before, the certainty that I already know how scratchy-soft his skin will feel.

This is ridiculous. I don't have time to be distracted by this . . . *boy*.

"You're right," I say, determined to put an end to the conversation. "Dylan is crazy, and at *that* moment, he might have hurt me." *And you.* "You helped me out. A lot."

He pulls to a stop at the last intersection in town, waiting for the red light to turn green, scowling at the empty road ahead.

"I just don't *need* to go to the hospital, and I don't *want* to go to the police. It has nothing to do with being afraid of anybody. I just . . . don't like police stations."

"Why? You got a criminal record or something?" he asks.

I barely resist the urge to roll my eyes. "Yes. I'm a car-jacker. Give me all your money and I'll consider sparing your life."

A surprised burst of laughter fills the car. The boy smiles, revealing crooked teeth that match his nose, making a crooked kind of sense on his face. "Then this really isn't your lucky night, *chica*. I just spent my last ten bucks on gas." I'm aware of an ache in my jaw, but it takes a moment to realize it's inspired by my own smile. "All I've got is a coupon for a car wash and half a bottle of Mountain Dew that's been in the backseat a few days."

"Well," I say, keeping my tone light. "I *am* thirsty. . . ."

"I already drank out of the bottle. It has my germs."

"Wouldn't want to catch those." I smile again, hoping we've left the subject of the police behind as he pulls through the intersection. "Guess I'll have to settle for a ride home." I take a moment to visualize the exact location of Ariel's house in my mind. "I live in Solvang, behind the Natural Foods. On El Camino."

"The road named after a road."

"You know where it is?"

"Yeah. I know. And I'll take you there, even though you know where *I* think you should go."

"I do. I . . . Thanks."

"You're welcome." He accelerates past a line of antebellum houses with lights burning on cozy porches, driving in a silence that gets more comfortable as we leave Los Olivos behind. "That store by your house has really good *pan*."

"Really?"

"Yeah. I'll bring you some next time I go," he says. "I only moved in with my brother a few days ago, but my sister-in-law already sent me to that store twice. The normal milk on our side of town isn't good enough for my niece. She has to have the organic, hormone-free, milked-by-free-range-farmers milk."

His easy assumption that we'll be friends, the warmth in his voice when he talks about his family, make me wonder how I could have thought he was dangerous—even for a moment.

He's actually sweet in a bossy kind of way. Ariel could use someone like him in her life. She and Gemma, her only friend, have been growing apart. It would be good for her to have someone else to turn to when she reclaims her body, even if her memories of meeting the boy with the crooked smile will be different from mine.

None of the bodies I inhabit recall anything about me, Romeo, or the work of the Ambassadors and Mercenaries. Their minds take the memories I make, modify them, and claim them as their own, keeping our secrets from the world.

"So do you have a name, *rubia*?" the boy asks, taking a left onto a narrow country highway.

I've spent shifts in people who spoke Spanish, but the ability left me when I was summoned back to the mist. Still, I can guess he's called me "blondie." A nickname. I think that will please Ariel. She's never had a nickname before—at least, not one she liked.

"Ariel. What about you?"

"Ben." He smiles. "Ariel, like the mermaid."

"Or the fairy in *The Tempest*."

He winces. "Stick with mermaid. I hate Shakespeare."

"Me too." I surprise myself with a laugh. "I mean, *hate* may be the wrong word, but I don't like the tragedies. Especially the love stories."

"I can barely understand what the people are saying." Ben shrugs. "But some of Shakespeare's sonnets are cool. We had to read them last year in Remedial Junior English for Dumb Kids."

"You don't seem dumb."

"Thanks," he says. "It was the word *remedial,* right? Made me sound smart?"

"It was more that you knew *The Tempest* was by Shakespeare," I say, "but remedial *is* a fancy word."

He laughs softly. "I like that."

"Like what?"

"The way you say *fancy.*"

"Thanks." I know I should feel uncomfortable with the hint of affection in his voice, but I don't. There's just something . . . natural about being with Ben.

"So which turn is it? I've never been this way in the dark." He slows as we pass the church at the edge of town and a playground dotted with plastic turrets.

The Castle Playground. Ariel played there when she was a kid, but her mother made her wait until sunset to walk from their house to the maze of slides and swings. She said she was worried about the sun hurting Ariel's raw skin, but she just wanted to avoid the busiest time at the park. Melanie didn't like it when the other kids stared and asked questions. It made her lips press into a thin line, made her jerk Ariel away from the others, tug her down the street, back to the house with the closed shades.

"It's the second street on the left," I say, finding it harder to swallow. I'm not looking forward to meeting Ariel's mother, not if the memories I have are reliable.

I comfort myself with the assurance that memories are always colored by perception. What Ariel remembers about her life will have been informed by her feelings and fears as much as by facts. There's a chance Melanie Dragland isn't as bad as I'm expecting.

"You okay?" Ben asks, slowing even more, as if he can sense my reluctance.

"I was just thinking about my mom. She's going to lose it when I walk in with blood everywhere."

"No worries. This is my sister-in-law's car. There are baby wipes and diapers in the backseat." He winks at me. "Baby wipes are magic. They clean everything—poop, puke, dirt, spilled juice, blood. We'll pull over and you can clean up before you go in."

Relief soothes the edges of my anxiety as he pulls to the side of the road a few blocks down from Ariel's house. "Thanks. Again."

"No problem." He cuts the ignition and reaches over the seat, grabbing a plastic bin. The air blooms with the smell of baby lotion as he tugs damp cloths from the dispenser and drops them into my hand. "I'm out past my new school-night curfew anyway." The way he hits the word *curfew* makes it clear he considers the idea ridiculous. "I might as well make the most of it and really piss my brother off."

"So you live with your brother?" I swipe at the side of my head, staining the pure white cloth pink and then red.

"Yeah. I used to live with my cousins in Lompoc. It seemed stupid to switch schools only a few months from graduation, but . . . it wasn't working out."

"Why not?"

He shrugs. "My cousins are older. They party a lot, and they're getting into things I'm not into."

"Like what?"

"Like gangs." He rolls his eyes. "They wanted me to get initiated; I wanted to live. It was a conflict of interest. Plus, my brother found out, and with him being a cop, there was no way staying there was going to fly. Even for a few more months."

"What about your parents? Are they . . ."

"My dad went back to Mexico when I was little. He used to send letters sometimes, but . . ." He turns to glance through the windshield, watching a cat scurry across the street. When he speaks again his voice is softer. "And my mom died about a year ago."

"I'm sorry."

"You're sorry a lot," he says, smiling as the cat disappears.

I reach for another wipe. "Not really."

"You *say* you're sorry a lot."

"I guess I don't mean I'm *sorry* as much as . . ." I pause, the wipe hovering between my forehead and cheek. "I guess I just . . . wish things were different, that people's lives weren't so hard."

"Me too," he says, a hitch in his voice. He turns and our eyes meet, and that sense of *knowing* him hits again, catching me in my empty gut. For a moment, the sadness and pain in his eyes is *my* pain, and I desperately want to make it better. I want to reach for him, hold him, whisper into the warm crook of his neck that everything is going to be okay, that I'll make it that way.

But I don't. Because I can't.

Because that whisper would be a lie. And because I know if I touch him again, I might forget who I'm not.

FIVE

I fist the damp wipe in my hand, reining in the part of me that aches for this boy with the big brown eyes.

I might feel an instant connection to Ben, but *I* don't matter, and Ariel isn't ready to love anyone. She pulled a car off the road and killed her first date, for god's sake. She needs to pull herself together, and Ben deserves a girl who won't load him down with emotional baggage.

Even after ten minutes, I can tell he's special, a kind, decent person in a world where people like him are becoming as rare as soul mates.

"Ariel?" he asks.

"What?"

"You missed a spot."

I lean over to look in the rearview mirror, swipe at a sticky place near my hairline.

"On the other side. Over by– Here, I'll get it." He pulls a wipe from the bin and brings it to my cheek, easing it over my jaw with the confidence of someone who has experience looking after people.

I freeze, mesmerized by his touch. It's been so long since anyone has touched me like this, with such . . . care. I always keep to myself in my temporary bodies. Living in borrowed skin doesn't encourage physical contact, at least not for me. I can't remember the last time I've taken comfort from someone's touch.

But at this moment, I do, so much so that it's painful. I don't want to think about how good this simple contact feels, or how long it will be before anyone touches me again.

Never. No one ever will, because you *don't exist.*

"There. Got it." He holds the wipe, now smeared with a streak of red, in the air between us. "You okay, Mermaid?"

"Yeah." My voice is rough. I clear my throat, smoothing out the wrinkles. This is the way things are. I know this. I've known from the beginning. "I'm fine."

"What happened? To that side of your face? And your ear?"

"What?" I've forgotten about the scars, forgotten I'm Ariel. Ben's matter-of-fact tone doesn't help. It's obvious he isn't repulsed by Ariel's face the way she assumes people–boys in particular–will be. "I . . . It was a long time ago. There was an accident with some grease when I was six. I've had surgeries. It's a lot better than it used to be."

"I got burned by a cigarette when I was kid," he says. "It hurt like crazy, and that was just a little thing. Nothing like that." He shakes his head. "That must have been hell."

He's offering empathy, not pity, something I know Ariel would appreciate, but I feel awkward accepting his compassion. I don't deserve it. I haven't suffered through Ariel's pain. My own physical suffering was brief—a few minutes on a cold stone floor with a knife cutting slivers of agony through my chest.

Still, I suppose I have my own scars. Even if no one can see them.

"I try not to think about it." I lift my eyes to Ben's. "I don't want to feel sorry for myself. I don't want other people to feel sorry for me either."

"I don't. I think you're tough."

"Oh yeah?" My lips curve. "And that's a good thing?"

"Tough is very good and you're very tough." His hand brushes against mine as he reaches into the back, making my pulse beat faster. "At least, tough for a girl named after a mermaid."

My smile fades. He isn't really talking about me, and the heart speeding in my chest isn't mine. I have to get out of this car. Ariel and Ben can become better friends at a later date. Preferably after I'm gone. I like Ben, but I don't like the way he makes me feel. *Me,* the bodiless soul who has no business feeling anything.

I am Ariel now, and I need to get home.

"We should probably go," I say. "It's getting late."

"Sure." Ben holds out a plastic bag he's fetched from the back and we throw the used cloths inside. "But if that psycho messes with you again, find me," he says. "I'll be in school starting tomorrow. You go to Solvang public, right? Or do you go to the private–"

"I go to SHS. Mom says she'd rather save her money for college than waste it on private school. But really, don't worry about Dylan. I just want to forget tonight ever happened."

"I don't," he says, voice soft, cautious. "If it hadn't happened, I wouldn't have met you."

Our eyes meet again and suddenly the car seems too small and his words too big. It would be so easy to bridge the distance between us. A word, a touch, it wouldn't take much to take this new friendship in another direction. Ben is interested, maybe he even feels what I feel, this connection that defies explanation.

But even if he does, it doesn't matter. Ariel isn't ready and I'm not able. This . . . whatever it is has to stop. Now.

"I'm overrated. Ask my mother," I say, making a joke, avoiding the possibility he's thrown between us. "Speaking of my mother . . ." I glance down the road, but the blue house from Ariel's memories isn't in sight just yet. "I should really get home."

Nurse will be worried if I don't contact her soon. I need her help locating the soul mates I've been sent for. She always knows where to find them, even in the most densely populated areas. In a small town like this she'll no doubt have already mapped the route from my new house to both of theirs.

"Right. Hint taken." Ben sounds hurt, but I pretend not to notice, pretend my chest isn't aching the way it did when I slid off his lap. He starts the car, pulls back onto the road. "I was supposed to be home an hour ago anyway."

"Why weren't you?" I ask, filling the silence for the last few feet of our journey.

"A friend and I had a fight. She's just . . . confusing," he says. "I don't know. I needed to drive. Think."

"Little fight or big fight?"

He pulls into my new driveway, shifts into park before pinning me with a hard look. "There was no blood. Or broken windows."

"So not a real fight at all."

His lips twitch, but he doesn't smile. "No, not a real fight. It's no big deal. We'll be cool by tomorrow. I can't afford *not* to be cool with her. She's the only other person I know at SHS. You gotta have friends, right?"

"I don't have many," I say, distracted by the light in the kitchen and the music drifting through the open window. Melanie is waiting up for her daughter, probably wanting to know all the details about her date. Wonderful. I smooth my hair away from my face and pray I've gotten enough of the blood off.

"That's weird."

"What's weird?"

"That you don't have many friends. You seem socially functional."

"Oh, I guess . . . I'm . . . just . . ."

I'm not Ariel. I'm an imposter, a girl from seven hundred years ago who's a little less damaged than this girl with the scarred face.

But only a little.

"You're just what?" he asks.

"Shy."

He smiles his real smile, the crooked one that is somehow more beautiful for its imperfection. "You don't seem shy. At all."

He's right. And Ariel isn't really shy; she's just . . . broken.

I'll have to work harder at impersonating her. The fact that she's never met Ben lulled me into relaxing my guard. I have to be more careful. Small, subtle changes in conduct that add up to a better life for her are the best way to get my job done without arousing concern about out-of-character behavior. I should know better than to let my own personality show too much.

I should know better than to make any of the mistakes I've made since jumping into this car.

"Well . . ." I shrug. "I guess the way we met broke the ice."

"Carjacking. Perfect icebreaker."

"Yeah. After that, shy seemed silly."

"I'm glad." Ben leans into the backseat again, grabs a wrinkled black sweatshirt, and presses it into my hands. "Here, this is a little stinky, but you should put it on. You've got blood on your shirt." He leans closer, the concerned look creeping back onto his face. "A . . . *lot* of blood. Are you sure you're okay?" His fingers reach out, whispering along my shoulder, making me flinch. Because it hurts even more now. His gentleness.

His eyebrows draw together, but he doesn't pull his hand away. "I'm not going to hurt you."

"I know," I whisper. Hurting me isn't what I'm worried about. At least, not in the way he means. He can't know that his care is the thing that hurts, the thing that makes something deep inside me cry out in a way it hasn't since I was real, since I was a girl with her own body and life and a sadness that felt bigger than the world.

"And I won't let anyone else hurt you either. I promise." His fingers drift to my cheek.

I know I should move away, reach for the door handle, get out of here before this moment gets any thicker, but I can't.

For some reason . . . I *can't*. I am lost in him, in the passion in his eyes, the softness of his touch, the conviction in his words.

"I have to go," I say, but I don't move. He doesn't either. He just stares at me, his eyes flicking from my lips to my eyes and back again.

"Then go," he says, as he leans closer.

"Okay."

Go, Juliet. Move! Now!

But I don't. I stay and let him come closer, closer, until I can feel the heat of his lips and imagine just how perfect they'll feel, how perfect he'll taste, how—

"Thanks for the shirt." I break the moment, lunge for the door handle, and half fall out of the car. My heart is pounding so hard it leaps in my throat as I pull the shirt over my head, hiding the evidence of how badly I've been hurt before bending back down to face Ben through the open window. "I'll see you tomorrow. Maybe we'll have some classes together."

When he speaks, his voice is as husky as mine. "Right. *Dulces sueños,* Mermaid."

Sweet dreams. Not likely. Not after a shift that's started like this one.

"You too." I turn and rush up the concrete steps and through the creaky screen door, cozy in my borrowed shirt if not my borrowed skin, the smell of ocean breeze and Ben following me in out of the night.

SIX

"That wasn't the same boy you left with." Ariel's mom—*my* mom—stands in the center of the kitchen, hands fluttering from the neck of her blue robe to the tie at her waist and back again. She leans to one side, peering around me through the screen door as Ben drives away.

Her blue eyes are a different color than Ariel's. But the rest of Melanie Dragland—white-blond hair, narrow nose, thin lips, willowy frame—is nearly identical, as if she created her daughter from a piece of her own flesh. She's pretty, or would be if it weren't for the tension that sours her features.

"What happened to Dylan?" she asks, voice rising. "And what are you wearing? What happened to your new shirt? And your makeup?" She sucks in a scandalized breath as she crosses the kitchen, wide eyes roaming over my face. "It looks like you rubbed it all off. All of it!"

"It's fine, Mom, I can—"

"It's not fine. I can see everything," she says, the pain in her voice making me flinch. The pain is *her* pain, but it would be so easy to take it personally. It would be so easy for Ariel to look into her mother's horrified eyes and believe that *she* is the thing that's horrible.

I would have fallen into the same trap if it hadn't been for my father. He was always there with a hug and a smile, balancing the cold consideration of my mother. In her eyes, I was simply a reminder of her failure to give my father a son. If they'd been my only reflection I would have gone mad.

It's no wonder Ariel has such a distorted view of herself. The mirror Melanie holds to her is warped, cruel. I have to find some way to change things in this house or I can't see Ariel's life improving in the near future.

I take a deep breath and try my best to keep my dislike for this woman from my voice. "Dylan and I went to a party on the beach. I got some spray on my face. I guess it washed my makeup off." My eyes roam around the kitchen as I think how to explain why Ben drove me home. Unfortunately, there isn't much to look at. Just white cabinets stenciled with blue Danish wooden shoes and windmills, cracked white countertops, and linoleum that was probably new around the time Melanie was born.

She obviously doesn't choose to spend her nurse's salary on home improvements. The kitchen feels cold and unlived in and smells of cheap coffee, bleach, and . . . cabbage. It doesn't bode well for the rest of the house.

"It's too cold to be down at the beach." Melanie crosses her arms over her chest. "It's barely fifty degrees *here,* and it's always colder on the coast."

"I know. I was freezing," I agree, the lies coming easier now. "So a friend gave me his sweatshirt, and a ride home."

Melanie shakes her head. "But what about Dylan? What happened?"

He's dead. Your daughter killed him, and now a monster is living in his body.

I lower my eyes, studying the brown stars on the linoleum, wishing Ariel had never met Dylan Stroud.

"I thought he really liked you," Melanie pushes, refusing to take the hint. "He actually came inside to say hello to your *mother.* That's kind of a big deal, isn't it? I thought boys didn't do that anymore."

"I guess." I shift my gaze to the ceiling, where lumps of paint bubble like an untreated rash. Ariel's memory tells me the style is called a popcorn ceiling. The artist within me is unimpressed.

"So? What happened?" Melanie's impatience is sharp in the air. This is the point when Ariel would usually scream for her mom to leave her alone and run to her room.

Instead, I meet her mother's eyes, willing her to let the subject drop. "After we were alone, I didn't like him. I asked a friend to take me home. The end."

"*You* didn't like *him?*"

"No, I didn't." I grit my teeth against the disbelief in Melanie's tone. "He was rude."

She sighs and rolls her eyes. "Ariel, real teenage boys aren't like characters in the books you read. They smell funny and are obsessed with video games and say dumb things. They're still learning, just like you. You can't expect a seventeen-year-old kid to—"

"I can expect whatever I want to expect."

"Fine," she snaps, not bothering to hide her anger. "If you want to be on the outside looking in for the rest of your life, then go ahead and spend your time painting dead animals and vampires and—"

"They're not vampires!" I shout, not certain what Melanie is talking about, but knowing Ariel hates it when she says things like that about her work. She hates that Melanie even sees her paintings, wishes she could lock the door to her room when she leaves and keep Melanie away from the pieces of her subconscious hanging on the wall.

"Your fantasies are never going to help you—"

"Wanting a boy who won't take bets on whether or not I'll sleep with him is a fantasy?" I wince as the words leave my mouth. I didn't plan to tell her about that, but her assumption that Ariel is a clueless idiot is infuriating.

"What?" Her eyes grow large, fear swimming in their depths. "Oh god, honey. You didn't . . ."

"No, I didn't. I found out it was a joke before . . . before." My temper fades a bit when Melanie's body sags with relief. Still, I'm not ready to let her off the hook. "But after that he was awful. *Really* awful. I know the difference between a normal boy and a bad person, Mom. You should trust me."

"Oh." She blinks. "Well, I do. Of course I do. . . ." Her teeth worry her bottom lip, her confusion making her look younger. "I just wanted you to have a good time. I was . . . I thought maybe . . . But if Dylan was a jerk, it's good you found another way home." Her hands clutch at her robe, tightening the knot until it seems she'll never get it undone. "But you could have called me, you know. I would have come to get you."

Does Ariel know? I don't think she does.

"Well, I kind of . . . lost my purse," I say. "And my cell phone, so I—"

"What?" Anger surges back into her voice. "Ariel! We still have another year on that phone before you're eligible for an upgrade."

Really? She's going to have a fit about *this*? After everything I've just said?

"You'll just have to figure out where you left it."

"I left it in Dylan's car," I say, wondering how Romeo is going to explain his wrecked car to his new "parents." Hopefully his welcome into his new family is going even less smoothly than my own. "I can't get it back."

"You *can* get it back."

"No, Mom. I can't. I'll pay for the phone myself, I—"

"With what? The money from the part-time job you never applied for?" She makes a sound that's more of a snort than a laugh. "I swear, Ariel, I—"

"I never applied because *you* said no one would hire me!" My voice rises to Ariel's usual, strident whine. If I don't lose my cool at this point, Melanie will surely suspect her daughter has been possessed.

"Probably not for counter service work, but you could've worked in a kitchen or something! Ah! This just . . . drives me crazy." She closes her eyes, sucks in a long, slow breath and lets it out, apparently unaware that there are antidiscrimination laws in modern America. Too bad there aren't any laws against discrimination in the home. "You know what? It isn't worth another fight. You're about to graduate and you can find a job next year. Maybe something part-time at the college."

Assuming Ariel overcomes the certainty that she's too hideous to be seen in public, and the general awkwardness and self-loathing that make most people her age consider her a social disease. At this point, that's a big assumption. I have to turn Melanie into an ally instead of another obstacle to overcome.

But not tonight. I'm exhausted and hungry, and Nurse is waiting for me.

"It's fine," Melanie continues. "I'll give you my phone, and I'll get an iPhone. I can get a good discount, and everyone else has one. I'm the only person at the hospital who isn't checking their email every ten seconds." She laughs, a strained sound that seems uncomfortable in her mouth. "So . . . don't worry about the phone. I'll leave mine on the counter for you in the morning."

"Thanks." At least she's trying. It's . . . a start. "I'm going to get something to eat. Do you want anything?"

Her upper lip curls, as if the thought of food is vaguely repellent. "No, I had a sandwich."

I turn to the refrigerator and tug open the door, searching for something to ease the ache in my stomach. Ariel doesn't have strong memories of food. She eats to live, doesn't live to eat. Good thing too, or the contents of the refrigerator—a few Chinese takeout containers, lunch meat, a jar of shriveled black olives, a hunk of orange cheese, three bottles of wine, and an old container of cottage cheese that's expired—would be enough to inspire a second suicide attempt.

Yuck. So much for taking comfort in food.

I reach for the cheese and the olives, then think better of

the olives and put them back. I have high standards when it comes to olives. My family grew them on our estate and pressed olive oil so fine I can still recall the smell of it spreading on a warm plate.

The memory makes my shoulders sag.

"Honey, are you sure you're okay?"

"I'm fine." I let the door drift closed and turn to find Melanie exactly where I left her, stranded in the middle of the kitchen, staring at me with a curious expression.

"You just seem . . . not yourself."

I freeze, considering my behavior since I came inside. Ariel and Melanie argue all the time, but Ariel usually loses her temper and runs for cover before things get as intense as they did tonight.

Maybe I've started off too strong.

I shrug. "It's been a rough night."

"I know. I'm just . . . I want you to . . ." She sighs and fists her robe once more. "I've never been good at this, but you know what I mean."

No, she hasn't, and I guess I do. She means that she cares, no matter how bad she is at showing it. But Ariel wouldn't know. Ariel would see this interaction as yet another time she's failed to be what Melanie wants her to be, another reason to get angry or give up and quit trying.

Still, that doesn't keep me from feeling bad for this woman. She isn't an awful person, or even the worst mother in the world. At least she waited up to make sure her daughter got home safely. My own mother couldn't have cared less, so long as I didn't attract scandal and stayed out of her sight.

"It's okay, Mom," I say, adding the words I suspect both of the women in this family need to hear more often. "I love you."

Her lips part before a smile slowly brightens her face. "I love you too." She reaches out and pulls me close, crushing our thin frames together for a moment that is equal parts awkward and wondrous. There is love in this hug, no matter how clumsy.

Maybe there's hope for this family. The realization helps me breathe a little easier . . . once Melanie releases her death grip. We pull apart and stand staring at each other—her hands fluttering back to her waist, mine clutching a hunk of rapidly warming cheese—until Melanie breaks the silence with a nervous laugh.

"Okay, I'll let you get to bed," she says. "I'm working the late shift tomorrow, so I'm going to sleep in. Is Gemma giving you a ride to school? Or do you need to take the car again?"

"I'm not sure." Gemma hasn't been picking Ariel up every day lately, but Ariel doesn't know why. "I'll try to call and ask," I say, inspired by my small success with Melanie. I might as well contact Ariel's friend and try to get that relationship back on track. The more put-together Ariel's life, the more attention I'll have to devote to my soul mates.

"Well, if you need to take the car, just go ahead and take it." She moves to the fridge, pulling out a half-empty bottle of white wine and fetching a plastic cup from the cabinet above. Lady Capulet would have fainted at the idea of sipping wine from anything except the finest glass from Venice. At least Melanie doesn't seem like an insufferable snob. Ariel could definitely have it worse. "I can get a ride to work with Wendy."

"Okay," I say, strangely touched by her concern for my transportation needs. "Good night, Mom."

"Good night, honey."

I return her smile before heading out of the kitchen,

munching my cheese as I go. It's disgusting, but at least I won't starve to death before dawn.

Straight ahead is a shadowed living room and to my left a narrow hallway. I turn down the hall, find my new room, and shut myself inside. It's small but bright and welcoming, with pale yellow walls and a white bedspread dripping with ruffles. It looks like a bed a younger girl would sleep in, and isn't something Ariel picked out.

Her aesthetic is represented in the artwork filling every free inch of wall space, haunting paintings of fairies sleeping in fall leaves, lonely trees atop epic mountains, young men in dark clothes with sad eyes, and an aging unicorn dying at the edge of a silent pool.

The last one takes my breath away. I find myself on the other side of the room, running fingers across the animal's detailed face. When I was a girl, everyone believed in unicorns. They're mentioned in the Bible, and their existence was taken as fact. Finding out that the creatures are myth was more difficult than I like to admit.

But the death of magic, of hope, is never easy.

Ariel has captured that beautifully. The painting makes me ache to pick up a brush. I lived to paint as a girl. Maybe I can steal some time for it while I'm here. At the very least, I have to finish the sets for the school play.

Thankfully, my talent and Ariel's seem to match up well. Certain skills—riding a horse, driving a car, performing other day-to-day tasks associated with life in a given era—seem to be physically ingrained and translate easily from one soul to the next. Talents, however, are a different story. A gift for mathematics or science, the ability to play an instrument or sing like an angel, are soul gifts, ones I've had difficulty emulating in the past. It will be nice to share a soul gift with my borrowed body.

The thought cheers me as I shove the last hunk of cheese into my mouth and step away from the painting, surveying the rest of my new domain. It isn't nearly as bad as Ariel's memories have led me to believe. The room is cramped but ordered, with a place for everything and everything in its place. A chest of drawers is wedged in tight against the bed and the opposite wall is filled by an empty easel and a white desk topped with a sleeping computer, a stack of textbooks, and a phone sitting in its cradle.

I'll use it to call Gemma, but there's one call I have to make first.

Above the desk hangs a mirror. It's a light, flimsy thing, and covered with animal stickers Ariel pasted there when she was younger, but it will work. I shift the books to the side and lean close to the mirror's surface, shutting my eyes, doing my best to clear my mind, to visualize the golden light Nurse and the other high Ambassadors inhabit when not on earth. Any moment I will hear her familiar voice. She's bodiless in her realm, but her voice is always the murmur of the woman who raised me.

Nurse borrowed that woman's body for only a few months, but somehow—through some trick of high Ambassador magic—she retained the voice. I suspect she knows I find it comforting, a piece of my past that travels with me through the years. I also suspect that's why she encourages me to call her Nurse instead of by her true name, though she says it's because her given name is too difficult for modern people to pronounce.

"Modern people" referring to the people of the fourteenth century.

For the hundredth time I wonder just how old Nurse and the other high Ambassadors and Mercenaries really are. Hundreds of years older than me? Thousands? Were they ever mortal? Or are they a completely different species from the converts they've each gathered throughout the centuries?

There's so much I don't know about the beings I serve. I know only that they are magical and good, and that they want me to be good. Nurse insists that my ignorance of their world is something I'll be grateful for someday, that it protects me from the Mercenaries in a way nothing else can, but sometimes . . . I wonder.

Sometimes . . . I doubt.

I doubt that lovers are worth fighting for. I've seen too many soul mates turn to darkness to believe that love conquers all.

I doubt that my efforts matter—there are others like me who will keep fighting if I stop. It isn't as if the fate of the world—or even true love—rests on my shoulders. Shakespeare made my story famous, but to the Ambassadors, I'm just one servant among many.

I doubt that I'm really Ambassador material. I've taken vows to serve goodness and light, but in my heart I am filled with hate. I hate Romeo, I hate stealing other people's bodies, and sometimes I even hate Nurse. For finding me on the floor of the tomb before it was too late, for giving a dying girl a chance at "life" that isn't really life at all.

Sometimes it seems wrong, what she's done. Sometimes I dread seeing that golden light stream from a mirror as much as I long for it. Sometimes I wish it wouldn't come, that the mirror would remain a mirror, that I would open my eyes and find that the madness of the past seven hundred years has been nothing but a dream.

But then, there was a time when I wished for forever with Romeo Montague.

I should have learned to be careful what I wish for.

I haven't.

My eyes fly open, confirming my fears. There is no golden light; there is no comforting voice. There is only a frightened young girl in a room full of shabby twenty-first-century furniture.

"No." I jump when I realize I've spoken aloud. I press my fingers to my lips, lean closer to the mirror, staring into my strange new eyes, praying for the light to come.

Please, please, please. I promise not to doubt, I promise to be better, finer, stronger. I promise and focus until I can feel electricity dancing inside my borrowed skull. But still . . . nothing. For the first time in hundreds of years and over thirty shifts: *nothing.*

"Nurse, please." I lay my hands flat against the cold glass, as if I can will her into the reflection with my touch. "It's Juliet. I'm here. Please. *Please.*"

Outside, thunder rumbles, sending a tremor through my bones.

Since the second I slipped into Ariel's body, something has seemed off about this shift. I dismissed it as bad luck—or perhaps my instincts warning me that Romeo was closer than I expected during those first moments—but now there is no comfort to be had. My line to the Ambassadors of Light and their guidance and support has been severed.

For the first time, I am completely alone on earth.

INTERMEZZO ONE

Romeo

I run from Solvang's town square, sprinting through the driving rain, imagining how the drops will needle my skin when I can feel them—a thousand bliss-filled stings, a million points of tiny, perfect pain. I open my mouth and let the cold stream inside, laughing until the water gurgles sickly in my throat—the sound of something dying.

No, the sound of something being born.

Alive, alive, alive.

The stories are true; the time has come. My time. Mine! Finally, after all these years, after an eternity of torture and a dozen lifetimes of lies, the mirrors are dark and the town empty of others like me. I haven't seen a single other Mercenary, and I would have. If they were here, *I would know.*

I will look for the black auras again tomorrow in the daylight, when more humans crawl across this precious town with its windmills and gingerbread roofs and endless string of pancake houses. But I am already certain, already sure. I am *alone.*

We are alone, my lady and I.

Juliet.

Her name still cuts at things inside me, brings phantoms of human emotion to haunt my stolen flesh. Some part of me remembers the exquisite ache of love, the crushing pain of loss.

I cling to the flutter in my chest, relishing the agony. It is terrible, beautiful. It spreads like the sweetest poison. The ghost of misery is a welcome friend. I crave the wretchedness it will bring, the writhing of my soul inside my stone prison. Pain is so much easier to recall than pleasure. I can't remember pleasure anymore, don't know if I'm capable of taking joy in anything, even if the specters make their predicted appearance, even if the spell works, even if—someday very, *very* soon—I can feel again, taste again, *live* again.

But if anyone can summon goodness inside me, it is her. My love, my enemy, my other half, my Juliet. Perhaps she can coax the knots from my soul, melt my frozen heart, banish my demons. Perhaps I will wake the morning after the spell that frees us and no longer delight in the suffering of others, no longer take pleasure in pain.

"And then we shall share true love's kiss, and live happily ever after." The words make me laugh. And laugh and laugh.

I laugh all the way to the edge of town, to the row of brittle, peeling houses where my new body lives. I laugh through the dented door, into a dingy room I can guess smells of smoke and sadness and death. I laugh when a man's voice yells from the room down the hall, threatening to "beat my ass" if I don't "shut the hell up."

I know the man will make good on his threat when he finds that his son has destroyed his car. I know Dylan's father will be relieved when I leave this shell and his son's corpse is all that remains. These thoughts make me laugh as well.

I laugh into my new room, where posters of other angry young men glare down at me from the walls. I laugh at this body's pathetic dreams of becoming a rock star, of becoming famous and making everyone "sorry." His dad for his loose fists, his mother for leaving, the entire stupid world sorry for daring to make him work for the things he desires.

I treasure his death, a warm stone in my fist, a bright, sparkling thing that keeps me smiling through yet another long, sleepless night. The two-hundred-thousandth such night or more. I've lost count. I could work the numbers, but I don't. There's no reason, not when the end is so very near.

Tomorrow. Tomorrow I will find her and teach her and she will love me and fear me and she will never be the same.

And neither, perhaps, will I.

SEVEN

I'm so cold I know I'll never be warm again. My fingers press against the heat gushing from my chest—pushing, clinging—as if I can hold my life inside me with trembling hands. But my hands aren't much larger than a child's. I didn't realize I was so small, so foolish.

Not until now, until it's too late to make a difference.

Too late.

"It's not too late, Juliet." Nurse leans over me, cupping my face in her dry, papery hands. "If you want to live, I can help. I know you still have love in your heart."

Do I? Do I have love in my heart? Can I hold anything inside me when I've been cut open and all my stupid little-girl dreams are spilling out onto the floor? I look into her soft gray eyes and say nothing. I don't know what to say. I'm not sure, not sure enough to promise, sure enough to swear.

But then the cold grows even colder and fear rises, a tide that will drown me if I hesitate a moment more. I raise my hand. I repeat the words she whispers, taking the oath, committing myself to the Ambassadors. I don't want to die. I want to live. I want to prove that my hands aren't so small. To prove I can fight.

The final words of the spell burn through my veins, making me cry out, scalding my soul from my human flesh. Nurse urges me to sleep, to rest until I'm needed, but I fight to keep my eyes open. I fail. My lids close, and behind them there is only the mist. And it is cold and endless and my body is gone. Nurse warned me it would be like this, but I didn't understand. I didn't dream . . .

I realize I am nothing and scream, panic racing through my formless being, banishing hope in a great wave of—

"Wake up. Wake up, niña." I awake to find . . . Ben. He lies beside me, hair rumpled from sleep, arms holding me tight, banishing the nightmare. With gentle hands he wipes the tears from my cheeks. "It's all right. I won't let anyone hurt you." His lips are warm against my forehead, sealing the promise with skin upon skin.

Relief floods through me, gratitude so profound it makes me shake. It's all been an awful dream. I sigh against his chest, finally protected, finally whole. "I love you."

"I love you too, sweet." The lips on my forehead grow hot . . . sticky. I pull back to see Ben's face, to wipe the damp away, and scream.

It's Romeo. And his mouth is full of blood.

He laughs as I scramble from his embrace, more red horror dripping from his lips. He's lapped my blood from the floor of the tomb, but the terrible secret won't stay inside him. "Soft, what light through *yonder window breaks? Break. Break. Break!"* His screeching reaches *a torturous crescendo and his teeth shatter into tiny daggers. They fly into my eyes, blinding me.*

I scream and scream and—

"Ariel! What's going on?"

My eyes blink against the harsh light and my heart races even faster. Where am I? I blink again. An angry woman stands at the door, blond hair sticking up on one side, eyes swollen from sleep. Who is she? What's happening? What—

"Answer me, honey." She crosses her arms and furrows her brow. "What's wrong? I thought you were hurt. Why were you screaming like that, Ariel?"

Ariel. That's right. The twenty-first century, California, the girl with the white-blond hair. Romeo in the car, and nothing in the mirror.

Nothing. Late, late into the night, using a dozen different mirrors, and still *nothing.* Nothing and more nothing until the absence of the golden light brought tears of frustration and fear, until I curled into bed in my bloody clothes, too tired to bother with the shower down the hall.

I pull the sheets to my chin, not wanting Melanie to see me in the clothes I wore last night. "I was just . . . I was having a bad dream."

She lets out a long, tired breath. "God. Some dream. I thought—"

The honk of a horn makes her turn to look over her shoulder, then back at me with a puzzled expression. "Is that Gemma already? What time is it? Why aren't you ready for school?"

Oh no. I forgot to set an alarm! I allowed my focus to be

eaten alive by worry, and now I'm going to be late for my first day of school. Unless . . .

"I'll be ready in five minutes. Will you tell her that I'll be right out?"

"I'm supposed to be sleeping," Melanie says. "I have to work until two a.m. tonight, Ariel."

"I know. I'm sorry. But please, Mom? Will you–"

"Fine." She sighs again and recrosses her arms, huddling against the morning. "But then I'm going back to bed and you need to get your act together. Senior year isn't over yet."

As soon as she turns to leave I leap from the bed, pulling off clothes and hurling them into the air, stumbling over my feet as I grab clean underwear and a pair of jeans from the drawers. Socks of two different colors come next, and then a white camisole. I spin, scramble over the bed, grab the first sweater my hands brush against from the closet and pull it over my head. It's pink, with brown yarn knots on the front. I grab brown shoes to match the knots, making some effort to look as if I'm not falling apart. Romeo could be at school today.

I swallow, my throat tight, the memory of my dream making me shiver. I can't let him know I'm afraid, can't let him see that I'm lost, abandoned. I hurry to the vanity, pull my brush through hair that still smells of baby wipes. Ben was right; they really do clean up everything.

Ben. My cheeks burn. I dreamt about him, too, about the way it would feel to . . . love him. I've never loved anyone but Romeo; I know I will never love anyone again, but still the dream felt so real.

"Ariel!" Melanie's shout startles me from my thoughts. "Move it! Gemma's waiting."

I throw the brush back onto the vanity, grateful that Ariel's hair is stick straight. It doesn't look as if I bled on it, wiped it clean with baby wipes, then slept on it while it was damp. I look pretty, considering I've dressed in less time than it takes most people to roll out of bed. I know Melanie won't be pleased to see me leaving the house without makeup, but what she doesn't know . . .

I wait until I hear her bedroom door slam before slipping out of my room and hurrying down the hall to the bathroom. I brush my teeth and smear on sunscreen, remembering that Ariel has to be careful to protect her skin, and am running through the kitchen less than five minutes from when I woke.

I grab my backpack and Melanie's cell and consider trying to find something to eat, but then remember the way the hunk of cheese rolled in my belly and dash out the door. There's a bakery not far from school. Maybe Gemma will want to stop there. We'll have time; I haven't kept her waiting for long. Five minutes isn't unreasonable.

Unfortunately, she doesn't seem to agree.

"What the hell were you thinking, Ree?" Her first words don't inspire faith in our lasting friendship; neither does the shocked look she shoots me from the driver's side as I slide into the cool leather seat. Gemma Sloop's sleek BMW is as luxurious as Ben's car is plain and worn, and Gemma herself makes me feel shabby in comparison.

Her rich chocolate-colored hair swings around her shoulders, gleaming even in the gray morning light, the jagged layers emphasizing the lovely planes of her face. A gypsy shirt encrusted with hundreds of stones flutters around her torso, and fitted jeans hug her narrow thighs. Hunks of sapphire too big to be real—but I know they are—sit in her earlobes, and another chunk perches on her right hand, gifts from her father for her sweet sixteen.

"And wow . . . no makeup." She shakes her head. "That's a choice. One I would recommend *not* making in the future, FYI. I haven't seen you look that scary since sixth grade."

"I didn't want to make you wait," I say, too stunned to be angry. I'd been prepared for Ariel's mother to be a monster, but not her best friend. *This* is Gemma, the girl Ariel is so terrified to lose?

"You could have brought it with you. I have mirrors in the car, Freak." Her tone is light, teasing, but I know the words would hurt Ariel. Ariel hates that word, *freak,* the nickname the kids at school gave her in fourth grade, after something awful happened. At recess. Something . . . The memory is fuzzy, and I can tell Ariel's tried hard to forget it. All I know is that was the moment she became the Freak, an outcast only another outcast would befriend.

To look at Gemma, it's hard to believe she's an outcast, but she is. Her parents own the largest winery in the area and employ most of the town as factory hands, vineyard workers, tasting-room experts, distributors, and seasonal help. Even if Gemma didn't dress like the daughter of a millionaire and speak her mind to the point of cruelty, school would be awkward. As it is, she's ostracized by almost everyone.

But she doesn't care. She insisted on staying in public school, even when her grades improved and her parents pressured her to go back to the private school in Los Olivos at the beginning of her freshman year. She's the type of person who only needs one friend, one follower, and sometimes doesn't even seem to need that.

"Whatever." She shifts into reverse and backs down the drive.

Rain pounds the roof as we slide from under the carport and spin in a tight circle before zipping down El Camino. The day is gray, colorless. It's no wonder I overslept. If it weren't for the nightmares, I'd wish I were still asleep. I'm so tired. I should be filled with Ambassador magic by now, feeling strong enough to take on the world—or at least the Mercenaries. But I don't. I feel . . . off, exhausted.

"I guess your new *boyfriend* doesn't care what you look like," Gemma says, hitting the word *boyfriend* hard enough to break a rock.

"What?"

"Melanie told me," she says. "I can't believe you told your mother—who you hate like ass sores—that you were going on a date, but didn't tell me."

"Oh." The date. That's why she's angry. Ariel decided not to tell Gemma until afterward, when she'd hopefully have a real story to tell.

" 'Oh.' That's all you have to say? 'Oh'?"

"Sorry. I didn't want to say anything unless we had a good time."

"Well, did you?" she asks, a twinkle in her eye. "Who's the guy? Where did you go? How late did you stay out? Did you finally see a penis in real life? Tell me everything. Immediately."

I surprise myself with a blush. "No." How much to say? I know Ariel won't want Gemma to know the date was a joke. "It was awful. Dylan's not—"

"Dylan, as in Dylan Stroud?" she asks, enthusiasm draining from her tone.

"Yeah."

"You went out with Dylan?" Her lips press together, the bright red of her lipstick making her mouth a crooked slash across her face. "Wasn't that . . . awkward?"

"It was," I say, not sure why the moment has become strained. "Like I said, it was awful."

"Right . . ." She turns her gaze back to the road. "Well, of course it was. I could have *told* you it would be if you'd given me the heads-up. He's *Dylan Stroud.* He's a sociopath."

"I know. He just seemed so nice at rehearsals."

"That's because he's pretending to be someone else," Gemma says, making a valid point. Ariel's crush on Dylan developed while she was watching him play Tony, the boy who falls in love with the little sister of the leader of the opposing street gang in *West Side Story.*

West Side Story, the musical based on Shakespeare's *Romeo and Juliet.* Which means that—should Romeo decide to continue with the drama club—he'll be playing *himself.* I'm sure he'll find the irony delicious.

"I mean, don't you think there's a reason a gorgeous guy like that doesn't have a girlfriend?" Gemma asks. "Or even some steady friends with benefits?"

"Because he's a jerk."

"He's insane. He and Jason both are, and their band is embarrassingly lame. Dylan can sing, but I swear he looks like he's having a seizure when he plays guitar." She turns left and then almost immediately right, taking us into the heart of Solvang's tourist district, a place Ariel thinks of as Disneyland for grown-ups who like wine.

The town is built to look like an old-fashioned Danish village, with wine-tasting rooms on every corner, testimony to the region's growing industry. Gemma's parents' tasting room is the largest, taking up two stories of a redbrick building on Mission Drive. We pass it on our right.

A heavy wooden sign advertising Sloop Vineyards sways in the wind, but Gemma doesn't slow down to look at it. She's far less impressed with her family than most of the other Sloops. It's one of the few things I'm finding likable about her thus far.

"You should just say no to Stroud," she says, obviously not ready to let the subject drop. "Crack is a better habit to start than Dylan."

"I know. We're not going to go out again."

"Good. He's not the kind of mistake anyone should repeat." She reaches over and kicks up the heat. "You want to go get a croissant? I'm starving."

"Yes. Please." Thank god. Food.

She drives in silence for a moment, before reaching out to poke me in the leg. When she speaks again, her voice is softer. "But you're okay, right? Your mom said some guy she'd never seen drove you home. I know you, and you wouldn't get into a car with some strange dude unless—"

"He's not strange. She didn't even meet him."

Gemma's eyebrows shoot into the air. "Oh, so you made a looovvee connection after all, did you? Who is it? Does he go to SHS or the priv-ass school? I can't believe you weren't—"

"No, it's nothing like that. He's just a friend." I hurry to correct her, turning to look out the window as she parks in front of the Windmill Bakery, a larger-than-life re-creation of a windmill with a dark tile roof that gleams black in the rain. "Really, I don't like anyone like that."

"Well, you could. You should," she says, shutting off the

car and reaching into the backseat to grab her purse. "Just not Dylan."

"I know. Thanks for worrying about me. I . . . I've missed you," I say, not wanting to let this opportunity to mend the rift between Ariel and Gemma pass me by. I might not care for her, but Ariel does, and it's not as if Ariel has friends to spare.

"Aw, man." The hard light in Gemma's eyes fades, and for a second I can see that she cares. Or that she wants to care.

But there's something wrong inside her, too, something damaged that makes her more like Ariel than I guessed at first. Ariel's memories don't give me any clue what that something might be, but it makes me feel for Gemma. Makes me smile when she squeezes my hand.

"I've missed you too. I'm sorry, I've just . . ." She sighs, her words trailing off. "There's been drama. Mostly with my dad, but also with this guy . . ."

"A guy? Like . . . a *guy* guy?" Ariel's memories tell me I shouldn't be surprised. Gemma always has a guy. Or two.

"Oh yeah. Definitely a *guy* guy. But it's a mess." She rolls her eyes and reaches for her door. I follow her out of the car, hurrying through the downpour and under the awning of the bakery. "We should talk. Catch up," she says, holding the door open as I dart inside. "I'll tell you all the shocking details. Want to meet back here for lunch?"

"Sounds good." Lunch actually sounds *great.* So does breakfast. The smell of sugar and fried dough fills my nose, making my stomach growl, reminding me that I've yet to eat a meal since I entered this body.

I lead the way across the red and white tiles to the counter, scanning the pastries in the brightly lit glass, searching for something that will stick with me through the morning.

And then I turn back to Gemma and I forget about food, forget about my long night, forget my exhaustion and fear, lost in the rosy glow surrounding her chest. It was too dark in the car, but in the glaring fluorescents there's no missing it. Her aura is stained such a vibrant pink it makes the bright blues and purples of her shirt look dull in comparison.

Seeing the auras of soul mates is one of my Ambassador-given gifts, a way to know when first love has become forever love. The energy of soul mates on the cusp is usually some shade of pink—light or dark, depending on how certain their feelings. Once my soul mates' auras both glow deep red, nothing can destroy their bond, not Mercenary interference, not the hardships of life, not even death. When that happens, my job is complete and I return to the mist with a victory for my side.

But I've never found a soul mate on my own. I've always needed Nurse's help.

Yet here she is, Ariel's best friend, one of the lovers I've been sent to protect.

A spark of hope flares to life inside me. Maybe *that's* why Nurse didn't come to me last night. Maybe she knows that Ariel is already intimately connected to one of the soul mates I've come for, maybe—

"Ariel. Wake up." Gemma snaps her fingers in front of my face. "What do you want? Nancy's waiting."

"Don't rush her, Gemma. I've got time, and school doesn't start for twenty minutes." The woman behind the counter—an older woman with finely wrinkled skin and a long gray braid coiled around her head so that it looks like a crown—smiles. "How about an egg and cheese croissant, Ariel? You look like you could use some protein."

I smile. I remember Nancy now. Ariel has a soft spot for her, and her croissants. "Yes, please. That sounds great."

"And a coffee for her too," Gemma adds. "She needs it."

Ariel doesn't drink coffee, but I don't disagree. It's definitely time to wake up. Gemma is the girl I've come for, and the sooner I figure out the identity of this mystery guy she's seeing–and why their relationship is "a mess"–the closer I'll be to accomplishing what I've been sent here to do.

"Dude." As we step to the side to wait for our order, Gemma gives the burned side of my face a long, hard look. "Your face really does look awful today. Maybe we should ditch homeroom and go back to your house for your makeup."

I bite my lip, refusing to give in to anger. Gemma's my job, and Ariel's friend. I'm not required to like her. Still, I can't help but wonder–not for the first time–why people like Gemma are lucky enough to get soul mates. It seems like it should be a privilege reserved for people who suck less.

"I mean, seriously," she continues, tapping one finger against her chin. "Your mom said she was going back to sleep so–" She breaks off, eyes going wide. Her ringed hand whips out to grab my arm. "Oh my god. There he is. That's him. The guy."

My other soul mate, delivered faster than my breakfast. The thought nearly makes me smile. I try to turn to get a look at him, but Gemma squeezes my arm until I flinch. "Don't turn around! He might still be pissed."

"Why is he–"

"I don't know." She shrugs, lowers her voice. "He said I was confusing and left in the middle of dinner to go drive around and think or something. He's like a girl. I swear."

Confusing. Drive around. Think.

A horrible suspicion curls in my gut, killing my hunger. A part of me knows who I'm going to see, even before I turn around.

"Crap. He's seen us. He's coming over." She drops my arm. "Don't be weird, okay?"

Don't be weird. How can I not be weird when I know . . . I *know* . . .

I turn and my eyes meet his, and that feeling of connection sizzles through the air between us, just like it did last night. But now I know the connection isn't just unwise or impossible, it's forbidden. I see the rosy glow burning through his red and black striped sweater and there is no room for doubt.

Ben is the other soul mate I've been sent to protect.

EIGHT

I want to run and hide. I want to jump over the counter and cower down behind the pastries with my arms over my head. I don't want to stand and watch and try to smile as Gemma flings herself at Ben, surprising him with a kiss on the cheek.

She presses against him, his arm goes around her waist, and something inside me screams like it's been set on fire. The embrace lasts less than a second before Ben pulls away, but the damage is done. He belongs to someone, to a girl I have to make sure he stays with forever.

It is unbearable. Intolerable. It's . . . my job.

These two are my job, and if I don't do it, one of them will die. In over thirty shifts, I've never seen two soul mates part peaceably. Either they commit to each other or one of them commits murder and becomes a Mercenary. That's the way it goes. Every. Single. Time.

There is no hope for me and Ben. But then, there never was.

"Hey, what's up?" Ben looks from me to Gemma and back again, shifts on his feet, shoves his hands into his pockets, as if he feels uncomfortable. Maybe he does. Maybe he's worried I'll tell Gemma that he nearly kissed me last night. Maybe he's afraid I'm about to ruin his relationship with the girl he loves.

Loves. He *loves* her. Whatever happened in the car last night was a fluke, a misstep. Or maybe only my imagination. Maybe Ben never intended to kiss me, maybe I took everything the wrong way.

"Things go okay with your mom last night?" he asks, as if he couldn't care less if Gemma knows we were alone together. Did I really imagine it? That connection so strong I dreamt about waking up in his arms?

"Yeah. Thanks." I nod, try to smile, show him I'm happy he's with my best friend.

"What?" Gemma spins, and her hair flies out to flick Ben in the face, making him flinch. "How do you two—"

"We met last night," Ben says. "Ariel carjacked me, and I gave her a ride home."

Gemma's eyebrows arch. "Really? So you're the one . . . Cool . . ." She trails off with a knowing nod. "So I guess I don't have to do the 'Ben, my special friend, Ariel, my best friend,' thing."

"Special friend." Ben is Gemma's special friend, her *soul mate.* Even seeing them standing there glowing like twin sunsets, I find it hard to wrap my mind around that all-important truth. Gemma is a pain with about as much empathy as a snake. And Ben is . . . Ben.

"Order up!" Nancy chirps from behind us.

"Thank god." Gemma moves past me to the counter. "I need coffee."

Ben and I face each other, and it's there again, that feeling that we both *know* this isn't how things are supposed to be. He takes a step toward me that I mirror with a step back. He stops, pins me with those fathomless brown eyes that see so much more than they should.

"I thought you didn't have many friends," he says.

"I don't. Just Gemma. We've been friends since we were little." I force a smile. "It's so great about you. And her. It's time she found a nice guy."

He cocks his head to the side and opens his mouth to speak, but Gemma beats him to it, sliding in between us, holding a cup out to Ben. "Here. You can have Ariel's coffee."

He shakes his head. "No. I don't want to take her drink."

"Take it, she doesn't care. Do you, Ariel?"

"No," Ben says. "I can just—"

"Take it," Gemma insists. "Ariel doesn't even like coffee, and I paid for it."

Ben's look grows dark. He crosses his arms, refuses to touch the coffee Gemma still clutches in her hand. "I don't want it, Gemma. And I'd like it if you'd listen when I talk. *Every* time I talk." He turns back to me before I can hide the shock on my face. "See you later, Ariel." And then he walks out of the bakery, leaving us staring after him in stunned silence.

"What was *that* about?" Gemma finally asks.

I don't know, but this isn't the way I like to see soul mates talking to each other. Not only is this job going to be miserable, it's going to be hard work getting Ben and Gemma back on the right track. "Do you think he's still mad about last night?" I ask. "About your fight?"

"I think something crawled up his butt and died is what I think."

"But what did you fight about?" I need to know what's gone wrong before I can help make it better. "Maybe he—"

"Screw him. Here, take this." She holds the coffee out to me. I take it, and she pulls the bag containing our breakfast out from under her arm. "Let's eat in the car. I need to go to my locker before homeroom."

I follow her out into the rain, praying I'll have another chance to pump her for information on the way to school. She might act like she doesn't care, but she *has* to be upset that she and Ben are fighting. But Gemma keeps her mouth full of food, and when we pull into the student parking lot I'm no closer to discovering what happened last night.

"Are you going to your locker?" she asks.

"Yeah, but I'm going to grab some juice first." The coffee's left me thirsty, nervous, and not much more awake than I was before. "You want to come to the cafeteria with me?"

Gemma makes a gagging sound. "I'd rather eat my own heart than set foot in that stink hole." She slams out of the car and pops up her umbrella. "Meet you outside homeroom."

"Okay." I hurry down the concrete path a few feet behind her, holding my backpack over my head to stay dry.

Within a few minutes, Solvang High School appears at the end of the curved path, six shabby brown buildings that would have been depressing to look at even if it weren't pouring rain. Groups of kids—shoulders hunched, identical frowns on their faces—cluster along the walkway. The students look less than thrilled by the rain but make no move to get closer to the shelter of the overhangs. Instead, they linger on park benches along the path, putting off the inevitable until the last minute, confirming that Ariel isn't the only teenager who thinks SHS is a prison.

No one says hello as I rush along. No one smiles or makes eye contact. It's as if I'm invisible. *Except* for the occasional shift of a body, the turn of a shoulder as someone moves to get out of my way, clearing the path to the cafeteria. The movements are subtle—easy to miss if your head were down and your hair were in your face—but the other kids are clearly aware of Ariel's presence. And they don't seem to hate her. They almost seem . . . afraid of her.

But why? I can't understand it. Ariel is anxious, awkward, and uncomfortable around just about everyone, but nothing in her memories gives me a clue why half the school treats her like a bomb about to explode.

I sigh as I shove my way through the heavy cafeteria door, and immediately wish I'd settled for a drink from the water fountain. The long room reeks of overcooked vegetables, burnt toast, and armpits. Unwashed armpits. *Long*-unwashed armpits.

Still, the juice in buckets of ice at the end of the line makes my mouth water. I grab a cracked melon-colored tray and start through the line. There are only a few people in front of me, and the cafeteria itself is nearly deserted. I slide my tray along—refusing lumps of eggs and greasy circles of sausage from the tired-looking cafeteria workers—and am nearly to the juice when I feel a change in the air.

Suddenly it's charged, electrified with danger. Romeo has arrived.

I know it's impossible, but I swear I can smell him coming, a faint odor of evil that cuts through the stink of the Solvang High breakfast. My stomach sucks in tight to my spine. I stand a little straighter, determined not to let him see any change in me.

Today is the same as any other day, this shift the same as any other.

I clutch my tray and turn, face carefully blank as I search for Romeo and find him all too quickly. He is striding across the cafeteria, followed by a shorter boy with honey-colored skin and jet-black hair that sticks up in spikes. The shorter boy wears dark blue jeans and a black button-down shirt, while Romeo has dressed Dylan's body all in black—black sweater, black jeans, and black motorcycle boots that give him another two inches of height, maybe more. His cheek is slightly bruised, as if—oddly—he hasn't quite healed from the accident, but he's still undeniably handsome.

But it isn't his looks or the bruise that make the air rush from my lungs. It's his hair, that unruly mop of brown curls. He's *curled* Dylan's hair, made it fall in soft waves around his forehead, made him look so much like—

I sway on my feet, lost in a crush of memories I was certain I'd burned away. I forget how to move, to speak, to breathe. *How* did I not notice this last night? Darkness, the threat of death, the shock and pain of entering a new body—none are adequate excuses. Nothing should have kept me from seeing how much Romeo resembles his old self, the boy I knew, the one who crept through my window with an expression just like that one.

No, *not* like that one. There was no glitter of madness in

his old eyes, no thinly veiled threat in the baring of his teeth. He's coming to me, in broad daylight, with this new friend— probably Jason, the one Gemma mentioned—to torment me, to break me down with some cruelty he's worked out during the night. It's the same as it always is, but so much worse.

Because I am alone, and Ben and Gemma are so strange, and he is . . . haunting.

I back away, fingers gripping my tray so hard my bones begin to ache. I don't want to look at him; I don't want to speak to him. But I have no choice. If I run, he'll know something is wrong. I never run, even when I should, even though the Ambassadors say it's better to run than to fight.

Instead, I put my tray back and walk toward him, meeting him head-on.

"Get me meat. Lots of it. Meat on meat," Romeo says to his friend before stopping in front of me. For some reason this makes the shorter boy snort with laughter. His dark eyes meet mine as he walks by, and I fight the urge to shiver. It's like looking into the face of a reptile, a predator born without human feeling. Even *Romeo's* eyes seem warm by comparison.

"So glad to see you," Romeo says, grinning like the madman he is. "I wanted to apologize. For last night."

Apologize? I look around, wondering for whose benefit he's putting on this show. There's no one within earshot, and his friend is already pushing a tray through the line fifteen feet away.

"Sincerely. I'm sorry. If I'd known, I never would have touched you."

"Known what?" I cross my arms, bracing myself for the inevitable punch line.

He leans close, his voice dropping to a whisper. "The world is different this time. You can feel it, can't you? You've noticed . . . things."

I narrow my eyes, searching his face. He's fishing. He might not know that I can't contact Nurse, but he knows something. Now it's just a matter of finding out what he knows without giving myself away. "I've noticed you don't seem to be healing as quickly as you should."

His fingers go to his cheek, pushing at his bruise. It's fainter than it was last night, but it's definitely there. He smiles, as if relishing the wound. "Perhaps my new father gave me a beating for wrecking my car."

I flinch. The thought of Romeo being beaten by anyone but me is unexpectedly disturbing. At least I know that every time I've struck him he deserved it.

"Or perhaps my gifts are fading," he continues. "Perhaps I've been abandoned by my cause. I believe it's likely. Look at this mess. . . ." He turns and lifts his carefully coiled curls, showcasing a dent in his skull, the one I made when I slammed his head into the glass roof of the car.

I gasp. And turn to make sure no one else has seen.

"Aw. I didn't think you cared." Romeo laughs, and slings a casual arm around my shoulder. "So tell me the truth, Jules. How goes it with you? Things rotten in the state of Denmark?"

"Wrong play." I shrug him off, refusing to think about how tired I am or how frightened by my inability to contact Nurse. I know better than to trust him. Romeo always has an agenda. *Always.* "I don't know what you're talking about."

"Oh, Juliet. Don't lie. I don't want to lie or fight anymore. I'm so weary of it, aren't you? Wouldn't you jump at the chance to put an end to it all?"

Romeo has said similar things before, when he's offered me the chance to join the Mercenaries. All I'd have to do is convince one soul mate to sacrifice his or her love to the Mercenary cause and I'd pay my way into their eternity. A waking eternity, where I would be free to do as I wished between missions. Romeo has reminded me a dozen times that the offer stands, but never with much conviction. He knows me well enough to realize I'm not capable of stealing an innocent soul.

"I've told you, I'm not–"

"I'm not talking about the Mercenaries. Or the Ambassadors." He leans even closer, until his lips are inches from my ear. "This shift is different. And if we play our cards correctly, it could be our last."

NINE

Romeo is waiting on the stage when Gemma and I walk into rehearsal that afternoon, smiling that smile that assures me my efforts to avoid him are futile.

Gemma chucks her backpack onto the floor and joins the dancers onstage without bothering to say good-bye, and Romeo's smile becomes a merry grimace. I turn and slip into the wings, determined to ignore him.

He's been relentless today, bent on winning confidences I refuse to give, shadowing my every move, forcing me to skip my lunch date with Gemma in the name of keeping him away from our soul mates. I apologized to her afterward, but we haven't had time to talk. We don't have class together in the afternoon, and texting isn't allowed on campus.

Hopefully I'll have the chance to smooth things over after practice.

The rehearsal music blares to life. Wrinkling my nose against the musty smell lingering in the wings, I gather my paints and set to work. The SHS theater smells like every other building I've had the misfortune to enter today—moldy and damp. White plastic buckets litter the backstage area, rapidly filling with yellowed water. I have to stop to empty them barely twenty minutes after I've started, tossing the water out the backstage door into the sodden grass. It's the wettest spring on record in central California. Fields of grapevines suffer in standing water, mudslides ooze down the hills, and roofs fail at an alarming rate.

"What the hell, Hannah?"

Tempers fail even faster.

"This is so stupid." Gemma's outraged voice carries to where I'm set up stage right, finishing Ariel's work on a series of flats meant to resemble a New York City street. I'm trying to enjoy it, but even painting can't offer comfort on a day like this. "Just let me have an eight count in the front row, and don't BS me about being too tall. I'm only five nine."

It's the hundredth fight I've overheard today. People at this school are chronically miserable and angry. But who am I to judge? I've certainly experienced my share of both emotions since this morning—misery at learning that Ben is destined to be with a girl like Gemma, anger that I still can't reach Nurse in any of the mirrors I've tried, including the bathroom mirrors at school.

"The choreography is set," Hannah says. The petite brunette directing the dance numbers studies at the Santa Barbara School of Ballet and is a passionate member of the I Hate Gemma club. Most people seem to be. Ariel is an uncertain quantity the other kids avoid; Gemma is a spoiled princess they want to rip from her throne. "We've only got three days until the show opens, we're not going to—"

"But there's no reason I should be in the back during the entire dance number," Gemma says. "I'm *Bernardo.*"

"Bernadette," Hannah corrects. Several girls are playing boys' parts. There aren't enough boys in the drama club to fill them all. It's quite a change from Shakespeare's time, when men played all the roles—male and female—and I can tell it amuses Romeo.

He laughs again, a high-pitched *hee hee hee* that makes my next stroke hit the canvas at the wrong angle. What the hell does he have to be so happy about? And why is he wasting time with me when he should be hard at work ruining Ben and Gemma's love?

Maybe he was telling the truth this morning and really does know a way out. Or maybe this is just a new way to ruin my afterlife, to trick me into doing something the Ambassadors can't forgive, something that will end what small semblance of existence I have left.

"Please, Mike." Gemma's voice rises, appealing to the student teacher helping with the drama club for the semester. Mike, a senior from Cal Poly, stands in the shadows on the other side of the stage. With his shaved head and multiple piercings, he looks more like a student than a teacher, but he's trying his best to offer guidance while Mr. Stark, the official sponsor, is busy.

"I think Gemma's right, Hannah," he says. "Why don't you give her a chance in the front?"

"But Miiiiikkke," Hannah whines, stretching his name into half a dozen syllables. "She's too tall."

"I am not. And I'm going to get stabbed to death in like two scenes. Can't I–"

"You girls work it out," Mr. Stark urges from the auditorium, where he's grading papers, clearly happy to let Hannah and Mike do the directing.

"You need to stay in the back," Hannah insists. "If you don't like it, you can quit. You're already going to miss the Saturday night performance, so–"

"That's *one* show out of six," Gemma protests. "And you said you'd fill in for me, tool."

"Maybe I've changed my mind, Sasquatch. I don't think it's fair for you to play a lead role when you're not going to be here for every performance."

Gemma growls with frustration. "Maybe you just wanted my part all along and are a nasty little bi–"

"Gemma, come on." Mike puts a calming hand on Gemma's back. Gemma takes a breath, relaxing slightly.

"Right, Gemma," Hannah says. "Everyone knows who the *witch* is around here."

"Girls! Please." Mr. Stark's seat squawks as he rises. "What's this about missing a performance, Gemma? When did this happen?"

"I have to miss Saturday night." Gemma sounds younger, nervous. I drop my brush in my water can and creep closer to the stage. "My parents are making me go to a rally in Santa Barbara Saturday night."

"Gemma, you made a commitment to this show."

Mr. Stark stands near the footlights, shaking his head. "You need to be here."

"I know. I swear, I know." The panic on Gemma's face surprises me. This seems important to her, despite the fact that she pretends to participate in drama club just to have an extra-curricular to put on her college resume. "But my dad is never going to let me out of it. I already begged a hundred thousand times."

"Can't Hannah fill in for her?" Mike asks. "She did all the choreography, and knows where Gemma's supposed to be on-stage."

"But Hannah's also the dream Maria in the dream ballet, and the best chorus dancer." Mr. Stark lets out a frustrated sigh. "It will be confusing for everyone to have her change roles for one night. I'm going to have to side with Hannah. It's not fair for Gemma to play a lead if she's not able to be here. Might as well cut the dream sequence and let Hannah step in as Bernadette now and–"

"But Mr. Stark!"

"I'm sorry, Gemma." Mr Stark pushes his glasses up his nose, looking more exhausted than sorry. "It would be different if we had an understudy who could take over for you, but we don't, and–"

"I'll do it," I say, stepping out onto the stage.

A strained silence falls over the cast, and twenty stunned glances crawl across my skin. Mr. Stark, Hannah, Gemma, all the other boys and girls in their dance rehearsal clothes– everyone stares at me like I've grown a second head. But then, a lot of them are in Mr. Stark's public speaking class, the one Ariel nearly failed because she's so petrified of getting up in front of a group of people.

No one knows how to respond. No one except Romeo, who laughs like I've told a fabulous joke. "I think that's a great idea. I'd love to see Ariel dance. And sing."

I can't sing, no matter what body I'm in. My voice is adequate on a good day and painful to listen to on a bad one. Romeo knows this, but I don't allow myself the luxury of glaring at him. I've already acted out of character by volunteering. Instead, I glance down at my feet, affecting Ariel's usual awkwardness. If I can pull this off, Gemma will owe me, and maybe she'll finally open up about what's happening with her and Ben.

"I don't have the best voice, but I know the music and words. I've been listening while I paint." It's true. Ariel has the show memorized. It would be hard not to after six weeks of rehearsal. "If Gemma teaches me the dance numbers, I can do it for one night. It'll be easier to pretend to be someone else than to . . . you know . . ."

"She could, Mr. Stark," Gemma says, though she doesn't sound entirely convinced. "I think it's a great idea."

"But she's never been onstage before," Mr. Stark says. "And singing voice aside, Ariel, there's a lot of dancing in the show. Can you dance?"

Can Ariel dance? She's never tried, but she's fairly coordinated and has been watching the others learn the choreography for weeks, and *I* can dance. I've already taken liberties with Ariel's personality. Might as well take one more in the name of winning Gemma's trust and devotion. "Sure. I can dance."

Hannah snorts—doubting my ability but unwilling to say anything outright—and turns to stare at Mr. Stark. The rest of the cast studies their shoes. Even Gemma doesn't say a word.

Mr. Stark sighs. "All right. It's not like this is Broadway." His glasses slip down to the end of his nose. "Look over the lines and music tonight and bring dance clothes tomorrow. You can shadow Gemma and learn the choreography in the next couple days. And give Gemma some time in the front, Hannah. She's one of the leads. The audience will want to see her in this scene."

"Thanks, Ariel. Thank you, Mr. Stark! You two are the best." Gemma gives me a giddy thumbs-up.

"Right." Mr. Stark shoves at his glasses and heads back to his seat. "Just be good this weekend, people, or I'll have to sponsor the yearbook instead of drama club next year. And I hate that layout program."

"All right, let's pick it up from just before Maria's entrance." Hannah wrinkles her nose at Gemma, who isn't hiding how pleased she is to have gotten the better of the other girl. "Shannon, back up the music."

I ease into the wings, ready to get back to work, but stop when I see someone crouched by the flats, washing a set of brushes in my dirty water. Even in the darkness, I know who it is.

Ben. Something in my gut twists and for a moment I'm dizzy, weightless, as if the floor has been ripped from beneath me, but I don't know which way to fall.

I shake my head. This has to stop. I can't go to pieces every time I see his face. I have to pull it together, be a good influence, make sure he commits to the love of his life and lives happily ever after.

"Hey, what's up?" I ask, managing a semi-normal tone.

"Hey." He stands up, fan brush in hand. "I came to help. If that's cool?"

I nod, try to smile. "Sure. That's great." It is. This is the perfect chance to make sure he knows I'm on Team Ben and Gemma, and maybe find some way to help make things better between them.

"I couldn't work art into my schedule, but the teacher said Ariel could probably use some help finishing the sets for the play. I figured that was you, so . . . yeah. . . ." He smiles. "You paint all these by yourself?"

"Yeah."

"You're crazy good."

I blush, even though most of the work isn't mine. "Thanks. You like to paint?"

"I live to paint," he says. "But I don't want to mess anything up. If you don't—"

"No, I can definitely use some help," I say. "And Gemma will love that you're here. She's onstage right now, but—"

"Yeah. I know. I heard." He turns, pulls another brush from the water and dries it on my towel. "That was cool of you to cover for her like that. I'd wet myself if I had to get up in front of a bunch of people."

I shrug and crouch down beside him to grab my palette, watching him mix cadmium white and a hint of yellow on his. "It's only for one night."

"It's still cool." He lifts his brush but hesitates before touching it to the flat. "Do you mind if I do some highlights on this side?"

"No. I mean, yeah, that's fine." I eye the area in question. His instincts are dead on. The bricks need something to counter the dark shadows I added. My respect for his skill grows as he works, adding texture and depth with deft touches of his brush.

"So I have a favor to ask," he says, visibly relaxing as he paints. I remember feeling like that, like the brush in your hand is a magic wand that banishes every care, leaches the worries from the day. "Come to dinner at my house tonight. My brother wants to meet you."

"Me?"

"Yeah. He was pissed when I came in late last night and he saw the broken window. He doesn't believe I was rescuing a damsel in distress," he says. "So I think you should come to dinner, show him your damselishness."

"My damselishness?"

He grins his crooked grin. "You'll like my family, and even if you hate them you'll love dinner. My sister-in-law is making ribs." He pauses, catching my eye. "You eat meat, right?"

"Yeah." Just the thought of ribs makes my mouth water. I missed lunch, and I've been so *hungry* since entering Ariel's body.

"So you have to come. Her ribs are crack for meat eaters."

I shoot him a look. "Sounds dangerous."

"Nah, I'll help you get your fix if you get addicted. She makes them all the time. My brother loves them, and she says food is the secret to a happy marriage."

"Food is the secret to a happy life." My stomach growls in agreement, making Ben laugh.

"See, you should come."

Ariel's mom is working late, so it isn't as if anyone's waiting for me at home, and spending more time with Ben and Gemma is definitely a good idea. "Okay," I say. "As long as Gemma doesn't mind."

Ben's next stroke hits too hard, leaving a clump of paint.

He reaches for his palette knife to scrape it off. "Um . . . Gemma's not . . . I didn't ask her."

"Why not?" What is wrong with these two? Soul mates usually can't get enough of each other. "Are you still fighting?"

"Not really. She's just . . ." He trails off with a shrug.

"Just what?"

"She's confusing," he says, sounding frustrated. "I mean, like, I had no idea you two were best friends. Gemma and I have been hanging out for a month and she never said a thing about you."

Ouch. That isn't going to make Ariel happy. "Well, I guess I'm not the most interesting person," I say, my joking tone falling flat.

"I think you're interesting. Best friends are always interesting. Who your friends are can say a lot about a person." Ben gives me a long look that makes my own brush feel awkward in my hand. "But you're too skinny. You should come eat."

"I . . . I'd love to." I wish I could leave it at that, but my time will be better spent with Gemma. Whatever's gone wrong with these two, it seems like she's the cause. Besides, spending more time alone with Ben probably isn't a good idea. "But I should go home and work on the understudy thing. I don't want to embarrass myself to death tomorrow."

"Cool. Some other time." His tone is easy, but his shrug isn't as loose. "But can I ask you something?"

"Sure." I add more shadows to the bricks on my side while Ben follows with the white and yellow. We're a good team. At this rate we'll have the bricks finished today, and Ben will have time to work some more creative touches into the background tomorrow while I'm rehearsing.

"Did Gemma tell you anything about me? About . . . us or whatever?"

"Um . . . no." I wish I could say something different. "She's been private lately. We haven't been talking as much. But I can tell she likes you."

"Really?" he asks, keeping his attention on his work.

"Yeah. It's obvious she cares about you." At least, it is to me, but Ben can't see Gemma's aura. Still, she *did* kiss him this morning, before he pulled away. He has to know that—

Something dances at the edge of my sight, a blur of blue— there and gone again faster than light reflecting on the water. It's the briefest flash, and I wouldn't turn to look . . . if it weren't for the smell that accompanies it. Rosemary and lavender, dust from a familiar field clinging to good satin, sunshine-warmed skin, and the impossible hint of sea salt, though Venice is a two day's journey by horse.

It's the smell of Verona, the smell of home, a scent that vibrates through my body, making my brush fall from my hand. Brown paint splatters across the floor, hitting my jeans and the bottom of the flat, leaving a mistake streaked across the bricks.

"What's wrong?" Ben asks, but I barely hear him over the blood rushing in my ears.

I spin so fast I nearly slip and fall, hurrying after the phantom scent, chasing it farther backstage, pushing aside thick red curtains that smell of damp and dust. But not the dust of home. That smell is gone, snatched away by sour water sitting in yellowed buckets marked *Processed Cheese* and *Thousand Island Dressing* and—

Another flash in the dark, royal blue slipping into the women's dressing room, the one Mr. Stark said was closed until they could patch the holes in the roof. It's a girl. She's moving slower now, slow enough for me to catch a glimpse of her fingers as they curl around the door, pulling it closed behind her. The smell comes again, mixed with honeyed bread and milk, triggering a pain in my stomach so strong it nearly makes me cry out. I remember licking that smell from my fingers, when I was small and Nurse would sneak a treat up to my room before supper. No other honey tastes like the honey from home, no other honey in the world.

I run to the door, pulse beating at my wrists and throat, and fling it open. What I see in the mirrors across the room makes my head spin, blurring the features of the girl in the reflection, twisting her open mouth into a bizarre half-moon.

But blurry vision or not, I can see the reddish-brown curls that fall nearly to the girl's waist, the wide, dark eyes that peer back into mine, the olive skin with cheeks pink from too much time in the sun.

It is . . . *me*. Myself. The body I was born into, the one I haven't seen in years but can never forget. No matter how hard I've tried.

"Love," she says. *"Now."*

The world spins faster as I stumble forward, scarcely able to walk a straight line but knowing I have to make it across the room. I have to touch her, press my hands against the mirror and pull her through the glass. I have to—

"Ariel?" I hear Ben come through the door behind me, but I don't stop. I can't. I can't lose sight of her, not for a second. No matter how dizzy I am. "Ariel, what are—" Ben breaks off as his arms wrap around my waist, holding me upright when my knees buckle. "What's wrong?"

I fist my hands in his sweater, willing the world to steady, but it doesn't. It reels like a child's toy set to spin on the floor, whirling so fast I squeeze my eyes closed to shut out the blurring colors. But still my head feels wrong, my skin too small, my lips numb, my fingers cramped, cold.

Perhaps I'm dying. Perhaps that brief vision of my old self was a sign that death—real death—has come for me at last.

"Hey, you've gotta calm down. Just try to breathe slower," Ben says, his voice soft in my ear. "I think you're hyperventilating."

Hyperventilating. The idea makes my chest hitch. I can't be doing this to myself, having some fit of vapors like the ones my cousin Rossa had every time she was lifted onto a horse. I'm not that type of girl. I don't lose control; I don't faint in the face of fear or danger.

I pull in a deeper breath and let it out, forcing all the air from my lungs before I draw another. Slowly—breath by breath—the spinning sensation fades, the warmth returns to the fingers clawed in Ben's sweater. Still, I leave them there as I glance at the mirror, knowing I'll need something to cling to if I see myself again.

I don't. There is only a tall, slim boy with dark hair holding an even slimmer girl with white hair and skin nearly as pale. The wide eyes that look back at me are still shocked, haunted. But they are blue eyes, not brown.

"Better?" Ben meets my eyes in the reflection, as if he knows it will be easier than talking face to face. I nod the slightest bit. Too much movement threatens to send the world spinning again.

"Do you want to go to the office? See if the school nurse is still here?" He shifts his arms, letting them drape about my waist in a way that's surprisingly familiar. The feeling that I've touched him before rushes back, and the words of the girl in the mirror ring in my ears. *Love now.*

Love. As if I'm capable of loving anyone. Now or anytime in the future. I must be losing my mind, finally giving in to—

"Ariel?" Ben's arms tighten around me. "I can come with you."

"No. I'm okay." I know I should step back, but I can't seem to get my hands to release his sweater.

Was it really a hallucination? Or is this some new Ambassador magic? And if so, why would I see myself? There is no "me" anymore. I died so long ago my bones must have turned to dust by now.

"You don't seem okay. Are you sure you don't want to talk? About . . . anything?"

I shake my head again. "No."

"Okay." His eyes leave the mirror as he turns to me. "But if you ever want to . . . I know you don't know me very well, but you can trust me. I can keep a secret."

The words make me shiver. And step away. There is no one I can trust with my secrets. No one.

"Hey, you want to get out of here?" he asks. "We can clean up the paints and go get a coffee or something. We can text Gemma and see if she wants to meet us when rehearsal is over."

A coffee is probably the last thing I need, but it sounds good. Safe. Warm. And Gemma will come join us, and maybe I can make something out of this mess of a day. I nod. "That sounds great. I . . ."

I forget what I'd planned to say, forget everything but the cold rush of fear. Romeo stands in the doorway, watching Ben and me with narrowed eyes. But it isn't Romeo who makes my hand fly to my mouth, stifling the scream rising in my throat. It's the *thing* behind him. A few feet beyond the rectangle of dressing-room light, crouched in the backstage darkness, is a monster, a creature from nightmares with a skeletal body, leathered skin, and two inhuman eyes drowning in creeping white. The curls that fall over its forehead are the same as the ones that earned Romeo strange looks in the halls today. Exactly the same.

It is Romeo. The *real* Romeo. But rotten. Wrong. A corpse come to life.

Before I can think of what to do, the thing vanishes, snapped away without a trace but for a whisper of decay that drifts through the air.

I swallow and fight to keep the panic from my voice. "Hi, Dylan," I say.

Ben turns, and his expression grows hard, angry. "What do you want?"

Romeo meets Ben's glare with a smile. "I wanted to apologize to you about your car window. I'll pay for the damage, of course. I just wasn't myself last night. *Lo siento, hermano.*"

"I'm not your brother, *chiflado*," Ben says, his tone leaving no doubt that *chiflado* isn't a friendly word.

Romeo laughs. "You're right. Of course." In the distance, I hear Hannah call Dylan's name. He glances over his shoulder, before turning back to us with a sad face. "I suppose I've got to go. See you both later."

"Not if we can help it," Ben says to Romeo's retreating back. He shifts his gaze to me, eyes softening once more. "He's full of crap. I've got two classes with him, and he didn't bother to apologize before. He only said that to look good in front of you."

"He'll never look good to me, no matter how many apologies he gives." My voice still trembles.

"I just can't believe his hand isn't more messed up. He should have broken—"

"I'm sorry, but I've got to get home." I have to try to contact Nurse again. Now.

"But I thought coffee sounded great."

"It did. It does. I just . . . I've got to go. I'm sorry." I edge toward the door. "But you and Gemma should go. I know she'd love that. Tell her I'll call her, okay?"

"Okay." Ben sounds confused, and he has every right to be, but I don't have time to explain, even if I could. Which I can't. I have no idea what's going on.

I grab my backpack from the floor and dash out the back of the theater into the downpour. I make it all the way to the student parking lot before I realize I don't have a ride home.

I curse and spin in an angry circle, kicking one of the puddles at my feet.

Gemma drove me. How could I have forgotten?

I briefly entertain the thought of going back to play practice but decide against it. Ben already thinks I'm unstable, maybe even flat-out crazy. I don't need to do anything to reinforce that opinion. I need him to trust me, to be a person he listens to and confides in. I have to find another way home. The bus, or my own two feet. It isn't *that* far. Maybe two miles, three at the most.

I start walking. And walk. And walk. And walk. Through the town and into the country, down the highway in the mud at the side of the road with cars splashing my legs as they drive by. By the time I reach the turnoff for El Camino, it's nearly dark and those three miles I've slogged through the rain feel like a hundred. There's no denying it, I'm not in top form. I still haven't achieved anything resembling supernatural strength.

Whether it's my poor diet since I arrived or the stress of this shift or something else entirely, I don't know, but I feel . . . wrong. I need Nurse, more than I have since my first days as an Ambassador. Surely she will come to me now. One of the mirrors in this house will work. It *has* to.

I let myself in the front door and drop my keys in the dish, shivering and exhausted and desperate to talk to someone who understands.

"Look who finally made it home. You look like a drowned rat."

But not *that* desperate. Not desperate enough to talk to the boy waiting for me in the hallway outside my room. Romeo slumps casually against the doorframe, grinning as if he has every right to be there.

I freeze, wishing I'd taken Ben up on that cup of coffee. At least then I'd be properly caffeinated, which might help when it comes time to fight for my life.

TEN

I run, hoping to make it to the living room or kitchen before he reaches me. The hallway is too cramped. There'll be no room to defend myself. It will be the car all over again, and this time I might not come out whole on the other side.

"Wait! Juliet, wait!"

I don't wait. I run faster, jumping over the red chair near the television and lunging for the front door. I have the knob in my hand when he grabs me from behind and spins me back into the room. I fall to my knees, groaning as the sharp corner of the coffee table jams into my stomach. Pain flashes through my midsection, but I'm back on my feet in seconds, bending my knees and lifting my fists, bracing myself for the inevitable attack.

"I didn't come to fight," Romeo shouts, raising his arms in a defensive position. "I want to talk. That's all I've wanted all day."

"Talk."

"Yes, talk. Chat? Have . . . verbal intercourse?" He winks, and I fight the urge to show him what I think of him with my middle finger.

"I don't want to talk."

"Oh, but you will. I have secrets to share."

"I don't care." I nod toward the door. "Get out. I'm not interested in your lies."

"Lies? When have I lied?" His hands drift to his sides, but his wary look remains. If I attack him, he'll be ready. I have to wait, to seize on a moment when his defenses are truly down. "I've never lied."

"And we killed ourselves to prove our perfect, timeless love." I spit the words with enough venom to poison a hundred young lovers, then curse myself for it. I shouldn't let him know how that false history still gets to me. I shouldn't give him such an easy victory.

His chin tilts down, but I can see the smile tugging at his lips. "Well, perhaps I did lie . . . just that once."

"Get out," I say through gritted teeth.

His eyes come back to mine. "But I honestly never dreamt Shakespeare's work would be so enduring." He wanders over to the table by the door and plucks a quarter from the key dish, tossing the coin in the air and catching it with an easy flick of his wrist. "I found his verse lovely, of course, but the tragedy of Romeo and Juliet itself is a rather immature work, more reminiscent of his comedies than—"

"Leave. Now." My every muscle is tensed and ready. What is he planning to do with that quarter? Hurl it at my face and hope to put an eye out? With Romeo anything can become a weapon—love, trust . . . loose change.

"And then what?" he asks. "You'll come give me a proper whipping? You know I enjoy your hands on me, Jules, no matter what they're doing there." He rolls the coin across his knuckles and back again while I try to keep my temper. "And knowing how close these bodies came to intimacy before we entered them, I've been dying to—"

Temper lost.

I reach for the closest weapon at hand, snatching the base of the lamp, yanking its cord free of the wall as I toss the shade to the ground. "Get out, or I will beat you. And I won't use my hands."

"Wait!" Romeo drops the coin, his smile slipping. "Please . . . hear me out. I haven't lied about anything that's mattered. I've always played fair. More than fair. In your heart you know that."

I roll my eyes.

"Please, I just want this to be over," he says. "We can put an end to it, without the sacrifice of a soul. But only here, only now. This is our one chance to take back what we lost."

"What you stole."

He sighs again. "You still believe it was all *my* doing?"

"You locked me in a tomb and left me to die."

"The past." He starts toward me but stops when I lift the lamp over my head. "The past can't be changed, but the future . . . the future can be yours. Life, love, everything you've longed for. You don't have to return to the mist. You can stay here. *I* can stay here with you."

I laugh. He's so absurd I can't help myself. "I don't want you with me. I want you to go to hell, where you belong."

"There is no hell," he says, lips tightening. "There is only the earth and the mist and the places where the high ones go, where they will *never* allow us to enter."

"Perhaps you haven't encountered hell yet, but your punishment is coming. Someday, you will suffer."

Fear flashes in Romeo's eyes, making me wonder if he's actually telling the truth. Maybe we are at the end of our long journey and he's genuinely afraid of what will come next.

"You want me to be punished. I understand that," he says. "But you don't have to wait for someday. I've *already* suffered. Every minute I've spent with you as my enemy has been an eternity of torment. Pretending to hate you, being forced to turn and kill innocent people, it is—"

"Enough." I shake my head, scattering his lies into the air. I've seen him revel in a kill. He's an abomination and takes pride in the fact. The only question is why he's suddenly working so hard to convince me otherwise. "Why are you here? What do you want?"

"I want your love."

"You will *never* have it," I say, exasperation thinning my voice. "Never."

"Hm." He has the nerve to look disappointed. In me. It's nearly enough to make me slam the lamp down on his skull. "Give me a chance to explain. It might make you rethink everything you—"

"I don't care what you—"

"I'll tell you the truth this time, everything about the world of the Mercenaries. There is nothing to prevent me," Romeo says, flicking on the companion to the lamp in my hand. Light blushes into the room, illuminating his features, revealing a look of such sincerity that something inside me demands that I listen. "For me, hell is a place on earth. I inhabit the mortal realm but enjoy none of the comforts of humanity. I wear any corpse I choose but am never a part of the world."

"I weep for you."

"Perhaps you would, if you understood." He falls onto the couch, his handsome face suddenly haggard. "I can no longer experience physical sensation. Nothing. Not ever. Not in these bodies we inhabit when we are called, not in the bodies I steal when I am alone. No taste, no smell, no touch. I believe the high Mercenaries allow me to see and hear only because I require those senses to function."

"No scent? None at all?"

"None," he says.

"Not even my *sweet breath*?" I ask, sarcasm ripening each word. "So you lied about that, as well?"

"A white lie." He shrugs. "As is the case with many compliments men give their women."

"I am not *your* woman, and I couldn't care less if—"

"Listen to me. Hear me." He jumps back to his feet. "I can feel no pleasure. Very little pain. No hunger, no thirst, not the sun or the rain on my skin, not the shiver of touch, not the pressure of a kiss. Wine passes through me without effect, not even to make me sleep. I can't sleep, not ever," he whispers, the madness in his eyes almost enough to make me believe him. Imagining an existence such as he describes makes my soul scream. "There is nothing but a deep, aching emptiness that I would do anything to escape."

"Then escape. Put an end to yourself." I refuse to pity him, not when he's brought it all upon himself. "I'll fetch you a knife from the kitchen. If you cut out your heart, that should–"

"I can't. The Mercenaries don't hesitate to punish their converts. The high ones will torture me if I try. They will trap me in a corpse but deny me the release of death, returning my senses only so that I might know what it feels like for a human body to rot all around me. I've seen it happen to others. They make us watch such things . . . as cautionary displays."

I fight to keep my face blank, to force the image of Romeo's real body–already rife with decay–from my mind. I can't think about what that vision might mean right now. I can't risk letting Romeo know my secrets.

"The only happiness I will ever have is what I steal. Now is the time to steal it, the time to take back what we lost." He steps closer, and this time, I let him. "I could have killed you a hundred times. If I had, I would have been granted a higher position in the order, but I couldn't end your life."

"Because I didn't let you."

"Because the part of me that remembers what it was like all those lifetimes ago still cares for you . . . loves you."

I choke on my next breath.

"I know you think you can't love me. But you must know how sorry I am. So sorry," he says, his voice thick, a shine in his stolen eyes.

Rage surges beneath my skin, so hot it feels as if it will burn me from the inside out. "Don't you dare cry for me. Don't you dare," I warn in a tight whisper.

"We must love each other again. Now." He continues as if he hasn't heard me. I shiver. *Love now.* I heard the same words earlier today, from my own lips. But surely she . . . *I* . . . couldn't mean that I'm supposed to love Romeo. It's . . . impossible. "I found the spell years ago—the one that will free us— but I had to wait until a sign came that it was time. I believe I've seen such a sign."

I bite my lip. The temptation to speak, to tell him the things I saw nearly rips me in two. But I can't. He is the enemy. He is my murderer, a monster, and a liar of unparalleled skill.

"For the first time in all my centuries," he says, "I'm certain they aren't listening. There isn't a single Mercenary wandering these streets. There should be a dozen or more in a town this size."

"Really? And how would you know?"

"Mercenary converts can see the auras of all transformed people. Black for our kind, gold for yours, pink and red for our darling lovers," he says, obviously pleased to share that he has some powers I do not. "But there are none of them here. This is *our* time. I can tell you the secrets I've learned. I can tell you how to reclaim a human life."

"And why would you do that?" I will my heart not to beat any faster, refuse to indulge the hope he's sparked inside me.

"You deserve it. You deserve an eternity of pleasure. And you can have it. All you have to do is trust me, and love me . . . just a little."

"Never. I will never, ever love you," I whisper, shocked that even a madman could believe such a thing possible.

"You could. I know it. I can see it in your eyes," he says, determination twitching in his jaw. "And if you can, we can be human again. With bodies that live and breathe, and the freedom to do as we please. Forever."

Forever. It's what he made me promise on our wedding night, the lie he begged me to tell. He's still so unchanged, despite his diseased mind and his hundreds of years of life. But I am not. Now the thought of forever makes me tired. Frightened. Sad. What is forever worth? When love is so fragile and even one human life so long?

"I don't want to live forever."

"You would," he says as I take a step back, closer to the kitchen, where the knives wait in the drawer next to the sink. "If you weren't a slave, you would."

"I'm no one's—"

"They aren't what they've told you they are. They aren't angels sent from heaven."

"They never said they were."

"They aren't the good ones either. Did they tell you that? They're just the losing team, the people who picked the wrong side of the coin." Another step and another, until he stands in the doorway to the kitchen and my back is pressed against the counter. I could have a knife in my hand in seconds. A part of me screams to arm myself before it's too late. The other part knows Romeo isn't here to attack me. He really has come to talk, to tell me this crazy story I shouldn't believe.

Shouldn't. Not . . . *couldn't.*

There are so many things Nurse hasn't told me. Why has she kept me in the dark? Why, if not to hide the fact that the Ambassadors aren't as pure and wonderful as I've been led to believe? What if Romeo is telling the truth? What if . . .

"They're using you," he says, playing to my secret fears. "And lying to you, and you will never, *ever* be free of them if you don't listen. This is a chance that comes but once in an afterlife. I can see that you're curious." He shakes his head sadly. "It makes me wonder what they've told you. Probably that they're protecting you with your ignorance. Saving you from the big bad wolves."

He knows. Somehow he knows what the Ambassadors tell their converts and is using that knowledge to manipulate me.

"Get out." The fact that he's tempted me—even for a moment—is terrifying.

"Don't believe their lies. If you make the wrong choice, your next trip to the mist will be your last. You will be trapped there forever, never human again, a prisoner of your own—"

"Get out of my house!"

"This isn't *your* house," he says. "No more than anything has been yours in hundreds of years. It may seem like a passing instant, but I *know* how the centuries stretch on, wrapping around you like a snake that refuses to squeeze the life out of you, no matter how you beg."

I keep my face still, trying not to give any sign that I know exactly what he's talking about, that the years I've spent as an Ambassador haven't passed as easily as he assumes.

"I know you think I'm a liar, but I promise you: this is our one—"

"Why?" I break. I can't help myself. I need to know what he knows. "Why now? Why is everything different? Why can't I contact Nurse in the mirror? Why am I so weak?"

He takes a deep breath and lets out a satisfied sigh. "So your powers are fading too. I thought maybe . . . But if it's the same for both of us, this must be the end." He jumps into the air, landing with a loud clap of his hands. "And to think a part of me still doubted."

He laughs his usual devilish laugh. I drop the lamp and reach for a knife. The butcher knife with the serrated edge, the one I can imagine swiping through the air to cut the grin from his wretched face.

"Out!" I brace myself, expecting him to come for me. But he doesn't. He turns and ambles to the front door, a swing in his step I don't care for. At all.

"We'll talk again soon. We have some time." He glances over his shoulder. "But think about what I've said, and don't be surprised if you have an unexpected visitor."

"You're not a visitor. You're a menace."

"I wasn't talking about me," Romeo says, a haunted note in his voice that makes the hairs at the back of my neck stand on end.

Is he having visions too? Of *his* corpse? *Mine?* Both? When I saw myself I wasn't rotted, but maybe he's seen something different. I'm dying to ask, but I bite my lip. I can't trust him. The past few minutes have made that clear. He's been pumping me for information, prepared to tell whatever lies it takes to get what he needs.

"If you have any questions, you can shoot me an email," he continues. "My contact information is on the cast sheet."

I shake my head numbly. He *has* to be joking. He can't really expect me to send him an *email*. About whether or not I can love him again, or am interested in an eternity apart from the Ambassadors. You don't *email* someone about something like that. You don't *email* a fiend who promised to love you, then locked you away in the dark and *murdered* you in cold blood.

But he doesn't understand. And he's not joking.

The hand holding the knife falls to my side. "You're insane. I won't work with you. Ever."

"Oh, I think you will. If you don't"—Romeo's eyebrows arch—"then I'll have to do what I've been sent here to do. If I'm not free by the end of this shift, I'll be renegotiating another term of service with the Mercenaries. I'm certain they'll be more *generous* if I bring a soul to our side while I'm here. It shouldn't be difficult. The girl is a train wreck. I'll have her turned against Ben before the week is out."

My hand clenches around the handle of the knife.

"Eternity, spent away from all those people she hates . . ." Romeo lingers, his fingers thrumming on the door. "It's not the worst carrot to dangle."

"Eternity in a prison of dead flesh," I say. "Doesn't sound that tempting."

"But she won't know the truth. She'll believe what I tell her. They always do, especially the young ones." He's calm, stating the facts, and I know Gemma well enough to worry he might be right. She loathes Dylan, but Romeo might be able to reach her if he tells the right lies, plays to the right fears.

"Take care, sweet." Romeo opens the door just as a bolt of lightning rips across the sky. The storm has progressed from threatening to raging, complete with thunder that booms out a warning for all living things to remain hidden away. I wince but don't close my eyes. I've learned the hard way not to take my attention off my former love. Not for a second. "Let me know when you're ready to move forward. I swear to you, we can have that happiness you've given so many lucky people."

"I'd rather die than make you happy."

Romeo stills, and an emotion remarkably like grief flits across his face. "I hope you'll change your mind. Soon." He inclines his head. "Good-bye, Juliet."

I grit my teeth and watch him go, refusing to wish him a good anything, even something as small as a farewell.

ELEVEN

Thirty minutes later—after failing to reach Nurse in the mirror yet again—I'm back in the kitchen with a peanut butter sandwich and a glass of milk. Melanie went to the store while I was at school, and the refrigerator is filled with more vaguely edible food. Just looking at the piles of slimy gray lunch meat wrapped in plastic makes me ill, but at least there is milk and fresh bread.

Milk. Bread. Peanut butter.

I chew, examining each taste as it evolves in my mouth. It's hardly a lavish dinner, but at least I can *taste* it. What would it be like to have that taken away? What would it be like not to feel the chill of the glass in my hand, or smell the wheat and roasted nuts? What would it be like not to have felt another person's touch in over seven hundred years?

It is . . . unimaginable, almost enough to summon a spark of pity.

"He could be lying," I remind myself, voice soft beneath the patter of the rain.

He could be, but he isn't. Not about that.

Maybe not about any of it. The more I turn things over in my head, the more I wonder things that are dangerous to wonder. What does Romeo know? Is there really some magic that can give me back my life? Do I dare to hear him out? Do I dare to consider–

The phone rings, making me jump guiltily. I push my chair back and hurry to grab the phone from the counter. "Hello?"

"Are you alone in the house?" an artificially deep voice asks.

My forehead wrinkles. "Who is this?"

"Are you alone . . . in the house?"

The voice isn't Romeo's, but I don't have the patience for prank calls. I'm not in the mood for torment from Romeo or anyone else. "I'm hanging up."

"No! Wait!" Gemma's tone rises to her normal register. "I'm sorry. I was just joking. I'm on my way to your place. Is your mom there?"

"No, she's working the night shift," I say, relief spreading through my chest. Perfect. I need to talk to Gemma, to focus on doing my job, even if I can't reach Nurse or the other Ambassadors. Gemma's visit is a sign that it's time to stop thinking about Romeo.

No good ever came from listening to the snake in the garden.

"Cool," Gemma says. "You want me to grab some burgers or something? I'd get pizza, but I don't want to get out of the car. This rain is dampening my will to live."

I glance at my half-eaten sandwich. I'm still starving. "A cheeseburger would be great. With fries, and a chocolate milk shake. Malted if they have it."

"Hungry, are we?" Gemma laughs. "I'll be there in fifteen. Pour me a glass of whatever cheap hooch your mom's got in the fridge. Chardonnay, not the pinot grigio crap."

I hang up. Fifteen minutes. It's just enough time to grab a shower and change out of my wet clothes. If I hurry. I run for the bathroom, gathering a pair of blue flannel pajamas with sheep on them while the water warms. It's a cool night and likely to get cooler if the rain doesn't stop.

I rush through my shower, concentrating on the shampoo, conditioner, and soap, clearing my mind, focusing on my job. By the time Gemma pulls into the carport and bursts into the kitchen, I'm calmer than I've been all day.

"Where's my wine, woman?" Gemma booms as she stumbles to the table with a load of brown bags and paper cups. The smell of warm meat and cheese, pickles and onions, drifts through the air, making my mouth water. Cheeseburgers. I'm fairly certain they're the most wonderful food invented by modern man.

"Hope you don't mind a plastic cup." I grab one from the cabinet before reaching into the fridge. "Is Viognier okay? The chardonnay's not open."

"Oh yes. Viognier pairs well with anything, dahling," she drawls. While I pour her drink, Gemma dumps cheeseburgers onto the table and settles into a chair with her sandwich. "I'm starving. That singing and dancing crap works up a fracking appetite. Which reminds me—" She squeals and turns, grabbing the plastic cup from my hand before I can set it down. "Thank you! Most awesome friend! You snuck out before I could tell you thank you, thank you, a thousand times *thank you*!"

I smile. Gemma's not so bad when she's happy. She's actually . . . charming, and I can see why Ariel enjoys spending time with her.

"You're welcome." I settle in across from her and reach for my burger. "Thanks so much, I was dying for some real food."

"No, thank *you*. The grease feast was the least I could do after you saved my life."

"It's not a big deal."

"It *is* a big deal. Especially for you." Gemma takes a gulp of her wine. "I know you're probably scared out of your mind, but we'll go through all the songs tonight and you'll learn the choreography super fast. You killed at Dance Dance Revolution when we were little, and this isn't much harder. Hannah has everyone changing lines and running around a lot, but the steps are easy. I wanted to do something harder, but buzzkill Mike said the boys look dumb if the girls' steps are too complicated. As if anything can make those losers look good."

"Mike?" I mumble around a mouthful of burger.

"You know, Mr. Stark's student teacher, the one with all the tats?"

"Oh right."

"You'd think with all the body art, he'd be cooler," she says. "But still, he's kind of hot, right? In a weird sort of way?"

"Gemma, he's practically a teacher." I don't bother to hide my distaste. She's in love with Ben; she shouldn't be considering the hotness of other guys. "That's gross."

She smiles. "Not as gross as crushing on Mr. Stark. I swear Hannah would lick his shiny bald head if she could." I make a face and Gemma laughs. "For real. She's such a kiss-ass. And all her little dancer friends are professionally lame." She shakes her head and throws a fry back into its box. "People here suck. I can't wait to graduate."

"But Ben seems cool," I say, watching her reaction. "He helped me with the sets today. He said he was going to ask you to go out for coffee after–"

"He did," she says, suddenly very interested in the bottom of her cup. "We went to the Windmill, but it was closed early, so we just sat in my car and talked. It was . . . good. I think we understand each other."

"That's great!" It's also a huge relief. Maybe this mission won't be as hard as I thought. "He's so nice."

"He really is. It's hard to believe he ever–" Gemma breaks off with a guilty look and takes another drink of her wine. "This is pretty good. Your mother's taste is improving."

"Hard to believe he ever what?" I ask, waiting for a second before pushing harder. "I thought we were going to talk."

"Do we have to?" Gemma whines, stuffing more fries in her mouth. "Can't we just sing about how the Sharks rock and how we're going to pound Jet face at the school dance? That song is fun. Let's sing."

"I'm still eating, and you're not supposed to sing within thirty minutes of eating."

"That's swimming, dork."

"No, it's singing, doofus."

Gemma cocks her head. "Well, well, aren't we sassy today."

I swallow and remind myself not to overdo it with the

confidence. I shrug and reach for my milk shake. "My best friend has been holding out on me. It makes me sassy."

"Understandable." Gemma sighs as she mops ketchup off her fingers with a napkin. "It's mostly my dad. He's been making my life hell. Did you hear that he's thinking of running for the Senate?"

"No. I haven't really—"

"Of course you haven't." She rolls her eyes. "Who has? Who cares? I mean, the entire government is corrupt anyway. It's beyond saving. We might as well burn Washington, blow up Fox News, and start over."

"But your dad doesn't agree."

"Of course not. He wants to be a Super-Important Big-Shot Douche, and doesn't care how miserable he has to make me to do it. He's gone completely over the edge."

"What do you mean?"

"I mean, getting on my Facebook to check for 'content' and stealing my cell phone every few days is no longer enough to entertain him," she says, the bitterness in her voice making me feel for her. "I think he read my diary."

"What!" I can't imagine anything more embarrassing than having someone else read your private thoughts. Especially a parent. "That's repulsive."

"That's Bob Sloop," Gemma says. "Anyway, something he read made him think I was doing drugs. He started looking around and he found some pot, the stuff I got from Niles a few months ago?"

"Niles . . ." The name doesn't ring any bells. I don't think Ariel met him.

"You know? The priv-ass school loser I was dating before Christmas? The one with the breath that smelled like dog food?" She waves her hand in the air before starting to stuff empty wrappers back into paper bags. "Whatever. It doesn't matter. Niles gave me some BC Bud before we broke up, as some kind of Christmas present or something. I had it in one of my old makeup bags and forgot about it. Dad found it and went crazy. I told him I'd only smoked a couple times and it wasn't a big deal, but he kept freaking out."

"What about your mom?" I ask. "She's let you drink wine since you were sixteen. Didn't she think—"

"I know, right? You'd think she'd be cool, but she's completely up Dad's butt about this Senate thing." Gemma crosses to the trash can and shoves the bags in with too much force. "She totally wants to move to Washington and socialize with a wider variety of snotty, ass-faced people. She didn't say *anything*, even when Dad made me go to this rehab group for 'troubled teens.' They both know I don't have a problem, they're just . . . assholes." She rolls her eyes again and flops back into her chair. "So yeah, that's where I've been every Monday and Wednesday morning. And why I stopped picking you up. Sorry."

"Oh, Gemma. You should have told me." I'm starting to feel for this girl. With a family like hers, it's amazing she's not more of a mess.

"I know." She shrugs. "It's just so stupid and I was so mad. I swear, I thought about running away from home and becoming a woman of the night or something just to ruin Dad's chances of getting elected." She tips her drink back, emptying the cup, and sets it back on the table with a sigh. "But then . . . I met Ben, and he made it bearable, you know? He started coming to the group about a month ago. He drove in from Lompoc until his brother made him move."

The news surprises me. "But Ben doesn't seem like he's got a drug problem. Not that you do, but–"

"No, he doesn't. He just got arrested."

My eyebrows shoot up. Ben? Arrested?

"He lost his temper and smashed some guy's face in."

"What?"

"And broke his nose," she says casually, as if it's no big deal. "And knocked out a couple of teeth."

"What!" I can't imagine Ben hitting someone, especially hard enough to break a bone. He seems so . . . gentle.

But what about that first moment in the car? What about the look on his face when Romeo called him his brother?

It's true. I don't know him as well as I think. Maybe I'm wrong about him. Maybe it's Ben's violence that's keeping him and Gemma apart, not anything to do with her at all.

"I know that sounds bad, but he'd *never* done anything like that before. It was just a horrible random night. He's a really decent guy, and I've never even seen him angry. At least, not angry like that . . ." She trails off, goes for a drink, and finds her cup empty. "Can I get more? Do you think your mom will notice?"

"She probably won't. And if she does . . ." I shrug.

Gemma smiles as she heads to the fridge. "Aren't you turning into a rebel? Maybe I can finally convince you to come raid the casks in the barn with me. It's fun. And I figured out how to turn off the security cameras so we won't get caught."

"Maybe," I say, dying to get back to the real story. "So . . . are you sure you feel safe? You know, with Ben?"

Gemma spins, wine bottle in hand. "Totally! And you should too. Please, don't think anything bad about him. This is why I didn't want to say anything about how we met until you saw how nice he is."

"No, I agree, he seems really–"

"He really *is*," she says, but something in her voice still doesn't sit well. "I was going to introduce you guys after he settled in with his brother, but we had that dumb fight." She lifts her right hand, as if to ward off any impending criticism. "But it wasn't because of him. It's me."

"Gemma, it can't be *all*–"

"No, it is. And I shouldn't have kissed him this morning. I knew it would piss him off." She sticks the wine back in the fridge and chucks her plastic cup into the sink, apparently rethinking her second glass of wine. "I don't even know why I did it," she says, voice softer. "Sometimes I think I'm crazy, you know? I just can't stop myself from doing the opposite of what I know I *should* do." She stares down at her feet, looking so young, so at odds with herself. Ben's right; Gemma isn't a bad person, she's just confusing, just–

A train wreck.

Romeo's words float through my mind, making me angry. Gemma might be troubled, but she isn't a wreck. There's still hope for her. And for Ben.

"You're not crazy."

"No, I probably am." She crosses her arms and leans against the kitchen counter. "I introduced Ben to my dad last week."

"That's not crazy. Why shouldn't you–"

"Ariel, wake up from happily-ever-after land. My dad had a heart attack, even before he did the background check and found out Ben's been arrested. It was awful. You know he's convinced Mexicans are taking over the 'real' America. Remember how he freaked out when they started having translators at parent-teacher night?"

"But doesn't your dad hire Mexican workers for the vineyards?"

"Of course he does, because he wants cheap labor. But that doesn't mean he can't also hate Mexicans living in the United States. Bob is a selfish paradox wrapped in an evil burrito, Ree." Gemma picks at one of the plumber magnets on the side of the fridge, peeling it off and then smashing it back on again. "I've shielded you from his loathsomeness, but I thought you knew that by now. Anyway, as soon as I got back from taking Ben home, Dad told me I couldn't see him again. And the sick thing is . . . I *knew* he would. But I brought Ben over anyway." She turns to me, dark eyes glittering. "I really am crazy."

"You're not crazy. Your dad is crazy, and wrong," I say. "Everyone here was from a different country at some point, and everyone makes mistakes."

I wish I could take a stronger stand for Ben, but I need to know what really happened first. Why did he break someone's nose? It's so strange to imagine him hurting anyone or anything, troubling in a way that goes beyond my usual concern about my soul mates.

"I know," Gemma says. "But I don't want to have that fight right now. I'm so close to going to college and getting away from him. And it would be pointless, anyway. Bob never listens or changes his mind. About anything." She crosses the room to steal the rest of my unfinished milk shake. "You should have seen how I begged him to let me skip his stupid rally Saturday night. But he didn't care because *my* life is never going to be as important as *his* life."

"But what about Ben? He really likes you." He doesn't just *like* her, he *loves* her, and Gemma seems more worried about her dad than the boy who's her soul mate. Ben is Gemma's One. She has to wake up and fight for him. Now.

"You think?" Gemma swallows, her face pale in the glare of the overhead lights. "But how do I know any guy is worth fighting my family and . . . everything else for? It's just scary. You know?"

Her words help me breathe easier. There's nothing that can strangle the life out of love faster than fear. If she's this afraid, no wonder she and Ben are having problems. She needs to get past her fear and concentrate on loving him, and I have to help her do it. No matter how much it hurts.

"I *guess* it's scary, but I bet it's also amazing. Meeting Ben could be the best thing that ever happened to you."

"Maybe, maybe not . . ." Gemma narrows her eyes. "But you can't be trusted. You've only known him for a day and a half. I can't believe he's the one who gave you a ride. How crazy is that? And how crazy are *you* for hitchhiking?" She chucks me on the arm. "You're just lucky Ben stopped instead of some psycho. But then, I guess you were in the car with a psycho already, so . . ."

"Ben and I had a good talk last night," I say, trying not to think about how good it was. "I think he's special. He'd be worth—"

"Okay, fine," she says, rolling her eyes. "I'll call him and invite him over to my place after school tomorrow."

"Great!"

"But I'm not going to tell Dad," she warns, pointing an accusing finger at me. "We'll sneak in the back gate after play practice. We can hit the barrels in the barn and celebrate your success as an understudy."

"We?"

"You're coming too, my lovely." Gemma grabs my hand and pulls me into the living room.

"But—"

"No buts. I've decided, and you know I'm the boss," she says, putting an end to the discussion. "Okay, so I've got the entire sound track for *West Side Story* with and without vocals. You want to sing with other people first or just go straight into it hard-core?"

"With the voices first." I watch her plug the phone into the sound system beneath the television, and try to tamp down the anxiety rising in my throat. It's just a little singing; how horrible can I be?

"Oh, come on, be hard-core, Ree!" Gemma turns back to me with a smile as music swells through the room. "Let's do it without the voices. You know all the words!"

"I know, but—"

"Sing!"

"But—"

"Sing!"

And so I do. And Gemma laughs, and finally I do too, giggling as my voice fights its way up and down. It cracks when I try to hold a note for too long but finds its way if I keep moving. I could be worse. At least I don't think I'll scar the audience for life.

By the time we finish going over some of the choreography and Gemma heads for her car, I've decided the night hasn't gone too badly. Gemma and Ariel are reconnecting, I'm making headway convincing Gemma to take her relationship with Ben seriously, and I have plans to spend time with both of them tomorrow.

And there are worse ways to spend time than with a friend, fried food, and singing and dancing like a fool. Sometimes it's easy to forget that fighting for love isn't all angst and despair and trying not to get killed. Sometimes it's an amazing job.

And sometimes it's not. Later, I lie in the dark, staring at the ceiling, doubt creeping in beneath the rhythm of the rain.

What if Romeo's right? What if this is your last shift? What if the next time you go to the mist you never come back? Or what if there's something worse than the mist . . . something unknown . . . ?

I close my eyes and pull the covers over my head, trying not to worry, determined not to dream.

TWELVE

"Get down, you two! Under the blanket!" Gemma hisses from the front seat as we pull up to the imposing back gate of the Sloop home the next afternoon.

The family compound is so large we can't even *see* the mansion from here. We'd have to drive miles to get to the house on the hill, through rolling vineyards and stands of fruit trees wilting in the never-ending rain. It's beginning to feel like the world will be swept away. Or at least Central California.

"Do we really have to do this?" Ben eyes the ratty Navajo blanket Gemma throws into the backseat. "I didn't hide under a blanket last time."

I shoot Gemma a questioning look that she avoids. So she

hasn't told him that she's been forbidden to see him. I don't know whether that's a good sign or bad one.

"Last time we weren't invading my father's turf," she says. "If anyone notices we've been in the cellars, I don't want my dad to find out you two were here this afternoon."

"A camera records everyone who comes through the gate," I say, forcing a smile as I lift the edge of the blanket. "Gemma's dad is kind of crazy about trespassers."

Ben lifts an eyebrow. "Okay, but if he's going to get so pissed, then—"

"He won't get pissed because we won't get caught," Gemma says.

"But—"

"Ben, are you going to play super-secret spy nicely? Or am I going to have to pull this car over and show you my ninja moves?"

"Don't make her show you the ninja moves." I try to keep the moment light. "They're scary, and I think my singing has traumatized everyone enough for one day."

Gemma snorts in agreement.

My voice didn't improve much during rehearsal this afternoon. Mr. Stark gave away most of my singing lines and urged me to talk my way through my one unavoidable solo. Thankfully, my feet proved nimbler than my tongue. I remembered all the choreography Gemma taught me, and put such passion into the fight scene with Tony that even Hannah agreed I'd make a decent Bernadette. At least for one night.

Of course, Romeo relished the opportunity to stab me with a prop knife and watch me pretend to die on the floor at his feet. Despite last night's insistence that he wants my love and forgiveness, I didn't miss the spark in his eye as he thrust his plastic weapon. A part of him—maybe a large part—still thrills to think of spilling my blood. It's something I'd be wise to remember next time he comes sniffing around, wanting to "work together."

"I think you did a great job, Mermaid," Ben says. "Considering it was your first rehearsal."

"No, I didn't. I can't sing."

Ben smiles. "You can. Just not as well as you paint."

I smile back. "Very diplomatic."

"Maybe Ben should run for Senate instead of my dad. Or maybe he's as tone-deaf as you are, Ree."

I poke my head over the seat and stick my tongue out at her, earning a laugh. Gemma reaches over, ruffling my hair. Things have been better between us today. I actually find myself starting to like her. A little.

Too bad that doesn't make it any easier to imagine Ben spending his life with her. I just want . . . more for him.

"Now get under the blanket, Benjamin," Gemma says. "Or you don't get any wine."

"I don't even like wine."

"You don't *know* if you like wine. You've never had wine."

"I have, I—"

"Boone's Farm doesn't count, Luna. Under the blanket."

"Gemma, I—"

Gemma makes a low "huuuaaaah" sound that I think is supposed to be a ninja cry and karate-chops the air near Ben's face.

Ben laughs. "*Dios mio.* Fine, crazy woman." He rolls his eyes but finally pulls the blanket up. Together we scoot down onto the floor behind the front seats as Gemma pulls up to the wrought-iron gate with the swirled *S* in the center and punches in the family's entry code.

Beneath the blanket, the air grows warm and filled with the smell of Ben. Even after a long day, he smells amazing. Like the ocean—salty and sweet at the same time—something vaguely food-ish that I can't put my finger on, and paint. He spent the afternoon finishing up the set while I shadowed Gemma, and didn't get all the paint off his hands. Specks of brown and white cover his gray T-shirt and freckle his knuckles and forearms.

I fight the strange urge to reach out and scrape the dried drops away with my finger, the way I would if they were on my own skin.

"This is still kind of crazy," Ben says. "I know we're underage, but it's not like we're going to take that much, right?"

"I know. Her dad is just weird."

"Her dad is more than weird. He freaks me out." Ben leans in to whisper the words close to my ear, making sure Gemma won't hear, and giving me a minor heart attack in the process. I wish I weren't so aware of his breath on my cheek, his lips so close they brush my hair when he talks. But I am. So aware that I have to fight to keep my breath slow and even. "And I don't like the way Gemma acts around him. It's like she's a different person."

"Gemma has a few personalities, but you'll learn to love them all." I smile, but Ben doesn't smile back. He just stares at me, a little too intently. I meet his gaze, unable to look away, unable to hide. "What's wrong?" I whisper.

"Nothing," he whispers back. "It's just . . . tight back here." He looks away, up to where Gemma drives slowly down the winding road.

"Well, we'll be at the barn soon."

"I thought Gemma said we were going to a wine cellar?"

"It's not really a cellar. It's a big barn where they keep all the wine barrels while they're aging. They stack them on top of each other in rows. Gemma and I used to play hide-and-seek there when we were little."

"So you two have been friends since you were kids."

"Since we were in second grade."

"Best friends," Ben says.

"She's my only friend."

"No, she's not."

I stare down at my knees, confused. Looking into Ben's eyes is . . . jarring, and makes me feel less like Ariel than I have all day. "I'm glad. I—"

"Hey! You two!" Gemma reaches back from the front seat and pokes a finger into the blanket, making a dent in our makeshift tent. "We're almost to the barn. When I say go, crawl out Ben's side and follow me. I can turn the cameras off on the way in. They don't record the entrance, just the barrels."

"Do they really have a problem with people sneaking in and stealing wine?" Ben asks.

"I don't think so," I say. "No one except Gemma, anyway."

"That's right. I am a menace to society *and* my own family, *muahaha*," she says, earning a snort from Ben, who obviously assumes I know he and Gemma are in a counseling group together. I wonder if he knows that she told me why he was there, and what he'll say when I finally have the chance to ask about the violence in his past.

"You ever shoplifted the hooch before, Mermaid?" he asks, nudging me with his elbow, oblivious to the direction of my thoughts.

"No, I've always been too nervous." I shift my weight,

trying to keep my right foot from going to sleep. "And I don't drink very often."

"Me either," Ben says. "It doesn't do much for me."

"Will you two quit talking about how you don't like to drink?" Gemma shuts off the car. "You're killing the buzz I don't even have yet. We're here to steal expensive wine, damn it. Now get in there and enjoy yourselves before I have to beat the fun into you."

Ben smiles and throws off the blanket, his hair wild around his face. I follow him out, slamming the door shut behind me, turning just in time to catch Gemma smoothing his hair behind his ear. The rain still drizzles the way it has all day, but it doesn't seem to bother them. They linger there together, Ben smiling at Gemma and Gemma smiling back, and for a moment, I see what they could be to each other—friends, lovers, the real deal.

The sight should lift my spirits, give me hope. Instead, my gut twists as Gemma takes Ben's hand and pulls him into the barn. An image of Ben and me in the dressing-room mirror—his arms around me, my hands fisted in his shirt—flashes on my mental screen, followed closely by a wave of something that feels a lot like envy.

Shameful, forbidden, maybe even *deadly* envy, so strong I rock on my feet.

What am I doing? How can I even *think* about feeling something like this? I can't be jealous of Gemma. I can't let myself keep thinking of Ben as . . . as . . .

My skin flushes hot and then cold, prickling with awareness, almost as if my moment of weakness is being observed. I turn in a circle, scanning the muddy parking area in back of the barn and the drooping vineyards beyond, searching for the source of the crawling sensation. But there's nothing. Just acres of bare vines with a gray sky above and black clouds moving in along the horizon—a sign of more storms to come.

"Come on, Ree. Move your skinny ass." Gemma's hiss comes from behind me, where she and Ben linger inside the metal door that serves as the entrance to the modern, very unbarnlike barn.

I hurry to join them, forcing a laugh when Gemma pinches my arm on my way by. Something like that would normally make Ariel laugh, so I do. It doesn't matter that I am uncomfortable and ashamed. Ariel would never covet her best friend's boyfriend—not even for a second—and I am an Ambassador who knows better. Who's known better from the start. From now on, I vow to remember it isn't part of my job to feel. My feelings don't matter.

"What's up?" Ben asks as we follow Gemma down the first row of barrels. They're stacked all the way to the ceiling and give off a pleasantly sour, woodsy scent.

"Nothing." I deliberately move closer to Gemma. "Just trying to figure out if that storm is coming our way."

"It is. My brother texted me during practice and told me to come straight home after," Ben said. "There's supposed to be a tornado watch or something."

"But Ben didn't go home right after practice, did you, Ben?" Gemma turns to run her red fingernails down Ben's arm. They match her tight red T-shirt and black and red striped dance pants and complete a look that is pure vixen. "What a bad boy you are."

"There's a reason I'm a troubled teen on Monday and Wednesday mornings, *mija*." He winks at her, but it's the look he shoots me over his shoulder that makes it hard to swallow. I tell myself it's because his words make me nervous, make me wonder if he's more dangerous than he seems. It certainly has nothing to do with the way the expression on his face changes him, gives him an edge, makes him look so . . . so much more . . .

"Are all these barrels the same type of wine? Or are they different?" I ask, determined not to even *think* words that start with *S* and end in *Y*.

"All of these are chardonnay, aged in French oak, for anywhere from six months to a year," Gemma says, putting on her tour guide voice, turning to motion to the barrels on either side of the aisle. "Chardonnay is Sloop Vineyard's biggest seller and twenty-six percent of the market share nationwide. Sloop also prides itself on its Bordeaux varietals, but you won't be seeing any of those on this tour." She cocks her head, flicking her hair around her face like a slightly deranged Barbie doll. "Those wines are aging in barn three near the Sloop family home, where Gemma Sloop's dickhead father might actually be working today."

Ben laughs. "You know a lot about this stuff."

"Dude, I was raised with a wine bottle in my mouth," Gemma says, dropping the perky persona. "Of course I do."

"You ever think of doing what your dad does?" he asks. "Making wine for a living?"

"I don't want to do anything my dad has ever done." For a moment Gemma's expression grows dark, almost . . . haunted. But then the big smile is back and she's urging us to "Come on!"

She darts to the left, down another row of barrels, toward a line of large upright tanks near the wall. She drops to the smooth concrete near one of the tanks and reaches underneath, pulling out a package of paper cups decorated with cartoon characters that she proceeds to fill from the spigot on the side of the tank.

Ben laughs when Gemma hands him a cup with a green monster on the side. "Nice. Very *fancy*," he says, catching my eye, checking to see if I've noticed he's used the word he said he likes to hear me say.

And I have. Of course I have.

I look at the ground, worried that my presence here is a bad idea. It could be my mind playing tricks on me again, but I would almost swear that Ben is *flirting*. With *me*. Right in front of his soul mate. Which is so bad that *bad* can't even begin to describe it.

"You know, I'm not sure I'm in the mood for wine after all." I make a face and put a hand on my stomach. "Maybe I'll just wait in the–"

"Don't even think about it, Ree." Gemma presses a cup with a pink monster on it into my hand. "It's the last semester of senior year. We're almost free and I want to celebrate with my best friend."

"Gemma, I–"

"Say 'yes, ma'am.'"

"Really, I don't–"

"Say it!"

I sigh. "Yes, ma'am."

"Now, you're going to drink, and you're going to like it."

So I drink, and Gemma is right–I *do* like it. The wine is smooth–sweet, but not too sweet–and leaves a buttery taste lingering on my tongue and warmth spreading through my chest.

It's been years since I've had a glass of wine. I haven't allowed myself the luxury. I can't afford to have my senses clouded even the slightest bit. But today it seems unavoidable. I take tiny sips—only one for every two of Ben's and Gemma's—but by the time we've been sitting on the floor for half an hour, I'm getting tipsy. My cheeks feel flushed, my lids droop, and my muscles are looser than I can remember.

I stretch, relishing the tingle in my toes.

"No more school talk," Gemma says, putting an end to our discussion as to whether or not the physics teacher realizes his nose hair touches his upper lip. "Let's play a game."

"I hate games," Ben says.

"I hate people. And yet, here I am, with both of you," Gemma counters with a grin. "How about I Never? Or do we want to go old-school with some Truth or Dare?"

"Not Truth or Dare. Please," I say, some fuzzy memory of Ariel's reminding me that she hates the game.

"I Never it is, then," Gemma says. "I'll start."

"But I don't know how to—"

"Shush." Gemma waves her hand, silencing Ben. "Listen and learn—I've never stolen wine from the Sloop vineyard." She tips her cup in our direction. "Now we all drink because we *have*. That's how it works. If you've never—you don't drink. If you have—you do. Easy." We all take a sip of our wine. I hold it in my mouth for a moment, relishing the taste before letting it slip down my throat with a sigh. "Your turn, Benjamin."

"Okay . . . I've never . . ." Ben stretches his legs out toward the center of the circle we've formed. It's darker inside the barn than it is outside, but I can still see the paint on his jeans. It's a different color than what he used today, a mix of lavender and dark blue that makes me wonder what he was painting the last time he wore them.

I'm suddenly possessed by the longing to see Ben's work, to see how it compares to Ariel's, how it compares to the landscapes and portraits I painted as a girl.

"Come on, Ben," Gemma urges, knocking his shoe with her black dance sneaker, making me jerk my eyes away from his legs. "While we're still young enough to remember the things we've never done."

Ben smiles. "I've never snuck out of my house in the middle of the night." He drinks, Gemma drinks, and I force my cup to remain in my lap. The thought's never crossed Ariel's mind. Where would she sneak off to? In a town like Solvang, when her best friend prefers to spend her evenings with the male of the species? My own exploits out my balcony and down the trellis don't matter.

"Your turn, Ree."

"I've never . . ."

"Something good," Gemma says. "Something even *I* don't know."

I sigh, head spinning pleasantly as I search Ariel's memories for something a little scandalous but not too intimate, and come up empty. I sense secrets in Ariel, but those are shadowy places in her mind, memories she's worked so hard to forget even I can't recall them. I give up, deciding I'll just have to lend her one of my scandals. "I've never hitchhiked after dark."

Gemma sticks out her tongue. "No fair. I already knew that." She doesn't drink. Ben doesn't either. I feel some small satisfaction in that as I take another sip of chardonnay.

"Okay, my turn again. I've never gone skinny-dipping."

Gemma and Ben drink, sharing a knowing smile over the edge of their cups.

I've never gone skinny-dipping. Ever. When did they? Did they go *together*?

Just how far has Gemma and Ben's relationship progressed? I know Gemma has been with a *lot* of guys from the private school. I've never seen her and Ben do anything but hold hands, but that smile is . . . telling.

I clear my throat and stare at my knees, refusing to admit that the thought of the two of them happy together in *that* way isn't a pleasant one.

"You've *never* ditched school? Not ever?" Ben nudges my tennis shoe, making me blush again. I've missed his question. Because I'm too busy thinking about things that are none of my business. They aren't, really, not unless some flaw in Ben and Gemma's sex life is responsible for keeping them from a full, auras-glowing-red commitment.

"No, Ree is the perfect daughter," Gemma says, a hint of meanness in her tone. "She never does anything Mommy doesn't like, including majoring in what she wants to major in at college."

"Where are you going next year?" Ben asks.

"Santa Barbara City College School of Nursing," Gemma supplies in a falsely chipper voice. "Because her *mother* went there for *her* nursing degree."

"Where did you want to go?" Ben pulls his legs in to his chest, ignoring Gemma.

"I don't know. I wasn't sure. I was thinking about art school," I say. "But nursing is a good field to get into."

"If you like blood and germs and wiping other people's

butts." Gemma snorts. "And doing what Mommy tells you, of course."

"Leave her alone," Ben says, heat in his tone. "Some of us have to think about how we're going to earn a living. Not everyone has a trust fund."

Silence falls over our corner of the barn. Gemma's expression hardens before a forced smile works its way across her face. "Totally right. I am *so* spoiled and out of touch. Forgive me." She tosses back the rest of her wine in one gulp.

Ben sighs. "Hey, I didn't mean it like that. I just–"

"No, it's cool." Gemma jumps to her feet. "I'm going to go grab some chips from my trunk. Anybody want pretzels or sour gummy bears? I hear they pair well with stolen chard."

"Gemma, I–"

"Last chance for snacks," Gemma says, cutting Ben off again. "Any takers? Going one, twice . . ."

"I'm good," I say.

"Me too." But Ben doesn't sound good. He sounds angry, frustrated.

"Okay, but don't try to steal my sour cream and onion chips when I get back because I won't be sharing. Help yourself to another glass if you want." She turns and disappears into the maze of barrels, leaving us alone.

I study Ben's tense profile, knowing this is my chance to urge him to forgive Gemma but unsure what to say. I feel so confused, my thoughts muddled by wine and concerns that go deeper than anything alcohol-related. Despite the brief moments of connection, Ben and Gemma just don't seem *right* together.

"Sorry," Ben says. "I don't like the way she talks to you."

"It's okay."

"No, really. I'm sorry."

"You don't have to be sorry."

"But I am."

"You're starting to sound like me," I say, getting to my feet and crossing to the tank, knowing I shouldn't drink any more but filling my pink cup to the top anyway. When I turn, Ben is behind me, holding out his green monster. I take it, trying not to notice when our fingers brush together.

"Okay. Then I'm *not* sorry. Somebody needs to remind Gemma that most of us are living in a different world."

I fill his cup, searching for the right words. "You always stand up for people?"

"Not all people," he says, taking his drink, but making no move to return to our spot on the floor. "Just the ones I don't think can stand up for themselves."

"*I* can stand up for myself." I look up into his eyes, willing him to believe me. He doesn't have to pity me, or Ariel.

"Yeah, I know." He moves closer, until I can feel the warmth of him through the T-shirt and sweatpants I threw on for rehearsal. "But you don't. Why?"

I hold his gaze—and my breath—as he takes a drink of his wine, his throat working the chilled liquid down. He licks his lips, and I fight to swallow.

"I'm not into conflict. And Gemma is my only friend."

"So you just let her walk all over you? I don't think that's really you." He narrows his eyes, as if he can see through my borrowed skin to my deepest, darkest secret. "I think there's a fighter in you, Mermaid. I was watching you from offstage today. I wouldn't ever want you to look at me the way you look at Dylan."

"I never would," I whisper. "Unless . . ."

"Unless what?"

"Unless you break my best friend's heart."

Ben's lips press together, but his gaze doesn't waver from mine. "I don't know what she's told you, but there is nothing going on between me and Gemma. Not in that way. We're friends. I think maybe she wanted it to be more for a little while, but–"

"But you love her." What is he saying? Is he out of his mind?

His eyebrows lift. "I do?"

Anxiety tightens my chest. How can he not realize he's in love? His aura is even rosier than it was the day before. "You *know* you do."

"I don't. I've never been in love." He pauses, considering me too carefully. "Have you?"

"I don't matter."

"Really?" He leans into me, until I can smell the wine sweet on his breath.

"Really." My heart beats faster, slamming in my chest.

"You do matter," he says, voice soft. "You matter to me."

THIRTEEN

"But I–I'm not–" I stumble over my words and fall into the first question that crosses my mind. "What happened when you were arrested? Why did you hit that guy?"

Ben doesn't blink. "He was beating up his girlfriend. Right in front of their house, where everybody in the neighborhood could see. No one else came out to stop it, so I did."

I should have known. He was coming to the rescue, as usual.

"I called the police, but I didn't think they would get there in time. She was pregnant. I'd seen her at the mailboxes a few times. . . ." He shakes his head, sadness on his face for this woman he barely knows. "She seemed so excited about the baby, even though her *pedazo de mierda* boyfriend was the father." He takes a drink of his wine, letting the silence wrap around us as he swallows. "Is that love, do you think?" he asks, sounding genuinely curious. "Being crazy about someone no matter how much they hurt you?"

"You know it's not."

"I don't," he says, shaking his head. "I've never seen it, not the way I imagine. Not even my brother and sister-in-law. He'd never hurt her, but he doesn't love her the way he should. He doesn't tell her everything he's thinking, doesn't look at her like she's the best thing that ever happened to him."

"Ben . . ." My heart squeezes in my chest, a beautiful ache that makes it even harder to breathe. I want to cup his sad face in my hands and tell him how glad I am that he really *is* a knight in shining armor, and a romantic, even if he doesn't know it. I want to tell him he's special and promise him he'll find someone who will love him the way he imagines.

But I can't promise that, not when his soul mate is Gemma. A girl with mood swings that make roller coasters seem tame, a mean streak, and a family biased against him, and who—at the moment—seems more preoccupied with potato chips than his feelings. And not when I've seen so many things that have weakened my own faith in love and happily-ever-after.

"They dropped the battery charge and let me off with counseling and twenty hours of community service, but . . ." He shrugs. "I guess you probably still think I'm a thug or something."

"No, you're . . . good." I reach out, unable to resist the urge to touch him. I scratch a bit of white paint off his arm, fingers lingering on his warm skin. His hand whispers along my cheek. My lips part and the smallest sound escapes, a barely audible betrayal of the way his touch makes me feel.

"Good enough for you to tell me the truth?" he asks.

For a moment, I think he means the *real* truth—*my* truth, not Ariel's—and something inside me thrills at the idea. To tell Ben my real name, my real thoughts, the real things "I Never" and the things that I have . . .

I want him to know me. Even though it's impossible. Dangerous.

"Why were you so upset yesterday?" he asks. "Was it because of Dylan?"

Dylan. The spark inside me dies. It always comes back to Romeo, to the miserable half-life he condemned us both to so long ago. I shake my head, trying to hold my sadness in, to bury it deep. "No. It was just a bad day."

"Please, tell me the truth," Ben whispers. "It's been driving me crazy. Every time I see Dylan in class he gives me this sick smile." His jaw clenches, and for a moment I see violence shimmer beneath his skin, see the face of the boy who broke a man's nose with his fists. "It's like he's got some kind of horrible secret."

"Who's got secrets?" Gemma asks.

Ben and I turn to find her standing a few feet away, watching us. I'm suddenly very aware that Ben's hand still hovers near my cheek. We shouldn't be standing so close, he shouldn't be touching me, I shouldn't be so conscious of his heat, his smell, his energy threading into mine.

Shouldn't. Shouldn't. Shouldn't. I'm breaking all the rules, even the ones I've sworn never to break. Whether he's ready to admit it or not, Ben is in love with Gemma. But that doesn't mean he can't find another girl tempting, the same way countless women have been tempted from their true loves by Romeo. With a look. A touch. A soft word.

No, you're . . . good.

Panic floods through me, burning away the rush I felt at Ben's touch. I duck my head, setting my cup on the edge of the vat as I slip away just in time, just seconds before another silhouette appears in the darkness behind Gemma.

"Ooo, I love secrets." Romeo ambles out into the light. I brace myself, waiting for Gemma to ask him what the hell he's doing here, to demand that he leave. Instead, she reaches into her bag, grabs a chip, and pops it into her mouth.

"Dylan snuck through the gate again," she says around a mouthful, as if this isn't a big deal, as if she didn't spend the entire car ride yesterday telling me that Dylan should be avoided at all costs. "Since he was already lurking by the door like a freak, I told him he might as well get a drink."

Romeo smiles and I feel Ben prickle beside me in response. "That's me. A freak for wine and secrets." His eyes shift to Ben, and when he speaks there's a challenge in his voice. "So come on, Benjamin. Tell all. *¡Cuéntame todo el chisme!*"

"Since when do you speak Spanish?" Gemma turns to Dylan, lifting an eyebrow.

"Since when are you two friends?" I ask, unable to help myself. This can't be happening. Gemma hates Dylan, and that's the way it should stay!

"We're not. He just comes over on the rare occasion when I don't want to drink alone." Gemma's eyes meet mine, but the girl I sang and danced with last night, the girl I've laughed with all afternoon, is gone. She's cold, guarded, and obviously angry.

Probably because she saw that loaded moment between Ben and me.

But that moment doesn't change the fact that she's lied to me—to Ariel—about her relationship with Dylan. Or the fact that she's invited him to join us when she knows my date with him was a horrible experience. She's thoughtless at best, mean-spirited and selfish at worst, and I want so much better for Ben. I want a generous, funny, sensitive girl who will treasure his love as her most priceless possession.

But I have Gemma. And I have to make this work or Romeo will win and someone will die.

But how to fix this? *How?* When Ben doesn't think he's in love, Gemma is angry and welcoming Romeo in her front door, and I've done nothing but put temptation in Ben's path that never should have been there. How to reverse the damage I've done? How to—

"That's Ariel's cup," Ben says as Romeo reaches the wine tank and grabs my discarded pink monster.

"That's okay. I've already got Ariel's germs." Romeo winks at me and takes a long, slow pull from the glass and I have my answer.

If Ariel is with Dylan, Ben will turn his attention back to Gemma where it belongs. And if Romeo is busy with me—working on that spell he's so desperate to cast—he won't have time to spend with Gemma, to get her drunk and spin tales of how wonderful immortality can be if she'll only sacrifice Ben to the Mercenary cause.

The decision is made, even though the thought of what I'm

about to do makes my flesh crawl. "Yeah. You probably do have my germs." I cross to Romeo, stopping only inches from where he's slouched against the wine tank. "But let's make sure. Just in case."

For a second, Romeo is thrown, his unshakable confidence wavering in the wake of my unexpected response. I try to enjoy that small victory as I wrap my fingers around the back of his neck and pull him to me, meeting his cold lips with mine. His mouth curves into a smile for a moment before he tosses his cup to the floor, wraps his arms tight around my waist, and kisses me like the world is ending and this is the last, breathless magic either of us will ever know.

His hands roam over the curve of my hip and his tongue slips between my teeth. I do my best not to gag, to pretend I'm enjoying this, to ignore the fact that being this close to Romeo makes me want to scream. To ignore the fact that Ben is watching, and that his soft sound of disgust makes me want to cry. For me. For him. For what can never, ever be.

"Well, well. *There's* a secret." Gemma sounds almost as repulsed as I feel. I pull my mouth from Romeo's, shifting my eyes to her, though I stay in Romeo's arms. "I think I'm going to go now. Ben, you coming?"

"Definitely. I'm definitely coming."

I turn to look at him, and it's all I can do not to burst into tears. The mixture of pain and disappointment, anger and despair, on his face cuts a hole in my heart deeper than the one Romeo put there with his knife. Ben looks so completely betrayed that I want to beg him to stay, confess that the kiss meant nothing and that I never would have touched Dylan if it weren't the only way to save Ben's life, a life that is impossibly precious to me after only two days.

But I can't say any of those things. Instead, I press closer to Romeo, twining an arm around his waist. This is what's best for Ben. Now he can write me off and turn his attention back to Gemma.

"Cool," Gemma says. "We can go hang out in the stables. I'll borrow the trainer's truck to take you home later." She digs into her pocket for her car keys and throws them at my and Romeo's feet. "You two can take my car out the back gate. I'll come back and erase the gate security tape after you're gone."

I meet her eyes, and the anger there makes me flinch. I didn't expect my kissing Dylan to make her even angrier. Her relationship with Ben is my top priority, but I don't want to ruin things between her and Ariel. "Wait, Gemma," I say. "Don't be mad. We wanted to tell you, but—"

She holds up a hand. "I don't want to talk about this now. Okay? Will you just go? You can park the car in front of the Windmill tomorrow morning. I'll get my mom to drop me off there before she goes to work." She turns and reaches a hand out to Ben. He takes it and holds on, following her through the discarded monster cups littering the concrete, making my spirits rise and my stomach plummet at the same time. I ignore my stomach. This is what has to happen. I have no other choice.

I stay in Romeo's arms until Ben and Gemma disappear down one shadowed row, then put my hands on his chest and shove. He lets me go with a laugh. "I guess this means you've changed your mind about loving me."

"Hardly." I grab the keys from the ground. "But I won't let you win this one."

"Then you must give me your love. If you want them both to live, if you want to live yourself, there is no other option."

I ignore him, gathering the cups from the ground. "What's going on with you and Gemma? With Dylan and Gemma?"

He waves his finger back and forth and makes a tsking sound. "No, no. No more scratching your back until you've scratched mine."

"When have you ever scratched my back?"

"Well . . ."

I hold up a hand. "Don't. Just . . . don't."

"I was only going to say that I helped you now, by sending that boy running back to Gemma's arms. I think he was starting to take an interest in someone else, in spite of these." He reaches for the scarred side of my face, but I step away. He smiles, an eager smile, as if anticipating some excellent game. "I like them, myself. Ugliness only makes beauty more striking. Don't you think?"

"Ariel isn't ugly. And I don't care what you like."

He shrugs. "It doesn't matter. Soon you'll have your own body back." He fiddles with the spigot, sending little bursts of wine to splatter onto the ground. "There's another way I've scratched your back. I discovered the spell, our way out."

"Stop that."

Romeo grins, flips the spigot to the on position, and walks away. I sigh as I turn it off and tuck the cups back under the steel tank. There's nothing left to keep my hands busy. I have to talk to him. At least enough to ensure he'll leave Ben and Gemma alone. "This is Mercenary magic?" I ask, trying to sound vaguely interested while I warn myself not to be drawn in.

"It is old magic," he says. "Original magic, before the Mercenaries and Ambassadors decided which side they were on.

Back when they were the very best of friends." His look becomes a leer. "Some of them were even lovers."

I roll my eyes. He's mad. This delusional story proves it. The Ambassadors and Mercenaries are bitter enemies.

As are you and Romeo, but once upon a time . . .

It's as if Romeo can hear my thoughts and knows the second weakness creeps into my mind. He sucks in a breath and begins his tale, words swift and sure. "Thousands of years ago, a group of ancients sought a way to escape the cycle of life and death. They were mystics of great power, and devised a spell that would grant their souls eternal life in the realms running parallel to the earth's reality, that would make them gods with worshippers bound to them by their magic. But the spell called for balance. For light and dark, good and evil.

"One half of the ancients took the power of goodness as the energy that would maintain their souls throughout the ages. The other half chose the evil of man as their fuel. They spilled each other's blood to work the spell, gambling their mortal lives in the quest for eternity. The magic worked, but not exactly as they'd thought."

He pauses, licking a bit of wine from his fingers with a strange smile.

"As the ages passed, the dark ones thrived on human wickedness. After a time, they were no longer consigned to their alternate realm, but lived forever on earth, poisoning humanity, bloating themselves on the evil they helped create, turning against the Ambassadors. For centuries, the light suffered, losing power, until they were forced to share their converts with death itself, to send them to the mist when they weren't needed. You are one of those souls, trapped between

{143}

life and death, never to be blessed with either. We are both slaves, forced into the worship of gods not of our choosing."

I cross my arms, shivering though the barn is warm and dry. Romeo looks on expectantly, as if waiting for my thanks for his outpouring. "So the Ambassadors are . . . vampires? Who feed on goodness? That's what you want me to believe?"

"You *must* believe," he says. "They use the good deeds of their converts to fuel their own eternity in their golden kingdom, never telling those converts that the evil they fight is one the Ambassadors helped create. Or that there is a way out of their service."

I shake my head. I don't want to believe him—god, I don't—but a part of me does. A part of me *believes.* Nurse's own words confirm every one of Romeo's. I have been forbidden to kill Romeo because murder "feeds the Mercenary cause." *Feeds.* Maybe literally *feeds* these magicians sustained by evil instead of good.

Anger and sadness and the familiar sting of betrayal surge inside me. Still, a voice within urges me to remember that Romeo is a liar out to help no one but himself. He requires my cooperation for this spell. That's the only reason he's bothering with this talk. Otherwise, he'd simply take what he wants, the way he always has.

"But their magic can't last forever. They can only hold their converts for so long," Romeo continues. "When the initial magic fades, they must either renew their converts' vows . . . or let the others take us."

"The others?" The air suddenly feels colder.

"You've seen them," he whispers. "I know you have."

I could lie. I could continue to deny everything, but I don't see what purpose it would serve. And Romeo is genuinely frightened. This man who has lived amid violence and death for centuries is spooked, and I need to know why.

"I've seen them. You and . . . myself," I say. "But how is that possible? Our bodies have been dead for—"

"They aren't our true forms," he says. "They are the specters of our souls, come to take us both to that hell you've been wishing for me."

"Hell," I repeat. The notion doesn't ring true. "If there is such a place—and you've insisted numerous times that there is not—why would I be taken there? What have I done that—"

"You've stepped outside the natural order, become a tiny dot of space-time cancer the universe must destroy in order to balance the cosmic equation."

"The universe as in . . . god?"

Romeo sighs. "The universe as in *the universe,* the primal forces of creation. Call it god if you must, but it is a nameless, mindless thing. It doesn't care about good or bad. All it cares about is balance and order. What the Ambassadors and Mercenaries have done violates that order, but it is we who will pay the price. If the specters—"

"But what are the specters? If the universe is mindless, then who controls them? Why do they—"

"They are parts of ourselves, left over from what we would have been, influenced by what we've become, but compelled by primal forces beyond human understanding," he says, obviously frustrated with my limited imagination. "All I know is that if they take us before we work this spell, we will go to that mist you've only lingered in until now, to that place outside of time where the universe dumps its waste. But the mist will not be a place of forgetting for us. We will be aware of every single moment that passes, conscious but bodiless and alone for all eternity."

I press my lips together. Yes, that sounds close enough to hell for me.

"The only way to escape that fate is to take control, to work the spell together and give the specters physical form, not simply psychic—"

"Have you seen your body? What it has become?"

He pales, runs a nervous hand through his loose curls. "Yes, well, I suppose wickedness does have its consequences. Hopefully the magic will fix . . . all that." I lift a dubious brow, and he does a poor impression of his come-hither smile. "They say love can work miracles."

I shake my head again, slowly, knowing that—even if everything he says is true—this is impossible. I can never love him, no matter how much I might fear the hell he describes. Fear can force obedience, but it can never transform a heart. But before I can say a word, laughter interrupts.

The laugh echoes through the long rows of barrels, drifting up to dance through the rafters of the barn, making us both turn toward the sound. At first I think Gemma has returned, but then it comes again, a rich, carefree giggle that's eerily familiar. I *know* that laugh. I've *felt* it thrum through my chest, tumble out my lips. It's *my* laughter. Someone has bottled the joy I felt as a girl and it's pouring into the air, sweeter than the wine I've stolen.

"It's her . . . you," Romeo whispers. He grabs my arm, fingers digging in too hard. "Don't welcome her, don't embrace her before we work the spell or she will have you. Hell will have you!"

More laughter, this time from the opposite direction.

Romeo and I stumble in our haste to turn around. My heart pounds, terror thick in my veins.

I catch a flash of blue and then my old body dances from between a row of barrels. She finds me with her slightly vacant eyes and smiles. *"Love. So close."* My mouth falls open. It's me. There's no doubt. But I'm not as I was; I'm not whole. There is a wound on my chest, blood drips down the front of my dress, and my smile is forced and strange.

Still, I am tempted to go to her, to take my old hand. Almost . . . compelled. I would go—despite Romeo's warning, despite my fear—if Romeo didn't grab my hand and shout for me to "Run!"

I see it a second later, the rotted corpse crouched in the darkness behind my body. *"Love."* The word is a growl—low and feral—that rumbles through the air, a warning we don't need to hear twice.

We turn and run, feet pounding faster than the rain pummeling the roof. Faster and faster, lunging to the left and then the right, racing down the rows, too terrified to stop and see how close the thing has gotten. I can hear it scrambling behind us, hands and feet slapping the slick floor, running like a beast, a nightmare.

Another turn to the left and suddenly, the door is in sight. I sprint for it with everything in me, hitting the metal bar just seconds before Romeo, hurling myself out into the storm. In seconds the rain has plastered my hair to my head, but I don't stop running until I reach Gemma's car. I fumble the keys from my pocket with trembling hands.

Romeo and I scramble inside, slamming the doors behind us. I hit the locks but still hurry to get the keys in the ignition. I won't feel safe until we are far, far away from the barn.

I turn the car around and guide it back onto the narrow road, pulling in long, deep breaths and letting them out slowly. I keep the car moving toward the gate at a semi-reasonable speed, only checking the rearview half as many times as I would like. I can't let fear take over. I have to keep my head, to think of some way to reach the Ambassadors.

They've never hurt me, never punished me, never shown me anything but kindness. I can't betray them now.

But what if he's right? What if—

"Do you want me to drive?" Romeo asks.

"No, I'm fine."

"You don't look fine, you look like you're going to murder that wheel."

I glance down, shocked by my white knuckles and the ropes of muscle straining against the backs of my hands. I relax my grip, but my thoughts only race faster as I punch the remote to open the gate and guide us back toward Solvang. Using that much strength, I should have broken the wheel, but I didn't, a reminder of my uncommon weakness.

Romeo is right. I'm different, *we're* different, and he may be my only chance at a tomorrow. But do I dare? Do I dare reach out to the enemy for help? Do I dare even ask him more about this spell?

"Are you ready now?" Romeo asks, as haunted as I've ever heard him. Even more than on the day he killed my cousin and learned he would be exiled from our home forever. "We can do this. Tonight."

He killed my cousin. He killed *me.* And over the centuries he's wrecked the lives and hearts of so many people. I cannot forget that. I *cannot.* He is a liar and a fiend and a monster.

"I know you hate me," he says. "But please . . . think on

this tonight. Sleep and see if you can dream of a life where I am not your enemy, where I am the man who loves you. You heard the specters. We must love each other, or we are doomed."

I laugh, a choked, desperate sound that makes me bite my lip.

"Leave me here," Romeo says, motioning to an empty produce stand at the edge of town. I pull in to the parking lot but don't turn off the car, don't look over at Romeo. Just driving him to safety feels wrong; how could it ever feel right to join forces with him in magic? "I'll walk home."

I nod. "You do that."

He sighs. "You have to try, Juliet, or it will be the death of us both. I'll give you a day to think," he says, catching my eye. "One day, without my interference with you or our young lovers. One day for you to spend in contemplation, as a show of my good faith. And then we act, before it's too late."

One day. It's more than he's ever given me before, but I already know it won't be enough. I will never love him or trust him, certainly not in twenty-four hours, but maybe . . . just maybe . . .

"One day."

Romeo beams as if I've handed him his life. "You won't regret this, Juliet. You are still the light in my darkness, the only beauty I've—"

"Stop."

He laughs. "A man has to try."

"You're not a man."

"But I could be again. Believe it." He clasps my hand, holds on even when I try to pull away. "*I* do. I believe." I meet his mad eyes and for a moment I see the spark of something human there. "Think, we could still make the story true, find our happiness. Even after death."

"Please, just go."

"Good-bye, my love, parting is such sweet sorrow, that I must say–"

"Leave," I say, then force myself to soften my voice. "Give me the day and I'll try. I promise."

"It's all that I ask." He slips out into the rain and heads across the parking lot with a slow, seductive stroll, oblivious to the cold and wet. I watch him go, and think maybe I should feel guilty for lying. But I don't.

I pull out without a backward glance, wheels spinning in my mind. If he keeps his word, I have twenty-four hours. Twenty-four hours to help Ben and Gemma finish the business of falling in love and put them safely beyond Romeo's reach. And when they are finished, we will be finished. Perhaps the Ambassadors will send me to the mist, or perhaps my old body will drag me there never to return. Either way, it will be over.

Maybe before sundown tomorrow.

FOURTEEN

The next morning I sit in the coffee shop, clutching a mug of tea and trying not to panic.

It looks like Gemma isn't going to show. I don't know why I'm surprised. She was so angry last night. I should have known that the text she sent me at two in the morning—promising she'd meet me at the bakery at seven—was simply to get me to stop calling.

I check the clock. Seven-thirty.

I try to tell myself it's okay, I can talk to her at school, but it makes me sick to waste a second of my day without Romeo. The pancake ball I ate churns in my stomach, a rock that refuses to be digested. It tastes different than Ariel remembers. At least, I think it does. Ariel's memories are thready today, a fog I can't see through, a scent I can't name. I'm too full of my own worries and fears, the Juliet inside me crowding out the girl I'm pretending to be.

My dreams were horrific again last night. Corpses come to life, blood on a blue dress, and the cold, immovable walls of the tomb where I once screamed for help until blood ran down my parched throat. And then . . . the mist, nothing but the mist, stretching on forever.

Forever.

What if Romeo's right? What if I'm a fool for spending one of my last days on earth attending to Ambassador business?

I glance up, bite my lip. Seven-thirty-three.

I can practically hear the clock tick from across the room. The bakery is unusually quiet. Far fewer customers come to claim their morning fare, and those who do sit in strained silence. It's almost as if the world at large can feel that two lives hang in the balance.

My eyes slide to where Nancy would usually be standing behind the counter. Instead, Nancy's daughter—a strong-faced woman with wiry black and gray hair pulled into a long braid—plucks bear claws from the case and delivers coffee into the hands of teachers, students, and shopkeepers. She looks sad, worried, as if she's having a hard time managing the few customers even with another woman I don't recognize helping her. Probably best if I give her one less person to worry about.

Just when I've given up and begun to gather my things, the bell above the door tinkles and Gemma shoves her way inside. She finds me in the corner booth and shoots me a glare that could melt bones as my jaw drops in shock.

Her aura is on *fire* this morning, burning a bright, strong red. Her time alone with Ben last night accomplished more than I'd hoped.

One soul mate down; one to go.

Ben must not be ready yet, or I wouldn't be sitting here. The moment both auras catch flame, I'm always pulled back to the mist. Unless . . .

If I see Ben today and his aura has changed as well, then I'll know there's no going back. I'll have to decide: join Romeo or let the specter of my soul take me. I know I should be afraid for my future, but all I can think about is Ben and how it kills me to think of him glowing the cherry-red-of-no-return for Gemma. For anyone except . . .

No. I won't think it. I *won't.*

"Hey." I force a smile, pushing my worries from my mind as Gemma stalks toward me. "I'm so glad you're here."

She stops next to the booth but doesn't sit down. She stands, arms crossed, looking down at me, making me squirm. "Yeah. I could tell. I just don't know what you're so happy about. Everyone else is totally freaked."

"Why?"

"Have you not turned on a television or computer in the past fifteen hours?" She rolls her eyes. "Wow, you must have been hot for Dylan last night not to–"

"I wasn't with Dylan last night, Gemma," I say. "And I want to explain what–"

"Nancy is *missing*," Gemma says, dismissing my explanation with an impatient wave before I can make it. "It's all over Facebook."

The thought throws me. "Missing?"

"Like officially a missing person, reported to the police, on the nightly news, would be coming to an Amber Alert near you if they did that for old people."

"Oh no." Her poor daughter; no wonder she looks so upset. "That's awful."

"Well, it's been an awful few days." Gemma's scowl deepens. "I can't believe you and Dylan . . . I mean, I expect lies from him, but I thought you were different. I thought that innocent act was real."

"Gemma, please," I say, keeping my tone gentle. "What about everything you said to me in the car? About staying away from Dylan? Wasn't that a lie?"

"That wasn't a lie. That was good advice." She looks out the rain-streaked glass next to my booth. It's another horrible, rainy, miserable day, and I'm beginning to think I'll never see the sun again. "But you're right, I guess. I've lied. You've lied. There's no one you can trust." Gemma's brightly stained lips droop at the edges. "I should have learned that a long time ago."

She's wearing fuchsia lipstick today, with a bright fuchsia sundress that falls all the way to the floor and a black shrug sweater with scraps of gauze whirling off in every direction. She's as bright and vibrant as ever, while Ariel is forgettable in another pink and brown sweater. Stripes this time. Ariel seems to have a dozen versions of the same sweater, equally plain and uninspired. She and Gemma are so different. It's amazing they've stayed friends for as long as they have.

But they *have,* and it doesn't matter what I think. I can't let Ariel lose this friendship. I could be gone by the end of the day.

"Gemma, please." I scoot to the edge of the booth and stand up, facing her. "I've never lied to you. I just wasn't thinking."

"No, you were," she says. "You were thinking I wouldn't like what you had to say."

"And you did the same thing," I say. "Can't we just forgive each other and—"

"I *know* I've done the same thing," Gemma says, anger creeping into her voice. "And I should have *kept* doing it."

"What do you mean?" I ask, confused by her words, her obvious anger. She's glowing with love; shouldn't she be . . . *happier*? Kinder?

"I should never have introduced you to Ben."

My lips part. How can she say that? When all I've done is try to help her and Ben get closer together?

And replayed every word he said a thousand times in your head.

"I'm not stupid, Ariel."

And held the memory of each time he touched you so tight to your chest you could barely breathe.

Gemma's mouth curves into a humorless smile. "It's tragically obvious."

And secretly thought Ben might be better off . . . with you.

"I know you have a crush on him."

"I do not." It's the truth. I have something much worse than a crush. I have sinful, traitorous, forbidden feelings. Feelings I've only had once before, seven hundred years ago when I fell in love for the first time. For what I'd assumed would be the *last* time . . .

God, can I really be . . . Can I . . .

I haven't dared to think about *that*, but now, there's no denying that it feels true. The thought of Ben burning red for Gemma makes me want to die. Why would that be unless . . . Unless . . .

I shake my head, dizzy with the unspeakable possibility.

"No. Ben is just a friend. I'm with Dylan. You saw that yourself last night."

"Making out with Dylan means nothing. Less than nothing." She curses beneath her breath. "I mean, how stupid do you think I am? I can see what you're trying to do and it's pathetic."

"What?"

She pauses, surveying me through narrowed eyes. "You heard me . . . you're pathetic."

I barely resist the urge to tell her to go to hell. "That's mean, Gemma."

"You know what's mean? Playing with other people's toys. Don't think I can't see you working Ben, trying to make him jealous." Her tone lilts up and down, each word more mocking than the last. "To make him so worried about poor Ariel that he needs to spend more time by your side, protecting you from your big, bad, abusive boyfriend. He told me about Dylan smashing in his window, and how you had some sort of fainting attack in the theater and he had to *hold* you." She laughs, the nastiest laugh I've ever heard. "I mean, *really,* Ariel . . . that's just . . . You should be embarrassed. When have you ever fainted? Ever?"

"Gemma, I don't know–"

"But Ben isn't interested in protecting you, and Dylan doesn't *love* you or whatever you're imagining," she says, hitching her purse over her shoulder. "He doesn't love anyone, and you're not capable of playing this kind of game. So quit trying to steal my life! It was a stupid life, even when it was mine."

Now I'm completely baffled. Gemma isn't making sense, and it's harder than ever to stomach that this cruel person is the girl Ben loves. Still, I fight for control, to keep my goal in mind, to remember that I'm doing this for Ben, to protect him. "Gemma, I'm not playing games. I promise. I just want–"

"Save it, Ariel." She backs away, shaking her head in disgust. "But you need to stop embarrassing yourself. Ben's not interested, and everyone knows Dylan only slept with you because of that bet."

Her words hit my chest, knocking the wind out of me. People know about the bet? Romeo told people Dylan and Ariel . . . I haven't heard a whisper of gossip at school, but then, how would I? When no one talks to Ariel except Gemma and Ben? And now they won't talk to her either. She'll come back to this body miserable and alone and shamed and it's all my fault.

I stare after Gemma, lost in a rush of emotion. "Please, Gemma–"

"Sorry, Ariel. I don't have time for your head games right now. I have some enormous decisions to make, and you need to work on being less of a freak."

I flinch. How can she say these things? To her best friend? To a girl who stepped miles outside her comfort zone to keep Gemma from being kicked out of the drama club production? To a girl who's said nothing but nice things *to* Gemma and *about* Gemma for as long as they've been friends? Gemma is a vindictive, selfish, spoiled girl who doesn't deserve Ariel and certainly doesn't deserve Ben's love.

I suddenly *hate* her. *Hate*. It's tempting to tell her so, to tell her that Ben won't even admit to being her boyfriend and doesn't think he's in love with her, to destroy any chance of reaching her with a few sharp, deadly words.

Instead, I fist my hands so tight my nails cut into my palms.

Gemma isn't just any girl. She's the soul mate I've been

sent to protect. Until Ben's aura is as bright as hers, I can't afford to burn any bridges. And as for Ariel . . . I have to let her make this decision, to hopefully work up the nerve to end things with this "friend" who reminds me more and more of my worst enemy.

"Later, Ariel," Gemma says, snatching her keys from the table as she backs away. "It's been real."

"Wait, Gemma!" I lower my voice as heads turn in our direction. "Gemma."

But secretly, I'm relieved to see her rush out the door and run through the rain to where I parked her car down the street. I don't know what I would have said, and in a way Gemma isn't my problem anymore. Her heart is secure. Once an aura goes red, there's no going back. Now I just have to find Ben and say whatever has to be said to help him finish falling for this girl who's just treated me like garbage.

The thought makes me want to weep with frustration, to rage at the universe for its unfairness. Instead, I grab my backpack and head for the door, ignoring the stares of the other students scattered throughout the coffee shop. I step outside and pause under the awning, cursing when I see how hard it's raining and realize I left my umbrella in the backseat of Gemma's car. Just another little thing to hate her for.

The door tinkles behind me. "Hey. What's up?" I turn to see Jason Kim, Dylan's friend, easing through the door. I hadn't noticed him inside, but then, snakes are good at camouflage. He lifts his chin as he comes to stand beside me, carrying the musty smell of leather along with him. Today he's wearing a brown motorcycle jacket with patches stitched on the arms, and jeans so dark they're nearly black.

His eyes track up and down, and he wrinkles his nose at my cheap sweater. "You're looking good."

"Thanks." I ignore his sarcastic tone and drop my gaze to the sidewalk. Ariel is afraid of this boy. She wouldn't want to attract any more of his attention. Maybe if I stand here under the awning staring at the ground long enough he'll get the hint and go away.

"You are *so* welcome." I can hear his grin even before I look up. His teeth shine so white they're almost blue. "You know, Dylan's been talking about you. A lot."

"Really?" My stomach cramps. Just what I need, more Romeo-inspired drama to deal with. For a man who says he wants to "work together," he's done his share to make my borrowed life a misery.

"Yeah. He had a really good time Monday night." He hesitates, smile spoiling into a smirk. "What about you? You have a good time?"

"It was fine."

"Fine?" His thin black eyebrows arch closer to his spiked hair. "That's it?"

"Yes, it was fine."

"Wow, I'd think a night like that . . ." He takes a step closer to the edge of the awning, holding a hand out to play in the water spilling down to the road. "For a guy that would be a huge deal. In the cool way. I think it should be the same for a girl. I'm all about women's rights. My mom's a lawyer."

I tilt my head to one side, trying to find some logic in what Jason has just said. He turns back to me, leaning so close I can smell the hint of coffee on his breath. "Dylan and the new guy. You did them both, right? On the same night?"

"What?" Romeo. I'm going to kill him.

"I didn't believe it at first. Dylan's my boy, but he's a liar." Jason's voice drops to a whisper. "But that Luna kid is in my gym class, and he said it was true too."

I don't believe it. Not for second. "You're lying."

"I swear that's what he said. And he seems like an honest guy. Don't you think?"

Behind us, the door dings—once, twice—teachers and students starting toward school. I give Jason my blankest stare. "Why are you talking to me?"

"We've gone to school together since third grade, Ariel," he says with a condescending laugh. "Why shouldn't I talk to you?"

"Because you've never talked to me before. Ever."

"I'm sorry." The falseness of the apology makes me want to punch him in the gut. "Did that hurt your feelings?"

"Not at all. I preferred it."

He grins, seeming to take the insult as some form of flirtation. "Cool. We don't have to talk. I just wanted to let you know that I'm *available* to you."

"Available to me," I repeat.

"I'm here to help meet your needs and achieve your goals," he says. "Ben and Dylan are cool with sharing. And hey, I'm cool with that too."

I shake my head, so repulsed I can't think of how to respond.

"My parents aren't home tonight. You could come over to my place after rehearsal and we—"

"Not if you were the last warm-blooded thing on the face of the earth."

Jason's laughter follows me down the street as I take off toward school. I grit my teeth, refusing to blink as the rain flicks at my eyes, refusing to look back over my shoulder or think any more about what Jason said. He's a creep and a liar. There's no way Ben would ever say anything to confirm a story like that. No way in hell. I don't doubt Ben for second. I trust that he's a good person with everything in me.

Just like you trusted that Romeo Montague would cherish you as his beloved bride.

I break into a run, sprinting for campus.

No. It isn't the same. I've only known Ben a few days, but he's already proved himself ten times the person Romeo ever was. Romeo never worried about other people's safety or well-being; he didn't talk lovingly of his family, or know what it was like to live through pain and loss. Romeo never saw the strength in me, never looked close enough to realize I was more than a pretty young girl, that I was a person with hopes and dreams and thoughts in my head. And Romeo might have praised my loveliness with lyrical poetry, but he never made me feel as beautiful as Ben did when he said four simple words.

You matter to me.

I rock to a stop in the middle of the sidewalk, the rain soaking me through, shaking as the inescapable truth rises up to meet me. I'm in love. With Ben. Another boy I can never have. Truly *never*, not even if I'm wicked and selfish enough to try to take him. This isn't my body, this isn't my life, and soon I'll be gone.

Loving him would be the worst thing I've ever done. Stupid, pointless, inexcus–

My cell phone trills in my backpack, a single upward scale I can barely hear over the rain. I jerk into motion, hurrying the last dozen feet to the school parking lot and ducking under the bus-stop awning at the southern edge. But when I pull the phone from my bag, it isn't ringing. Instead, the screen glows blue with a message. It's from Romeo. So much for my twenty-four hours . . .

But then I read what he's written. And shiver.

Meet me backstage in fifteen minutes. If you see me before then, we are enemies, as always. Circumstances have changed. You are being watched.

We are not alone. The one who made me is here.

FIFTEEN

The second bell rings as I reach campus and the last of the students still plodding in from the parking lot quicken their steps down the path. I join them—just until I've passed Mr. Stark, who's on morning duty—then cut to the right, slinking around the school office building, hunched over so the top of my head won't be seen in the principal's window. The ground is spongy and slick. It oozes beneath my feet, making sucking sounds each time it's forced to release my boot.

By the time I creep around Building A and make my way to the back entrance of the theater, my sweater is sodden and my boots are covered in mud. I shake the damp off as best I can and reach for the door. It opens with a barely audible groan. Inside, the theater is dark, except for the ghost light perched on the stage on the other side of the curtains. It penetrates the deep red velvet, casting the backstage in a hellish glow.

The heavy door clunks shut behind me, sealing me inside with the eerie light and the peculiarly still air of places that are usually filled with noise. Apprehension lifts the hairs on the back of my neck.

Squeezing the soggy strap of my backpack, I pad toward the dressing room, boots nearly silent on the paint-spattered floor. This afternoon Ben and I are supposed to paint over the mess we've made working on the flats, cover the floor with a fresh coat of black before the dress rehearsal tonight.

I wonder if he'll show up, or if he'll decide he'd rather not spend any more time with me.

I tug open the dressing room door but almost immediately close it again, letting it ease shut but for the barest inch. Someone is inside. The light is on, and I caught a flash of movement in the corner. I have no idea who—or what—is in there, but I don't want to be seen. My meeting with Romeo will have to be relocated.

Unless Romeo has already arrived . . .

I peek through the crack in the door, angling my head until I can see the far corner of the room and the sink where I wash up after painting. His back is turned, his shoulders hunched as he scrubs something clean in the sink, but I recognize Ben the second I lay eyes on him. My gaze roams over his wild hair, the strong line of his back, his narrow hips hugged by paint-spattered jeans. My heart lurches and my mouth goes dry.

There he is, the boy I love, his aura still rosy, but not red.

Just looking at him makes my fingers ache to touch his face, to curl around his neck, to pull his lips to mine and tell him all my secrets in a kiss. I want to feel his arms around me, the comfort of his bones resting against mine. I want to look into his eyes and see that there is nothing in the world but the two of us and that is enough. That is . . . everything.

Everything. Just like Romeo was before that last night, before he pulled me from the nightmare of my living tomb only to plunge a knife through the heart he'd sworn to treasure.

I shiver, fear soaking through my wet skin, chilling my core.

How can I *think* of loving someone again? How have I let this happen? Even if it weren't forbidden, haven't I learned my lesson? Haven't I learned that love can't be trusted, especially love like mine, love that burns away every last bit of sense in the fire of its devotion?

You can trust me. Ben's words whisper through my mind. Maybe I can. Maybe I can trust Ben—even if I can't trust love— but it doesn't matter. Ben can never, *ever* be mine.

My throat squeezes tight and the backs of my eyes flare with sudden heat. I step away, pulling the door softly closed as I go. I turn and creep through the near-darkness, the faint flare of crimson in the air a condemnation of my weakness, a confirmation of my sin-filled soul. I don't deserve Ben's trust or friendship. I am truly awful. I've put him and Gemma in unforgivable danger. I have to fix my mistake; I have to make his aura burn or spend eternity with guilt pressing down all around me.

I'm so focused on my shame, my regret, that I don't realize I'm not alone until fingers clutch my arm, pulling me into the narrow space between the curtains. Romeo's hand comes down on my mouth, stifling the scream that would have slipped from my lips.

"Shh," he hisses. "He could find us any second." His face is far too close to mine, his breath hot in my ear. I catch the faint hint of something heady, metallic, something that reminds me of aged meat, but it isn't something Romeo has eaten. The smell is coming from beneath his clothes, his flesh a steak that's starting to spoil.

Forcing myself not to gag, I nod and turn my head, twisting from his grasp. I take a step back, breathing through my mouth, staring up into Romeo's wide eyes. In the dim light they are great black circles, his pupils a disease that's beginning to spread.

He is . . . *not right,* even more so than usual. I have to get him out of here. I don't want him anywhere near Ben in this condition–or any condition. My lips part, but he stops me with a trembling hand.

"There isn't time," he says, voice strained.

"But I–"

"He's here. The one who made me. That's why there aren't any other Mercenaries in this town. They don't linger when one of the high ones comes for a visit. He's been hiding his aura from me with magic, but I saw it last night. I'm sure I did, and I think he knows." He grips my arms, fingers squeezing, pressing the cold, wet fabric tight to my skin. "He's watching, waiting for me to turn one of these children, ready to force me to kill you a second time and finally advance through the Mercenary ranks."

"Who? How do you–"

"We can still escape, but time is short," he says, oddly

{166}

breathless, as if he's just finished running a great distance. "Soon our chance will have passed us by. We have to work the spell before it's too late."

I shake my head. "I don't—"

"You can love me. You did before, you can again." His eyes dart to the side and back to me, mouth trembling as if he can't decide whether to laugh or cry. "We can go now. Immediately."

I wince as his fingers dig deeper, regretting the decision to meet him more with every passing second. He's finally lost what's left of his mind. "Why don't we go outside? I can't see y—"

"It is not necessary that you see. It is necessary that you *take action*," he says, shaking me once, as if that sharp motion will force my brain to make sense of his rambling. "What more do you need?"

I shrug him off, breaking his hold before he can shake me again. "I need you to make sense, or I'm going to leave."

His clawed fingers fist in the air before falling to his side. He takes a deep breath, visibly forcing himself to calm down. "You're right." He crosses his arms, licks his lips. "You have to know everything about the spell. I'll tell you, but you have to promise we'll go right after. Promise. *Swear* it." He reaches for me, but I lift a hand, warning him not to touch me again.

"I won't promise anything until I understand what I'm promising."

Romeo laughs, a hysterical sound that's smothered by the curtains. "Like the first time? When you swore to serve a cause you *still* don't understand seven hundred years later?"

I press my lips together, keenly aware of the passage of time. Ben will have to get to class soon. He seems to be skipping homeroom, but first period starts in twenty minutes. He'll pass right by these curtains on his way out. I have to be finished with Romeo before that happens. "Then educate me. Quickly, if time is so precious."

"Not every Ambassador or Mercenary gets a chance like this, but we were once bound by love, a force that has its own magic," he says. "If we love again, speak the words of the spell I've stolen, and seal our promises with blood—the way the Ambassadors and Mercenaries did thousands of years ago—then we can take their magic for ourselves. We can heal our souls, make real those spectral bodies, and live forever. All we have to do is love again, the way the specters have told us."

"But why would they help us?" I ask, his words not ringing true. "If their purpose is to take us to the mist and end this imbalance you say was created, then—"

"I don't think they want to do the job they were sent for," he says. "I think they want us to claim them again, to make them—"

"But won't magic like you're proposing create more imbalance? Won't we be in the same—"

"I don't know, Juliet," he snaps. "And I don't *care*. Whatever awaits us after the spell can't be worse than staying here, waiting for a monster to drag me to hell or a Mercenary to find out what I've been talking about with you and do worse."

I bite my lip. The bell signaling the end of homeroom is about to ring, and I don't intend to be in the theater when it does. "You said you'd give me a day to think."

"There is no time to spare," he says, voice rising. "I love you. Just love me in return, and let's get on with it." He tosses out the word as if it's an ingredient in a recipe, as if he isn't asking for the moon.

Love. Love *him*. It's impossible. Even if this spell is our only way out. Even if I risk my soul, betray my vows, and spill my blood, it's impossible. I'm in love with Ben. "I can't."

"We're soul mates," he says. "We are forever. Our kind of love cannot be destroyed."

"It can. It was. You destroyed it the day you bartered my life to the Mercenaries."

"What was I supposed to do, Juliet?" he shouts, so loud I worry Ben will hear him through the door of the dressing room.

"Quiet!" I hiss. "I thought you said—"

"Please, tell me." His voice drops to a harsh whisper. "What other option did I have?"

"What other option?" I clench my hands at my side, frustration making my arms vibrate. "You had a *hundred* other options, a thousand—"

"I was *banished* from the city, never to return upon penalty of death," he says. "My father had disowned me and my new wife's family were my mortal enemies. I was sixteen years old, with no money, no friends outside Verona, and no skills with which to earn a living. I was a rich man's son. How was I to feed *myself,* let alone a wife and the inevitable children? *How?*"

I shake my head, refusing to try to understand his motives for the ultimate betrayal. Nothing can justify what he did. *Nothing.* "We could have found a way. We were young. We had our health and our minds and our love, we could have—"

"We would have starved to death," his says. "We would have *died* in the streets or been murdered on the road by highwaymen for the jewels in your shoes before we reached Mantua." He stops, looking at me, eyes filled with sadness. "You would have died cursing my name, cursing the day you met me and the day I killed your cousin. You would have died poisoned with hate, and it would have destroyed my soul. And yours. I couldn't bear the thought of it. I loved you too much. I swear that I did, that I *do* . . . or at least, that I will again if you'll give me the chance."

My chest tightens, aches. It's too easy to imagine the fate he describes, too horribly easy, but I'll eat my own tongue before I'll agree he had no other choice. If working for the Ambassadors has taught me anything, it's that there's always a choice between good and evil. "If that's what you believed, then you should have left me."

"What?" He blinks, as if the thought never entered his mind.

"You should have left me with my family in Verona."

He shakes his head, dismissing me. "You would have ended yourself in despair."

"Maybe, but it would have been my choice. *My* death."

He pauses, then speaks in a whisper. "Who's to say it wasn't?"

"And there was a chance I would have lived." I speak through gritted teeth, ignoring his insinuation that I somehow *chose* to be murdered. "Maybe I would have realized that a coward like you isn't worth dying for."

He snorts. "You forget the time in which we lived, sweet. You would have been ruined, a wife discarded after one night, a—"

"Better ruined than—" I break off, something in his face making my blood run even colder. "You knew. That night. Before we . . ." I fight to swallow past the lump in my throat. "You knew that you were going to give me to them."

He shrugs, but his eyes stay on the floor, as if he's ashamed to look me in the face. "The past is meaningless."

"It is not." My lip curls. "It is a testimony to what a monster you are."

"We're wasting time. It doesn't matter what you think of my choices." He curses, drives his fingers through his hair. "You must love me or spend eternity in *hell. Those* are *your* choices."

"Then I will go to hell," I say, knowing the second the words leave my lips that they are true. I won't work this spell. I won't betray the Ambassadors. Even if they *have* been using me, they have used me to do good, to make the world a better place. I won't betray that, and I won't aid Romeo in reclaiming his life. I've been *forbidden* to kill him, but I haven't been ordered to help him live.

The thought makes me feel suddenly lighter. Even hell doesn't sound as bad, knowing Romeo will suffer the same fate.

"You will not," he growls.

"Oh, I will. And you will too." I smile. "It isn't so nice, is it? Having someone else decide whether you will live or die?"

His hands strike like snakes, reaching around to the back of my neck, fisting in my wet hair. My eyes squeeze shut at the flash of pain, but I refuse to cry out. I can't make a sound, can't do anything to attract Ben's attention. "I will not let you or your destructive tendencies defeat my chance along with yours. I forbid it." Romeo pulls my face close to his, whispering the words against my cheek. "You will love me. You will see." His lips come down upon mine and I taste the stink of him.

I gag and push at his chest. "Let me go!"

He holds my hair tighter. "Our destinies are one, our fate is—"

Suddenly the harsh backstage lights blare to life, blinding in their intensity. Romeo's grip loosens and I shove him—hard—willing to sacrifice Ariel's hair in the name of gaining my freedom. The sacrifice isn't necessary. Romeo's fingers go limp and slide from my hair without resistance.

I stumble away, throat working, doing my best not to be sick. Now that I can see him in the light, it's even clearer that Romeo's power is fading. I can see it in the faint blue tinge around his lips, the black beneath his eyes, the sagging of the skin on his face. Anyone else looking would see a boy who hasn't slept well or partied too hard the night before. But I know the truth. Death is already stealing into this body, driving Romeo out of his mind with fear.

Still, he manages to work up a laugh as his eyes rake up and down my soaked frame. "You still love me. You can't help yourself." He takes a step forward.

"Don't touch me!" I warn, raising my fists.

"Get away from her! Now!" Ben's voice comes from behind me, near the wall where he's just hit the lights. As afraid as I am for his safety, I'm equally glad to see him. I back away, keeping one eye on Romeo as I move toward Ben.

"You love me, you—"

"I don't. And I won't. Ever." I can't lie, even for the sake of convincing Ben I'm with Dylan.

"You heard her." Ben takes my hand, pulling me behind him. "She isn't interested anymore," he says, a thinly veiled threat in his tone.

Romeo laughs. "Then why . . ." His smile fades as his eyes flick back and forth between Ben and me, and a strangled sound escapes his throat. "What have you done?" Romeo turns his full attention to me. "What have you done!" Shock and betrayal sharpen his features, making him appear even more haggard.

"Leave, *pendejo*," Ben warns.

"No." Romeo's rage banishes his despair. He steps forward, pointing an accusing finger at my chest. "You will always be mine. This changes nothing. You are mine!" He lunges for me, but Ben moves faster, palms finding Romeo's shoulders and shoving–hard.

Romeo stumbles backward, falling to one knee before regaining his balance. Ben's hand wraps around my waist, urging me toward the door. I turn, trying to keep Romeo in my line of sight, but Ben holds tight.

"Come on," he says. "Let's get–"

His words end in a huff of breath as Romeo grabs him from behind and spins him back into the theater, tackling him with a scream of rage. They fall to the ground in a tangle of arms and legs and tight fists. "I'll kill you. I'll kill you myself!" Romeo's fist comes at Ben's face, but Ben dodges to the left, leaving Romeo nothing to punch but floor.

I run forward, reaching them just as Romeo's knuckles slam into the wooden planks hard enough to make them crack. I reach for his arms, but he's already busy with his leg. He sweeps his foot in a circle, knocking me to the floor. I fall as Romeo turns and dives for Ben again.

Ben's ready for him this time. He grabs Romeo's shoulders and rolls to the ground, kneeing Romeo in the gut, hitting hard enough to lift his feet off the floor. Even before he lands, Ben's at him with his fists, pounding at Romeo's face, chest, stomach–any body part unlucky enough to come into range. He's terrifyingly fast, brutal, holding nothing back. If Romeo were in top form, Ben wouldn't be able to land half his blows, but in his present state Romeo isn't faring well. There's a chance Ben could damage Romeo, and his own future along with him. I have to end this. Now.

"Ben, stop!" I scream. "Stop!"

But he doesn't seem to hear me. He's lost in the fight, his bright eyes shadowed in a way I've never seen before. I'm going to have to stop him myself, hope he'll come to his senses if I pull him away.

I've just taken a step forward when the door to the theater opens and a male voice cries out. "What's going on in here? Ben! Dylan! Stop this right now!" Mr. Stark—with Mike, the student teacher, close on his heels—runs into the theater. Together, they pull Romeo and Ben apart, revealing the mess they've made of each other.

I suck in a breath, fingers flying to my lips. Romeo's eye is swollen, and blood leaks from the side of his mouth. Ben's face looks better, but he can't seem to stand up straight, even with Mike holding his arm.

"We're going to the office. Now!" Mr. Stark pulls a glaring Romeo toward the door. "You too, Ariel," he adds before heading out into the rain. Mike and Ben follow. As they come closer, Ben's eyes meet mine, making a promise, a vow that he would do the same thing again in a heartbeat. That he will destroy anyone who tries to hurt me. Anyone who dares to threaten the girl he . . . the girl he . . .

Oh no. It can't be. He can't feel *that*. Even if he *thinks* he does.

It's impossible. *Gemma* is his soul mate; she's the one he's been glowing for since the night I arrived, and probably long before.

"Don't say you're sorry," he says, stopping beside me.

"But . . ." But I am. So, so sorry. It doesn't matter if the Ambassadors are liars. I can't believe I've done this, put Ben's chance at a lifetime love at risk.

"Come on, guys. Let's go." Mike looks nervous, out of his element policing kids only a few years younger than himself.

As we trudge outside, I keep my eyes on the ground, misery flooding into every borrowed cell. My own feelings I can deny, destroy, or at the very least, control. But what am I going to do now?

If Ben isn't just tempted, if he thinks he's in love with the wrong girl?

SIXTEEN

The rain rattles down on the metal roof covering the path, an ominous drum solo that accompanies our walk to the office, where the principal will decide our punishment for fighting on school grounds. I suppose I'll be included in the punishment. I tried to join in and am the reason for the fight, though I'm still not sure what pushed Romeo over the edge.

Was it simply my refusal to work the spell? Or did he see something in my eyes? Something that gave my feelings for Ben away?

If he did, we're all in bigger trouble than a trip to the office can ever produce. Once Romeo recovers from his jealousy, he'll find a way to use this information against me, against Ben and Gemma. He promised he'd go after them if I didn't play nice. The thought makes me drag my feet. Mike slows beside me. He's released Ben, allowing him to walk, while Mr. Stark pulls a cursing Romeo forcibly down the path.

"You two will be fine," Mike says. "Mr. Stark knows Dylan is trouble. He wouldn't have given him a part in the play if more guys who could sing had tried out."

"Right." I force a smile. It's nice of him to try to make us feel better.

"And . . . I don't know . . ." Mike's eyes meet mine. "Well, I don't know what you've heard, but I try to do the right thing. I'll speak up for you guys."

I stumble on a crack in the sidewalk and just barely catch myself before I fall. What's he talking about? What does he think I've heard?

"You okay?" Mike asks, stopping beside me.

I nod. "Yeah. Thanks." I stare into his green eyes, searching for something I hope I won't find.

Romeo said the Mercenary who made him is here, hiding, watching us. The monster could be inside anyone, even this seemingly kind man. This man who is suddenly very concerned about what I may have "heard."

"I think I've heard just about everything." I hold his gaze for a long moment, until a curtain drops behind his eyes. The authority-figure facade fades, leaving an equal standing beside me, assessing me with newfound respect, trying to judge just how much of a threat I truly am.

"Are you two coming?" Ben asks.

Mike turns to him. "Go on ahead. We'll be there in a second."

Ben hesitates, but then I guess he decides he's in enough

trouble and continues down the path. Mike waits until Ben turns, then speaks in a whisper. "Does he know?"

"Know what?" My breath comes faster. Could Mike really be one of them? One of the high Mercenaries, standing right next to me, asking if one of the people I've been sent for knows there are immortal bad guys after his soul?

He crosses his arms and his look grows decidedly less friendly. "You know what. Just tell me if you told Ben."

"No." I stand tall, refusing to show fear. "But I won't let anyone hurt him."

Mike sighs. "If you tell him, there's no way that—"

Before he can complete his threat, a scream cuts through the gray morning, making me flinch. It's a girl's cry—high and frightened, a shrill sound that vibrates along my skin. I spin, searching for the source, letting out a cry of my own when I find it.

"What's wrong?" Mike asks.

I shake my head, pulse pounding louder than the rain, drowning out everything but the sound of her scream as it comes again and again.

At the edge of campus, I see my old form, running through the field behind the theater building. She struggles through the high grass toward the shelter of the trees, slippers sticking in the mud, stumbling and falling only to scramble to her feet once more. She's moving fast for a girl hampered by heavy skirts and underclothes, but she won't be fast enough.

The thing behind her has nothing to impede its progress. It runs like an animal, capering up the hill as if this chase is a game it will see through to its bloody conclusion. Romeo's corpse appears even more skeletal with its tattered bits of clothing soaked by the downpour. I can count every rib, see the way its pelvic bones shift as it runs, swiftly closing in on my old self.

I don't know why he's chasing her if Romeo is the one he's been sent for, but I'm not going to let him have her. My mind tells me I should fear the soul specter sent to claim me, but my gut screams for me to help her, to protect her, to go to her. Now.

"Ariel! Where are you going?" Mike calls after me, confusion in his tone. Whether it's real—and he honestly can't see or hear what I do—or for the benefit of those listening, I don't care.

All that matters is that I reach myself in time.

I sprint across the sodden school grounds, arms working, fists flying up beside my eyes, feet skipping from one patch of grass to another. Faster and faster, until my legs cramp and my stomach knots, but I don't stop, I don't falter. I run straight for the creature scampering up the hill, this time the hunter instead of the hunted.

The rain comes harder, making it impossible to see more than a few feet ahead, but I keep going. I hear her cries and the eager snarls from the beast as it closes in. It's drawing out the chase, torturing its prey, feeding on her fear as surely as it will feed on her blood.

I fall, my sweater snagging on a twisted branch and holding tight. Instead of fighting to free myself, I tug the sweater off and leave it, running on in my brown tank top. The skin on my arms puckers in the cold and my teeth chatter so loudly I can no longer hear her screams.

My screams. Hers. Mine. Hers.

I don't know anymore. I don't know what's real or true. I only know that as I reach the end of the trees and the land opens up onto a vast vineyard, a part of me isn't surprised to see my body and Romeo's waiting for me. They stand hand in hand, as if the chase has been a game for them both, as if they own the world that slopes in graceful folds all around them. My old dress is still soaked and bloody, and Romeo is a slack-jawed horror, but the two figures are united in a way Romeo and I haven't been for centuries.

"*Run away,*" the Romeo creature groans. I brace myself, thinking it intends to chase me back through the woods, but then my old body laughs.

"Don't *run away*," she says. "*Love.*" My eyes meet hers and once again I sense a hollowness inside her, a feeling that something necessary is missing.

"What do you mean?" I ask, voice shaking. "I can't love Romeo. I just—"

"*Love,*" she repeats, as if she hasn't heard me, and before I can say another word, they're gone. Vanished in a blink. My eyes sweep along the rows of vines in every direction, but there is nothing. They've disappeared and I've lost her again. I've lost myself.

I should be glad. According to Romeo, that body is a psychic manifestation sent to consume me. But I'm not glad. A wounded sound tears from my throat as I fall to my knees. I can't do what she says. I can't love Romeo. I can't. I hate him. I will always hate him. My heart squeezes in my chest, trying to collapse into itself and disappear, to escape this strange agony.

Love. Hate. Love.

I feel as if I'm being torn apart. My stomach lurches and the world tilts unsteadily on its axis, and I find myself wondering if maybe this is all in my head. *All of it.*

What if everything I believe to be real is simply a creation of my mind? Maybe I was never Juliet. Maybe I never died in a tomb or fought my ex-love through the ages. Maybe I'm just Ariel Dragland, eighteen, a girl who's suffered a head injury and is now certifiably insane.

"No. I'm not mad, I'm not," I sob, only realizing that tears are streaming down my face when the words come out more gurgle than shout.

I suck in a breath and choke on it, swiping at my running nose and dripping eyes, angry at the nose for its pert, upturned slope, hating these big blue eyes and the rough scars that mark my stolen skin. I hate this body—not because of the scars, but because it isn't *mine*. It *isn't*. I'm not crazy, not yet. I'm simply sick to the bone of having nothing that is *mine,* not my mission, not my choices, not even my own flesh and blood. I *hate* it.

I hate traveling through time, watching the world transform so radically yet stay so much the same. I hate the world for creating monsters like Romeo and the greed and fear and evil that give him and people like him something to kill for. I hate the Mercenaries for stealing my brief flash of happiness. I hate Nurse for not telling me the truth about who and what she is, about what *I* am. I hate the Ambassadors for trapping me with my own compassion, for forcing me to work for the good of humanity even when humanity seems the furthest thing from good. I hate that I've spent so many years fighting for love when my own love was stolen away. So brief and then gone, never to have a second chance.

Most of all, I hate the hope that continues to spring to life inside me only to die again and again, as if I haven't lived through enough misery to know that hope is for fools.

Tears and more tears, enough to fill the world, rush down my face, making it feel like the rain is still falling, though it has stopped for a moment, leaving the air cold and lonely. I try to pull myself up, but I can't, can't find my way through rage and despair to something good enough to get me to my feet.

And then he's there behind me, wrapping his arms around my waist and pulling me to him, my back tight to his chest. "It's okay," he says, holding me when I try to move away. "It's okay."

"It's not okay," I sob. "It will never be okay."

"It is. You're tough, remember?"

"I'm not."

"You are. You stood up to him. You're strong."

I shake my head. I'm not. I'm weak and selfish. I hate and I covet and I'm far too aware of Ben's skin on mine, of the way his arms circle my waist, the way his warmth surrounds me, banishing the chill. I want him to be mine. I want to know that I belong here with him, that the arms I cling to will never let me go.

"You are," he whispers, propping his chin on my shoulder, as if being close to me is the most natural thing in the world. "It's one of the things I love the most about you."

A strained sound—half laugh, half sob—bursts from my throat. My fears have been confirmed, but a part of me wants to weep with relief. He thinks he loves me; he said the words. Even though I know they aren't true, they are still precious. "You can't love me." I do my best to keep the regret from my voice. "You love Gemma."

"I don't love Gemma. I *have* never, and *will* never love Gemma," he says, mimicking the words I said to Romeo less than an hour ago, right down to the stubborn refusal in his tone. "I love you."

"You don't even know me."

"I know you," he says, with a quiet assurance that threatens to make my tears start all over again. "I know you're strong and as beautiful on the inside as you are on the outside. I know you like to eat and hate Shakespeare—at least the love stories—and would do anything for a friend. I know you're an artist, and you made a wall of bricks look like it should be hanging in a museum. I know you've been through hell, but you didn't let it eat you up inside." He pauses, hugs me a little closer. "And I know you make me think the hell I've been through was worth it . . . if it's what made me recognize heaven when it jumped into my car."

My throat squeezes so tight I can scarcely breathe. Everything he's said—almost all of it—is about me, the real me, the soul inside this body. Ben *sees* me. He knows me. Is there even a chance . . .

No, there isn't. I've had my chance. One soul mate, one chance, and that's the end of it. I wasn't summoned into this time for myself. I was summoned because Gemma and Ben are soul mates—the color in their auras confirms it beyond a shadow of doubt.

"No," I say, tears stinging my eyes. "You may think . . . But you don't. Not really."

"I *know* what I feel. But if you don't feel the same way . . ." The pain in his voice makes the tears run again. I can't stand the thought of hurting him any more than I have, but there's no other choice. He has to forget me.

"I don't."

"You're lying," he whispers. "Just like you lied yesterday when you kissed that asshole. You didn't want to touch him; I could tell. You were doing it for Gemma, weren't you?"

"*She's* the one you're supposed to be with."

"How the hell do you figure that?" he asks, anger creeping into his voice. "She was *never* even my girlfriend. Sure, we made out *one time* at one of her family's barns near my house, but it didn't feel right. And it didn't go any further than kissing. I swear to you. Even before I met you, I knew Gemma and I were going to end up being just friends, and maybe not even friends. She's a *lunatica,* and she's definitely not my soul mate or whatever."

I turn, shifting until I can see his face. The intensity in his eyes makes me forget the argument I was forming, forget everything but how much I want to believe him. Even the deep, nearly auburn glow of his aura—the blush that confirms his love for another—can't convince me to move away. I'm not sure anything could. Not right now, not when he's so close, that fire burning in his eyes reminding me so much of myself, of the way I love.

"And I told her when we went for coffee that I wasn't interested. She knows that. She knew it last night. All we did was talk and feed the horses carrots, because you're the person I want to be with," he whispers, pushing my rain-soaked hair away from my face. "I knew that when you started fighting me for the gas pedal. I think I was in love with you by the time I dropped you off at your house."

"But—"

"I hated that you and Gemma were friends because I knew it would hurt my chances with you," he says, pushing on, his determination simmering in every word. "And last night, thinking about you being with Dylan . . . I couldn't sleep. I couldn't stand thinking that you were with him, that he might be touching you, kissing you . . . I just—I—" He breaks off with a sigh.

"I'm not doing this right, and I know I sound crazy, but . . . I love you. I could see myself loving you for a long time."

My breath rushes out. "I wish I could see that too." The tears flow faster. His words are breaking my heart into jagged pieces that stab away inside of me. Having him so close but so impossibly out of reach feels as if it really might kill me.

"Whatever happened to make you so sad . . ." Ben's words trail off as his face drifts closer to mine. Closer, closer, until I can feel his warmth against my lips. "I would do anything to make it better." Closer, until our exhalations meet and mingle and I pull a piece of him inside me with my next breath. "I want to be the person you come to for . . . everything."

So close our lips will touch if either of us moves an inch. "We can't do this," I whisper.

"We can." His hand comes to my cheek, cupping my face with a gentle insistence that sends sparks shivering over my skin. "I love you. I'll prove it, if you'll give me a chance."

And then he kisses me and any thought of protest vanishes with the press of his lips against mine. He is . . . *perfect*, as perfect as I knew he would be. His kiss fills me up like sunshine, burning away every bad thing, beating back the darkness that's weighed so heavy inside me since the day I learned there would be no happy ending. Not for me.

But in this moment, with his arms wrapped around me and his taste on my lips, his breath my breath, I swear I've been wrong. There is such a thing as happiness, and he whispers my name and holds me safe.

But who will hold Ben safe if Romeo convinces Gemma she should kill him? Her aura might be red, but she's not beyond Mercenary reach, not until Ben burns just as brightly for her.

My blood chills, moves sluggishly in my veins. Romeo can do it. Gemma is vulnerable; she's angry with me, and likely to get angrier when Ben tells her how he feels about Ariel. And he *will* tell her. He can't know that she won't understand, that his confession will put his life in danger. If this shift proceeds like every other, if he and Gemma don't end up together, they will perish apart.

And I'm not willing to risk Ben's life on the chance that this time will be different.

I turn my mouth from his, ignoring the howl of protest from my selfish soul. "I can't." I stand and stumble away, shivering in the sudden chill.

"Please, Ariel, I–"

"I can't do this. I don't love you."

Hurt flashes in his eyes. "You wouldn't have kissed me like that if–"

"It was just a kiss. It doesn't mean I love you, and I *know* you don't love me." I jab the words in his direction, doing my best to get through to him. "We barely even know each other, and three days ago you were probably saying you were in love with my best friend."

"No, I wasn't. I swear, I told her I wasn't into her, even before you and I met. She just wouldn't *listen* to me. Or she would, but then she came up and kissed me like we hadn't talked about being friends. She's just crazy, Ariel, I–"

"I don't care."

"Please, don't do this." He reaches for me, a gesture of such supplication it makes my chest ache. "I know it's hard to believe me. *I* wouldn't believe me if I were you. But if you'll just give me some time, I–"

"I don't believe you. I never will." I take another step back. "We should get back to school. We're going to be in even bigger trouble than–"

"Olvida la escuela," he says, anger in his eyes. "This is more important than–"

"Go back to school, Ben." I cross my arms tight, doing my best to hold myself together. "Find Gemma and tell her you want to work it out. We can pretend this never happened."

"No." Ben's lips press together in a stubborn line I want to trace with my shaking fingers.

"You have to," I plead. "Do whatever it takes to convince her you're worth it, or you *will* regret it."

"No, I won't."

"You will. I promise you will." Overhead, the sky darkens and thunder rumbles, echoing across the valley below. When Ben's eyes look to the sky, I slip past him and back into the woods. "Love her . . . or run as far away from both of us as fast as you can."

"What are you talking about?" He trails me, ignoring the hand I hold in the air, demanding that he stop.

"Love her." Lightning flashes like a warning to keep my secrets. A warning I ignore. "Or leave Solvang and don't ever come back."

"What?"

"You're in danger if you and Gemma don't stay together. Just . . . be careful. Okay?" I see the confusion on his face but push on before he can speak. "I know you don't understand, but I couldn't live with myself if I didn't try to warn you. I wish someone had warned me." My voice wavers as my steps grow faster. "I wish I had listened."

"Ariel. I don't–"

"Please listen, Ben. Please. We will never be together. *Never,* no matter what. It's more impossible than you could ever imagine. The best thing you can do is forget we ever met." Without another word, I turn and walk away, heading in the opposite direction of the school. I can't go back there. I can't risk seeing Romeo with the taste of Ben still on my lips.

SEVENTEEN

I walk home in the rain—again—this time wearing nothing but jeans and a tank top. I'm freezing, shivering until my jaw locks up and my bones ache, every second a painful reminder of how fragile I've become.

Finally, I decide to hitch a ride. The scariest people in this town won't get out of school for another six hours. I should be safe. I've had my thumb out for less than five minutes when a car pulls over.

Unfortunately, it's familiar car. With a very familiar, very *angry* woman in the driver's seat.

Ariel's mother leans over to open the passenger's door. "Ariel Dragland, what are you doing out here?" Her voice rises to a note so high it makes me wince. "What is wrong with you?"

"Mom, I . . ." Caught skipping school and hitchhiking. This isn't going to end well. I can see a vein on Melanie's forehead beginning to bulge. "I th-thought you were at w-w–"

"I *was* at work. Before the school called and said you'd been in a fight and run off into the woods with some boy." She snaps her fingers and flutters one impatient hand. "Get in the car! You're going to freeze to death and the seats are getting wet!"

I slide into the seat and pull the door shut behind me. The heat blowing from the vents feels as if it will burn my numb skin, but I'm grateful for it. As soon as I buckle my seat belt, I hold my fingers in front of the plastic slats, hoping the warmth will seep through my hands into the rest of me.

Melanie stares. "You're blue. You're going to catch pneumonia."

"I'm sorry," I say, clenching my jaw tighter, trying not to shiver.

"You'd better be." She shifts into drive and pulls slowly back onto the street. Water churns around the wheels, splashing as high as my window. "What is going on? Why did you leave school? Why were you in a *fight*? Where is your sweater?"

"It got ripped on a tree branch, so I left it in the woods," I say, answering the only question that seems possible at the moment.

"You left it in the woods," she repeats, voice flat. "With that boy? The one who was kicked out of the other school?"

I shake my head. "Ben wasn't kicked out of school. He came here to live with his brother."

"Well, he's probably going to get kicked out of *this* school," she says, squinting through the windshield as the rain picks up. "And you might too. Do you get that? Do you understand how serious this is? You might not graduate."

"I'll graduate." It's only three months until graduation, and Ariel's grades—with the exception of public speaking—are excellent. There's no way she'll be kicked out of school because of *one* mistake, *one* in four years of being a perfect, invisible, low-maintenance student.

"Ariel, don't you dare act like you haven't messed up big-time," Melanie snaps. "We've got a meeting with the principal *and* the superintendent tomorrow morning to talk about what happened, and it doesn't look good for you. Fighting on school grounds is a big deal. You're *absolutely* going to get suspended. You might even get expelled."

"What? But I wasn't fighting. I was just—"

"Don't act surprised. You're not that stupid." Melanie jerks the wheel to the right and the car sloshes down El Camino, where standing water covers everything but the middle of the road. "What did you think would happen when you and your boyfriend attacked Dylan and then ditched school right in front of—"

"We didn't attack anyone," I say, not wasting time debating whether Ben is my boyfriend. It seems Romeo's revenge has already begun. He certainly didn't waste any time. "Dylan attacked *me*. Ben saw him and—"

"That's not what I was told. The principal said—"

"The principal wasn't there." I shift to face her as she pulls into the carport. "And all she knows is whatever Dylan told her. Which isn't the truth. He's a liar, and—"

"He's not the one who ran off into the woods, Ariel."

"So what?" I ask, struggling to keep my volume down. "I was upset. Haven't you ever been upset?"

"Sure I have," she says, shutting off the car with an angry twist of her wrist. "I'm upset right now, but I'm not running away from my responsibilities."

"Well, maybe you should have," I snap back. "If your responsibilities are so awful."

"Don't you dare try to turn this around on me." She reaches back to grab her purse from behind my seat, jerking it into her lap the way she used to jerk Ariel from the playground. Angrily. Resentfully. "You're the one who messed up, and–"

"And you're the one who messed up when you got pregnant when you were nineteen." They aren't words Ariel would use out loud, but I don't try to stop them from coming. I don't know how much longer I have in this body, and it's time someone told the truth that's been festering unspoken between them for far too long.

"No, it wasn't easy having you by myself," she says. "I had no one to help me. *No one.* I had barely started my life and–"

"And then I messed it up." The accusation in Melanie's tone makes mine harsh, cutting. It's impossible to sit here and listen to this woman ask me to feel pity for her. I had enough of that from my own mother, enough of the guilt and the feeling that my very birth was something I should apologize for.

"Ariel, please, I never–"

"And then I messed it up again when I got in your way in the kitchen." A part of me knows I'm taking this too far, but I can't help myself. "And you've never let me forget it."

Melanie pales, her lips going white beneath the flecks of

lipstick still clinging to her mouth. "How . . . I . . ." She swallows. "That's not fair."

"You know what's not fair?" I ask, my voice a liquid whisper. "It's not fair that you tell me I'm too ugly to go outside without makeup. It's not fair that you act like no one will hire me because of my face."

She clutches her purse tight to her stomach. "I never said that. That's not what—"

"It's not fair that you think I'll never have a boyfriend because I'm so hideous." I push on, ignoring the tears streaming down my cheeks. I don't know who I'm crying for—myself, Ariel, or all the mothers and daughters who can't find a way to love each other. All I know is that this feels more important than just another borrowed moment in someone else's skin. "But I'm not hideous, Mom. You're the only one who sees me that way."

"I do not, I—"

"Some people think I look just fine. Some people even think I'm pretty."

People like Ben. Ben, who wiped the blood from Ariel's face without hesitation. Ben, who kissed her thin lips as if they were magical, sacred. Ben, who might very well stay in love with Ariel when the soul he's really fallen for is gone.

The idea is an imperfect flower blooming in my mind. People don't always end up with their true love. There are hundreds of perfectly suited pairs who never reach the place in their relationship that attracts the attention of the light and the dark. Once Romeo and I have been summoned, it's always been too late for a peaceful parting, but what if . . .

What if I take Romeo out of the equation? Would Gemma

go to Stanford in a few months, leaving Ben and Ariel to see where their life—and love—will take them? An eye for an eye is surely fair, no matter what Nurse says. And Nurse isn't here, and the Ambassadors can't be trusted, and I can't fathom a world without Ben.

Even if I can't be in the world with him.

Even if I have to give him to another girl to love.

I clutch my own stomach, trying to keep my insides from spilling out onto the floor. It's an almost unbearable thought, but what if . . .

"I think you're beautiful. I've always told you that," Melanie whispers. I look up to see silent tears running down her face, a perfect mirror of my own grief.

I want to do something to make the tears stop, but I can't. I can't force the lie from my throat. "No, you haven't," I say. "I can't remember a single time. Not one single time in my entire life."

Melanie's face crumples, every soft line around her eyes and mouth cloning itself until her expression is wrinkled with misery. "I . . . I'm sorry." Her lips curl away from her teeth as she begins to sob—silently at first and then in low, choked bellows that make my throat hurt just to hear them.

She *is* sorry. She really is. And I am too.

I reach for her, putting my arm around her back, my forehead on her thin shoulder. "I'm sorry. I just don't want it to be like this anymore. I want to be different. I want *us* to be different."

Melanie's hand lands lightly on my arm. "I love you. You know that, right?" She pulls away, her tear-streaked face stark, earnest, "I have *always* loved you. Even when I wished I had more time or more money or more help . . . I never regretted my decision." She sucks in a breath and reaches for a crumpled napkin sitting in the cup holder between us. "But you're right . . . I have regretted other things. Too much, maybe. I just . . . I always thought . . ."

"Thought what?"

Her red eyes fill with tears again. "I always thought you hated me. For all the pain I'd caused you. When you were little you'd scream and reach for me in the hospital, but I couldn't take you out of the bed. I couldn't hold you, and I thought . . . I swear I saw you decide to hate me right there."

"Mom, no. Of course I didn't. I *don't*." God, I never would have thought . . .

I suddenly feel like a fool, a cruel fool who only sees the world from her own point of view. Just like Gemma. It makes me wonder what else I've seen through warped glass. What if I had tried to talk to my own mother all those years ago instead of lashing out and running away? Could things have been better? Might we have discovered we weren't so different or distant as we thought?

For the first time since I was a girl, I long for the chance to see my mother's face, to look into her eyes and see if it was hate or fear or regret that made them so cold. I'll never know if I could have reached Lady Capulet, but I can reach Melanie. Right here. Right now.

"It wasn't your fault," I say, willing her to believe me. "It was an accident."

"No, it wasn't." She sniffs, swiping at her nose with the tight ball the napkin has become. "I mean, it was, but I'd had three glasses of wine on an empty stomach. I wasn't drunk, but . . ." She sniffs again and her next breath catches in her throat. "But if I hadn't had that last glass, maybe I wouldn't have lost my grip. Maybe I wouldn't have spilled it. Maybe I wouldn't have carried the stupid pot to the sink in the first—"

"Mom. Stop." I reach for her hand, but she waves me away.

"But it's true." She curls her spine, hiding her face. "You should know the truth. You—"

"Mom. I don't care." I lean down to catch her eyes, to make certain she knows Ariel doesn't harbor the slightest resentment. At least, not about the accident. "And you can't do this to yourself. All those maybes aren't going to change anything. You've made mistakes; I've made mistakes. The important thing is we don't have to keep making them. We can stop worrying about who hates who and just try to love each other."

She looks up, eyebrows arching. "You really don't . . . you don't think I'm awful?"

I meet her gaze—so vulnerable and hopeful—and know that I don't. And Ariel won't either. She never has. All she has ever wanted is her mother's love, her approval. "No. I don't."

Melanie sobs softly, and fresh tears fill her eyes. "I . . . That's good to hear." She sniffs, then laughs at the sound. "When did you get so smart?"

"I've been studying. I hear you have to be smart to make it as a nurse slash artist."

She smiles. "I do love you, Ariel."

"I love you too, Mom."

"But I don't want you to get pregnant," she says, the abrupt change in direction making me blink. "Not until you're married and you really feel you're ready."

"Okay," I say, embarrassed by the conversation.

"I'm serious." She takes my hand, squeezes it too tight. "We can go to the clinic now. I know they'd fit you in and you can get a prescription for birth control pills. Or they have IUDs if you want something more long term that you don't have to think about every day. They're perfectly safe. But either way, you need to use a condom too to protect against disease because—"

"Mom, please. I'm not in any danger. I promise. Ben and I aren't even . . ." What are Ben and I? I don't know, and that's a subject I know is better left alone. "We're friends."

"I just want you to be careful." Her forehead wrinkles. "Especially with this boy. He sounds rough."

"He's not rough." I sigh, wishing we'd stopped while we were ahead.

"I mean, I know Dylan's no angel, but he's never been arrested. Mrs. Felix said Ben has a police record, Ariel," Melanie says, stuffing her used napkin in her purse. "The only reason they let him enroll in SHS was because his brother and a couple of other people from the sheriff's office vouched for him."

"But I know why he was arrested," I say, struggling to be patient with her concerns. "He had this neighbor whose boyfriend was beating her up. He called the police, but he was afraid they wouldn't get there in time. And the police dropped the battery charge, so—"

"Oh, well, great." Melanie rolls her eyes.

"He was only protecting her."

"Like he was protecting you today?"

"Ye-es." Something in her voice makes me certain my answer won't satisfy her.

"Ariel . . . violent people usually have a good excuse for why they're violent. But even a good excuse is just an excuse."

The argument I've been composing dies on my lips. *Even a good excuse is just an excuse.* Is she right? I have every reason to kill Romeo, but can any reason excuse murder? Or is my love for Ben, my fear for his safety, simply a lie dressed up as justification, violence disguised as justice?

"You might want to step away and think about that before you and Ben take your friendship any further," Melanie says.

"Ben's a good person."

I, on the other hand . . .

"I'm not saying he's not." She sighs and reaches for her door. "But when we go for that meeting tomorrow, you need to think about your future."

"I don't understand." I follow her. The second I leave the car, my skin breaks out in goose bumps. I'm still soaking wet. I need a warm shower, not another lecture.

"I'm saying you need to make sure Mrs. Felix and Mr. Neville know Ben and Dylan aren't the kind of people you usually hang around with." She wrenches open the screen door and slides her key into the lock. "Ben may be a criminal, but you're not."

"He's not a—"

"You're a good kid who—"

"So what are you saying?" I interrupt, pausing on the steps instead of following her into the kitchen when she opens the door. "I should blame him? Throw him to the wolves?"

"No." Melanie turns back to me with a frustrated sigh. "But Dylan is saying that you two planned this attack."

"Like I said before, he's lying."

"Well, he's apparently got a witness who heard you saying that you and Ben were planning to corner him in the theater today before school."

"What?" A witness? I'm guessing that's Jason Kim, the only person in school as full of lies as Romeo. "That's impossible.

Dylan's just convinced one of his friends to say that so he won't get in trouble. He's a horrible person, Mom."

Melanie waves her hand. "Will you come inside? You're making me cold just looking at you."

"You believe me, don't you?" I ask, hesitating on the last stair.

"I believe you," Melanie says, making me sag with relief and take the last few steps into the house. Inside, the kitchen smells as sour as always, but at least it's warm. And there's bread and peanut butter in the pantry. No matter how upset and confused I am, I have to keep eating. I have to keep my strength up.

I head toward the cabinets, hoping Melanie will get the hint that we should end this conversation if I start making a sandwich.

"But Ariel . . ." She drops her purse on the counter and crosses her arms.

"But what?" I ask, fetching a plate and a knife.

"I'm not sure what everyone else is going to think. You and Gemma have been friends for almost your entire lives."

"Gemma?"

She bites her lip, obviously not wanting to tell me what she knows.

"Please, Mom, I don't—"

"Gemma's the one who said she heard you planning to hurt Dylan. She says you said something to her this morning at the bakery."

"Gemma," I repeat dumbly. Why would she lie for Romeo? Because she's mad at me, or is it something more?

She lied about her true opinion of Dylan from day one, and welcomed him into the barn yesterday. Who knows how close she's grown to Romeo? She's been listening to his lies for at least a day, maybe longer. For all I know she could be getting ready to drive a knife into Ben's heart at this very second, while I'm wasting time making a peanut butter sandwich.

The knife in my hand clatters to the counter.

"I have to go back to school," I say, heading for the door. Melanie stops me with a hand on my arm.

"Ariel, you can't."

"I have to. I have to see Gemma and find out why she's lying."

"Honey, I'm so sorry she–"

"It's fine. I don't care, we just . . ." I take a breath, trying to keep the hysteria from my voice. "Gemma and I have to talk." About how she's never going to lay a hand on Ben, how I'll kill her if she even *thinks* about making that kind of bargain. Gemma will *never* become a Mercenary. I'll make sure of it– one way or another.

"Please, Mom." I shrug her off and reach for one of the coats hanging on the pegs by the door. If I can't be dry, I can at least be warmer. "Can you just take me back to school? Or let me borrow the car for a few hours?"

"Ariel, you're not allowed back onto school grounds until the meeting tomorrow."

"But I have to go." I *have* to go back. I have to get to Gemma before Romeo sways her completely to his side. She's already telling outrageous lies for him; how much further is she willing to go?

"We can't," Melanie says, her voice admirably patient. "Why don't you go take a shower and warm up? I'll make you a peanut butter and banana sandwich, and while you're eating you can tell me exactly what happened. All about Ben and Dylan and Gemma and the rest of it. People telling that many lies always have holes in their stories. We'll find them and be ready to point them out in the meeting tomorrow and everything will be fine."

I shake my head, struggling to think straight, wishing a talk could solve this problem.

Melanie wraps her arm around me, pulling me close. "Come on, you'll feel better after you're clean and dry. And I bet between the two of us we can think of lots of ways to make Gemma suffer for being such a complete b-word." My head snaps in her direction. She smiles at the surprise on my face, trouble sparking in her usually tired eyes. "What? You know I never really liked her. Her mother is a snob, and I honestly think Gemma is suffering from a nasty case of borderline personality disorder. And she treats you like a puppy. One she likes to kick."

"She does," I say, not caring anymore that Ariel is so attached to Gemma. She'll just have to get *un*attached. Gemma isn't best friend material. And despite that red glow, she isn't soul mate material either.

My decision is made. The Ambassadors can take her glowing aura and shove it. I'm not going to do anything to help Gemma get closer to Ben. I don't care what they do to me. They can come for me, strip me of my power, and send me to the mist, but I'm going to take care of Gemma before they do. Maybe I'll lock her and Dylan away in some dark, cramped cellar—someplace similar to the tomb where I spent my last days—and let them fester there together until I make sure Ben is far away from both of them.

"But from the look on your face, I'm guessing the puppy

has learned to bite." Melanie gives me another hug. "Go on, shower."

I hesitate, clenching the jacket in my hand. I still feel driven to find Gemma, but if what Melanie's saying is true–if I'm not going to be allowed back on campus until tomorrow's meeting–chances are that Ben won't be allowed back on campus either. That means he's probably safe at home, secure under the watchful eye of his would-be-dictator brother. A phone call will confirm it.

Maybe his brother will even let me talk to him, let me tell him I was wrong, that maybe he and I . . . he and *Ariel* . . .

Bliss and misery, expectation and despair–this situation is all that, wrapped up in an impossible package. Still, the thought of talking to Ben lifts my spirits, makes me feel there's something in the world worth looking forward to, worth fighting for. But this time I'll be fighting to extinguish his glow, just as many a Mercenary has done before me. If I haven't switched sides, I'm definitely dancing on the line.

One, two, three, one, two, three–careful, or I'll stumble into the dark.

"Okay." A little drunk on my decision, I hang up my coat and head out of the kitchen, spinning back around at the last moment. Melanie is watching me leave, a relaxed look on her face that makes me smile. I've failed in many ways, but I haven't failed completely. Ariel and her mom are going to have a different life now, a better life. I'm sure of it. "Thanks."

"You're welcome. And in case you were wondering, you're not grounded."

"Oh . . . good." I didn't consider the possibility of being grounded. Ariel's never done anything worthy of a grounding before.

She shrugs and smiles. "We've made it eighteen years. I don't see any reason to start with the grounding now. And you're right, it's time I start trusting you more." She points a warning finger at my chest. "As long as trusting you doesn't involve any more calls from the principal, or running off into the woods and making me worry that you're dead. Or hitchhiking. Especially hitchhiking. That's a good way to get killed by a sex pervert."

I could hitchhike from here to New York City and probably not encounter anyone as evil as the boy we'll be sitting with in the principal's office tomorrow, but still . . . I appreciate the fact that someone cares enough to worry. Even if it isn't really about me.

"No more. I promise," I say, hoping Romeo will allow me to keep that promise.

I hurry down the hall, darting into the bathroom to start the water before heading to my room to fire up the computer. I open the Internet browser and type in *Luna, Solvang,* sagging with relief when I see that Ben's brother is listed. I've never gotten Ben's cell number. Professions of love, a kiss I'll never forget—but no phone number. We're going at this backward, but it feels so right; it has since the first day. It doesn't matter that his aura is glowing for another girl. He and Ariel can be happy together. I know it.

And in the meantime, maybe it's okay to let myself love him. Even if it isn't forever. I pluck the phone from its cradle and dial.

"Hello?" A woman's voice answers on the second ring. Ben's sister-in-law, I'm guessing.

"Hello. Hi, this is Ariel Dragland." I clear my throat. "I was wondering if I could speak with Ben?"

"Of course! Ben has said so many nice things about you," she says. "Let me get him." The sound on the other end is muffled as she calls Ben's name. When she comes back on the line, her voice is a hushed whisper. "Don't give up on him, okay? He's talking to Gemma right now, but I think he'll be grateful for the interruption."

Oh no. Gemma. Why isn't she at school? "Gemma's there?"

"Yes, but Ben's making it *very* clear he's not interested in being friends anymore. In a nice way, but still, very clear," she says. "I've been eavesdropping while the baby's sleeping. I just couldn't help myself. He's such a good kid, and I really want him to find someone who—"

She breaks off with a worried *humh*. "Hold on a second, Ariel." She puts the phone down with a soft thunk. I listen to her footsteps fade away and hear her calling for Ben again at a distance. Once, twice, three times, her cries getting higher and more panicked with every shout. I know something's wrong even before she comes back on the line.

"I'm sorry, Ariel," she says. "I've got to go. Ben's left the house."

Left the house. With Gemma. Oh god, oh no.

"I'm going to have to call his brother." She sighs. "I'm sorry. But call back later. Don't give up on Ben. He's got such a good heart."

"I know," I whisper. "I won't give up." *Not ever,* I add silently. I'll find him. I'll keep Gemma from hurting him, and do whatever it takes to keep him safe.

I hang up and run for Ariel's window but freeze with my fingers on the pane. I can't do this. I can't sneak out of the house. It would destroy the fragile new beginning between

Melanie and Ariel, betray the trust Melanie has obviously worked hard to give me. To give her daughter, the one who'll be reclaiming this body—maybe very, *very* soon if Gemma is intending to sacrifice Ben today.

Sacrifice. Ben. There's no time to waste caring about Ariel Dragland.

Still, for some reason my feet carry me away from the window, back down the hall into the kitchen, where Melanie is putting away the bread. She turns to smile at me, but the smile fades when she sees my face. "What is it? What's wrong?"

"Ben needs me. I have to go to him, Mom."

Melanie shakes her head. "Ariel, I don't think that's a good idea. You two have already had a traumatic day. I think you should give him some time and—"

"There isn't any time. I have to see him. Please, Mom," I beg. "Let me take the car. Please."

She hesitates only a second. "No, Ariel. You need to stay home. You're stressed and exhausted and—"

"I love him, Mom," I say, the words catching in my throat, so true it hurts to speak them. "And he loves me. He told me he loved me, but I was too scared to say it back. And now I'm afraid I won't get the chance. I think he might be . . ." What lie to tell, what cover story to explain how desperately I need to go to Ben? "I think he might be running away. I need to stop him, and let him know we can get through the thing at school tomorrow. That we can get through anything."

Melanie stares at me for a long moment before she speaks. "Go change into some dry clothes." Hope dies inside me. I'm going to have to sneak out the window. I have no other choice. "And then you can have the keys."

"I can?" I ask, shocked.

"Yes, you can. But you're going to take my cell phone and answer the second I call and wear your rain clothes and not drive too fast or do anything stupid with this boy."

"I won't. I won't!" I dash across the kitchen and give Melanie a quick hug. "Thank you, Mom."

"You're welcome," she says. "He's lucky to have you."

I look up at her, wishing I could tell her how much her words mean to me. Instead, I hug her one last time and run from the room, determined to change clothes faster than anyone has ever changed before.

Hold on, Ben. I'm coming.

EIGHTEEN

Where are they? Where has she taken him? Where would I go if I were Gemma and wanted a nice, private place for a murder?

Murder. Ben's blood on the floor, Ben's sightless eyes staring up at—

I swallow and grip the wheel tighter. Maybe they're just talking. Maybe things aren't as dire as I fear. Surely Gemma can't have been turned completely. Just yesterday, she seemed to care for Ben. Just this morning, she warned me away from him. No matter what Romeo promised her, no matter what Ben might have said this afternoon, surely she isn't ready to take his life. At least, not yet.

I cling to that hope as I steer through the streets of Solvang, searching for any sign of Gemma's or Ben's car. The rain pounds so hard the windshield wipers can't keep up, barely swiping away one sheet of rain before another riot of wet takes its place. I have to lean forward, strain to see the flooding streets.

School hasn't let out yet, and half the businesses have closed early. The usual tourists have been scared away by the crazy weather, and the town feels eerily deserted. The emptiness makes my anxiety spike higher and higher.

Where are they? Where have they gone?

I paw through Ariel's memories, searching for any clue as to where Gemma might go, but I can't find anything solid to hold on to. Ariel's life still feels so much more distant than it should. I've let my own desires take up too much space inside this skin. I'm crowding out information I need to keep Ben safe.

He *has* to be safe. What will I do if he isn't? What will I do if I'm too late? What if Romeo has—

Romeo. I might not know Gemma as well as I'd like, but I know Romeo. I know the way he works, know the places he encourages his converts to go. He likes isolated locations with a touch of the macabre. Cemeteries, deserted buildings, the ruins of ancient churches. There aren't any church ruins in Solvang. There are plenty of cemeteries, but it's raining so hard that they wouldn't be ideal. Maybe a deserted building, someplace where Gemma knows she won't be observed.

Someplace where she can turn off the security cameras and clean up the mess at her leisure.

One of her father's barns! But not on the Sloop grounds like yesterday. She won't want to be seen driving Ben through the gate, and my gut tells me he wouldn't hide under a blanket a second time. But the Sloops own a lot of land, miles of vineyards spread out all over the area, clear down to the ocean. Most of those vineyards have outbuildings to store farm equipment. And didn't Ben say something about being with Gemma at a barn?

We made out one time at one of her family's barns, near my house.

I turn on Ben's road, hoping my gut is steering me in the right direction. I can't imagine Ben wanting to go anywhere with Gemma. Unless she's holding a gun on him, she probably suggested someplace close.

Unless she's holding a gun . . . Her father has quite a collection. It wouldn't be hard for her to get her hands on one. I should have grabbed something more serious than a paint knife, but Melanie was in the kitchen, standing right in front of the knife drawer.

I drive faster, scanning the small placards on either side of the road, the ones that name the grape varietal growing in a field and often identify which winery the grapes belong to. The Sloops always have theirs marked and are one of the few companies that bother putting fences around their property. There's really no reason to. The only people who wander into the fields are drunk tourists wanting their pictures taken with the vines, and they rarely hurt anything.

I guess even the Sloops know that on some level. The vineyard of chardonnay grapes about a mile past Ben's house is surrounded by a barbed-wire fence, but no gate blocks the muddy road leading into the fields. I brake hard, sending the back of the car skidding before the wheels catch and turn down the narrow lane. There are tire marks in the soggy earth, and they look fresh.

A few minutes later, the land dips down, revealing a low spot in the field where the grapevines are half underwater. I brake, second-guessing my instincts until I see the tracks swerving out of the mud on the other side of the standing water. Someone has driven through here recently, and almost got stuck on the way through. Globs of mud cover the grapevines near the tracks, testimony to how the tires spun as they fought their way out of the flooded area.

Maybe Romeo told Gemma to meet him here for just this reason, knowing that should the rain continue to fall, they'll all be flooded in on the other side, giving them plenty of time to kill Ben and complete the spell to bind Gemma to the Mercenaries before anyone reaches their location.

I eye the water. It isn't moving. I won't be swept away if I try to cross on foot, but I have no idea how much farther Gemma has driven. Some of the fields are miles across, and I can't see a barn from here. What if I go on foot and I'm too late, what if those minutes I could have gained in the car make the difference between life and death?

My foot shifts to the gas pedal and the car eases down the hill. Water rises up the side. Up, up, until I hold my breath, wondering if I'm going to make it. Will the engine stall? Will the tires float up off the ground? Melanie's tiny Hyundai doesn't weigh much, and the water is rising, rising, until I could reach out the window and touch it. The car makes a sputtering sound, and I feel the wheels spin uselessly for a second before catching the ground again.

"Please, please, please," I mutter, leaning forward in my seat, willing the car to roll just a few more feet. . . .

The wheels spin, then catch, spin, then catch, and finally hit the road on the other side, spraying mud as the car fights its way out of the flood. And then I'm moving again, up the small rise, down into a shallower stand of water, and then up once more. About a hundred feet away, I see it. A small barn, and Gemma's BMW parked around the side.

Relief and fear burst inside me, overloading my nervous system, making me shake as I pull to the side of the road about fifty feet away and cut the engine. I don't want them to hear me if they haven't already. I take only a second to flip up the hood of my raincoat and pat my pocket—ensuring the paint knife is still there—before stepping out into the downpour. Thunder crashes and the rain slams against my head and shoulders, tiny fists warning me to get inside and leave nature to its own devices.

I walk as quickly as I dare up the hill toward the barn entrance. There's no door, and the structure isn't that big. Depending on where Ben and Gemma are standing, they might have seen me already. My gut tells me to move slowly, to try not to attract attention. Just in case.

But it's hard to slow my steps, to keep from breaking into a run. I have to see Ben. I have to touch him, feel the warmth of his skin and know that he's still alive.

Please, please, please. Please let him be okay. I don't know what I'll do if he isn't, whether I'll be able to stop myself from falling on Gemma with this ridiculous weapon and finding some way to end her. I'm afraid I'll kill her if she's hurt him, no matter what the consequences for my soul or Ariel's body.

The seconds tick by with ruthless slowness, each slippery step an eternity. And then a car engine guns to life, and time stands still.

I spin to the right, making the turn just in time to see Gemma's BMW leap from the mud and bear down on me. I catch a glimpse of her pale face behind the wheel, meet her eyes for a moment that leaves no doubt that she's seen me, before the rain smears her reflection. Then all I can see is gray steel and the grille of the car and mud flying from tires that spin faster and faster with no sign of stopping.

I jump to the side without a second to spare, the moment so close I feel the heat of the engine on my legs. The rear tires spatter me with filth as Gemma speeds away. Raindrops pound into the puddles like quarters hurled from outer space. I lie in the muck, shaking with fear, unable to move, unable to pull myself up off the ground.

She's left. She almost ran me over. Why would she do that? Why, if she doesn't already have Ben's blood on her hands?

A sob rises in my throat. I don't know if I can do it. I don't know if I can go in there and look down at another dead body. Not the body of some soul mate I barely knew, but the body of a boy I love. A boy I pushed away when I should have drawn him close and kept him safe. A boy so good and—

Hands close around my arms, lifting me off the ground, making me want to scream with relief. I know those hands. Even before his face appears above mine, I know it's Ben pulling me out of the rain.

Ben. Alive. Alive!

We barely make it under the cover of the barn's roof before I hurl myself at him, twining my arms around his neck, feathering kisses across his face—his cheek, his chin, his lips, his nose, his lips. *His lips.* Warm, scratchy with the hint of stubble, soft and beautiful and blissful and Ben.

Ben, Ben, Ben. I could say his name a thousand times and

never get tired of the sound of it. I could kiss him like this for hours, days, years. But first, there's something he has to know.

I pull my mouth from his. "I love you." And I do. I've already had a soul mate, Ben's aura is glowing for another, and these aren't my lips that speak or my arms that hold him. But it is my heart and my truth. He *is* my love. My impossible, doomed, undeniable love.

"And I love you." He cups my face in his shaking hands. "I'm so glad–I can't believe– She almost ran you over!"

"What about you? Are you okay? Did she hurt you?" My hands run over his shoulders, down to his chest, feeling the pulse of his heart beneath his damp sweater. It's black this time, flecked with drops of red. I touch a drop with one finger, and my knees nearly buckle with relief. Paint. Not blood.

"I'm fine, but–"

"But nothing!" I squeeze his shoulders, brush his damp hair out of his eyes. "I told you to be careful with–"

"She wanted to go someplace where we could talk in private," Ben says. "My sister-in-law kept showing up on the porch offering snacks so she could listen to what we were saying. It was embarrassing, and I knew this barn was close. Then the phone rang, and Marianne went to get it, so we got in Gemma's car. I thought I'd be about twenty minutes, and be back before she noticed we were gone." He hugs me closer as the thunder booms again. I let my arms twine back around his neck. "But as soon as we turned off, I knew I shouldn't have left. Gemma just . . . *perdio la mente.* You wouldn't believe the stuff she was saying."

Oh, I might. "Like what?"

"Like . . . crazy stuff. Apparently she and Dylan are . . ."

"Friends?"

"More like *friends*." He snorts beneath his breath. "It's just a physical thing, I guess, but she said it's been going on for a while. She said you knew all about it."

"I didn't." I shake my head. But I should have guessed. From what I know of Gemma, she doesn't hang around with boys for purely friendly purposes.

"I knew you didn't," he says. "I told her that. But she said that's the reason you went out with Dylan and the reason you and I . . . connected. She thinks you're trying to steal her identity because you're too messed up to create your own. And she's convinced you tricked me into beating Dylan up and . . . just a bunch of stuff that's so far out there I don't see how she could say it with a straight face."

I roll my eyes. If Ariel and Gemma were in a race to see who was more messed up, Gemma would be the front runner by a lap or three.

"I told her you didn't *trick* me into anything." His forehead drops to mine. "And I told her how I feel. About you."

I pull away, looking up at him. "You did? Even though–"

"I was hoping you'd come around." His lips quirk into one of his crooked smiles. "But even if you hadn't, it's still the way I feel. It's not going to change."

"What did she say?"

He slides his hands up and down my back in a way that's one part comforting and another part incredibly distracting. "She told me she was in love too. With some *other* guy."

"What?" My brow furrows.

"She wouldn't name names, but I guess there's a third guy in the picture. One who's 'worth the trouble.' She says they're in love and he's convinced her to change her life, and that she doesn't want to play games anymore. She actually had the guts to say she was trying to protect me. From you. That you're crazy and have all this 'deeply buried rage' no one else knows about and on and on until I just started laughing."

"You didn't." My lips curve despite my worries.

"I did. And then I told her I liked your deeply buried rage and everything else about you. That's when she really lost it." He shrugs, a movement that brings me even closer, until I can feel our stomachs press together as we pull in our next breath. "I couldn't care less. Gemma is nothing to me. I never felt this way about her. I've never felt this way about anyone."

"Me either." Even in the days when I worshipped Romeo, I didn't feel like this.

I didn't feel I could tell him anything and he'd try to understand. I didn't believe he saw through to the heart of me and loved me for my strengths *and* my weaknesses. Romeo lifted me up to dizzy places with his adoration, but he never held me with such gentle recognition, never made my feet feel planted on solid ground. Planted in a place where something real and wonderful could grow, something more amazing than "forever."

One human life, a human heart freely given–it's the greatest gift anyone can give. And Ben wants to give his to me. The last of the pink in his aura deepens before my eyes, until the heart of him burns a rich wine-red. It's a light going on in the darkness in more ways than one.

My hand slides from his neck to press against my chest. I've never been able to see my own aura–I assumed I didn't have one after my death–but what if . . . what if . . . what if I am glowing as brightly as Ben?

It would certainly explain why Romeo was so thrilled when the lights first came on in the theater. He must have seen my aura and thought I was glowing for *him*. And then he saw me with Ben. That's why he was suddenly so intent on asserting his claim, why he—

What have you done? This changes nothing.

What have I done? I've fallen in love with someone else—true love, burning-heart love. And it changes everything.

"Do you think a person can have more than one soul mate?" I ask, my pulse racing as I wait for Ben's answer.

He cocks his head. "Why? You thinking of replacing me already?"

Something inside me lightens, just because he's so certain. So certain that I am the One. His One. "No. No, I just . . . I thought I was in love once. A long time ago when I was . . . younger." Several hundred years younger. "I was so sure that was it, my one chance, but now . . ."

"Gemma said Dylan was your first date."

I bite my lip, not wanting to lie, but too afraid to tell the whole truth. "I met the other boy at a party. We never went on a date. He would sneak into my house at night and we'd talk, but it only lasted for a few days. Five days after I met him he . . . left town."

"You've only known me three days."

The realization makes me start. It's true, but it seems I've known Ben forever. I've felt that way since the night we met. It's as if some part of me has been waiting to meet him my entire life, my entire afterlife.

"I knew that first night," Ben whispers. "That first hour. Right after I wiped the blood off your face, I just thought—this is it, this is . . ."

"What?"

"This is the girl I'm going to spend my life with. I could

see it," he says, a vulnerable look in his eyes that makes it hard to swallow.

Maybe he really *did* fall in love with me, *me,* that first night. Before I saw him in the light, before I knew his aura was colorless before we met. Maybe Ben isn't the soul mate I've been sent to protect after all. Maybe I've been sent for Gemma and *someone else.* Maybe the other boy she's seeing, the one she told Ben was worth the trouble.

"I don't need any more time to know that I've never felt like this before and never will again," Ben says, banishing thoughts of anything but him as his hands smooth over my hips. "But I don't care if you have."

My eyebrows arch. "You don't?"

"No. I don't care if I'm not the first." His head tilts and his lips move within a whisper of mine. "As long as I'm the last." And then he kisses me, until the world spins and my blood races and there is nothing but Ben.

And he is perfect and right and good and I love him. I don't care if this is impossible. I don't care if it's forbidden. I *know* it isn't wrong. There's nothing wrong in the way he makes me ache, nothing wrong in the way his heart speeds along with mine, nothing wrong with his hands on the buttons of my raincoat, working at the barriers that separate us from each other. I want his skin on my skin, I want—

Skin. The terry-cloth liner of the raincoat slithers along my arms as it falls to the ground, reminding me of the scars peeking out from beneath the T-shirt I threw on before I left the house. Scars. Skin. This isn't *my* skin.

"Wait." I choke out the word as I stumble back, hands flying to cover my mouth.

This isn't my body. Ben and I might be soul mates, but I

have no physical form of my own. I don't belong here and I'll never be able to stay. Despite the strangeness of this shift, despite the miracle of falling in love again, I can't promise Ben this body's future. I can never be with him, even for a night. Ariel's soul is out there in the mist. She will be coming back. Sooner or later. Maybe sooner, if Romeo has discovered that Ben isn't Gemma's soul mate after all.

Somewhere out there, Romeo could have found Gemma's real love and be making progress convincing him to slay Gemma in return for immortality. Ben and I could have a day, maybe less. And then I'll be gone and Ariel will be here in my place. If I use her body as my own, I'll be an abomination. I'll step over the line I'm dancing on and become one of the monsters. When the time comes for Ariel and Ben to be together, it has to be Ariel's decision.

I dig the heels of my borrowed hands into my borrowed eyes and fight the despair the thought of leaving Ben inspires, try to ignore the jealousy that curdles in my mouth when I imagine Ariel's lips against his.

"I'm sorry," Ben says, still breathing fast. "I wasn't even thinking. We can wait. We can wait as long as you want. We can wait until we're married if you want."

"Married." I sob the word.

"Yeah. Married. Why not? Someday?" He takes my wrists, pulls my hands away from my eyes. The love in his makes tears roll down my face. "I love you. I want to do everything with you. I want to marry you and have kids with you and get old with you. And then I want to die the day before you do, so I never have to live without you."

I can't say a word. I only cry harder. What have I done?

How could I have let this happen? How could I have opened Ben up to the kind of pain he'll feel when I'm gone? He and Ariel seemed possible together before, but now that I know it's *me* Ben's fallen so hard for, I know he'll be able to tell something is wrong. He'll recognize the difference of Ariel's soul being in this body instead of mine. And it will tear him apart, wondering what has happened, wondering if love is as real as he thought if a soul connection can disappear so suddenly.

"Why are you crying?"

"Because I . . . I can't be with you. No matter how much I want to be."

"Why?" The word seems torn from his chest, as if the thought of not being with me is life-threatening.

"I can't tell you. You'll never believe me."

"I'll believe. I swear I will." He reaches for me, but I step away, closer to where the rain falls outside the barn door. "Anything you tell me, no matter how—"

"You don't understand. It's . . . I'm not the person you think I am."

"Yes, you are." He reaches for me again and this time I let him wrap his arms around me. It's too painful not to. "I know you. I love you, Ariel. I—"

"I'm *not* Ariel."

Ben shakes his head, brow furrowing. "I don't understand."

"I'm not . . ."

I'm not Ariel Dragland. My name is Juliet, and I've spent centuries jumping in and out of other people's bodies, fighting for love, trying to save soul mates from Romeo, the man who killed me. Yes, that Juliet. That Romeo. He's in Dylan's body. And I'm only borrowing this body for a short time.

Then I'll be gone, and the soul that really lives here will come take my place. But no matter what she remembers, she'll never love you the way I do. Never.

I swallow. It's impossible. He'll never believe me. No one ever has, no one ever will. "I'm . . . I'm sorry."

"Don't you dare. Don't run away from me." He holds me tight, his fingers pressing into my back. "I'm listening. You're not Ariel. Then what should I call you? I don't care. I'll love you no matter what name you want me to use."

If only it were so simple. A rose by any other name would still smell as impossible. It's a body I need, not a name.

A body. The word floats across my mind, and temptation dances behind it, luring me with smoky fingers. If I work the spell and reclaim my old form, could Ben love me in another body? Would he be able to look into my eyes and see my soul and believe? No matter how impossible it seems?

"Mermaid?" His hand sweeps across my forehead, fingers teasing over bone. "What's going on in there?"

I look up into his sweet face. "Nothing." I can't do it. Saving myself would mean saving Romeo, and Romeo deserves to die.

He could die just as easily after *the spell as before. Especially if he has a little help . . .*

And here I am again. Back to murder, but this time contemplating killing to keep my love, not simply to save him.

"We should go," I say, taking his hand. "I barely made it through the water twenty minutes ago and the rain hasn't let up. It might–"

"Oh shit," Ben says, gazing over my shoulder. I turn to look, echoing his curse as I see what's become of Melanie's car. The water has risen rapidly. The trunk is already under and the hood will join it before too long. There's no way Ben and I will be able to drive out of here now.

And Melanie is going to kill me.

"I have to call my mom. Did you bring your cell phone?" I ask. "Mine is in the car, but I can try to—"

"Don't bother." Ben pulls his from his pocket and holds it up between us. "No service out here. I checked when Gemma started going psycho. I was going to call my brother."

I sigh. "I guess we should try to walk. Your house isn't—"

Lightning flashes, and thunder booms seconds behind, a warning that makes us take a cautious step away from the door.

"It's not safe to walk through that right now," Ben says. His hands come down on my shoulders and squeeze. "Guess you're stuck with me for a while."

"Guess so." If I were a normal girl, being trapped in a cozy barn with the boy I love would be heaven. But I'm not a normal girl. And my one shot at becoming something close to one is slipping through my fingers. Ben is slipping through my fingers.

I turn and wrap my arms around his waist, press my cheek to his chest, close my eyes, and hold on tight.

INTERMEZZO TWO

Romeo

Blood, blood everywhere but not a drop to drink. It spills from the old woman's puckered throat, gushes down the filthy dress he's kept her in these two days, pooling on the floor, the last of her human warmth stolen away by stone. He's chosen a tomb as the location for the ritual to slay the high Ambassador, a mausoleum not far from town.

For nostalgic reasons. For a Gothic flourish. For laughs.

He isn't laughing now.

He yanks her hair, pulling her head back, making the slash below her chin gape wider. It grins at me, a wink between friends. There is no magic here, no golden light spilling into the darkness, no mournful wail as an ancient is cast out of paradise.

The woman from the bakery wasn't lying when she said she didn't know what we were talking about, that she'd never heard of the Ambassadors of Light. Despite the golden glow that filled her aura in life, Nancy isn't the woman he's looking for.

He was *wrong, wrong, wrong,* after he'd been so *sure, sure, sure.*

Hee. Hee. Hee.

"Is that a smile, Romeo?" he asks, voice as cold as the knife he still clutches in his red hand. "I can't imagine why you'd be smiling."

"I can't either." Some hard kernel of deeply buried sanity urges me to stitch up the grin ripping across my cheeks. But I don't. I smile wider, letting the infection spread.

She doesn't love me. She loves another. She blushes like a rose in bloom, though I ripped her up from the roots long ago. She is *my* soul mate. She should never burn for anyone but me. It makes me want to kill her. Kill him. Kill everyone in this town, anyone who has ever born witness to their new love, their heated glances and lingering sighs.

But beneath the lust for blood, beneath the hate, beneath the fear and the anger, there is something else. For a moment, that one shining moment this morning when I thought the glow around Juliet's heart was for me, I felt . . . happiness. No, more than happiness. I felt . . . *hope,* the spark of something pure, flashing like lightning through dry air, setting things crackling inside me.

"Well . . ." He heaves a great sigh and tosses the knife to the floor, where it lands with a dull clank. "This is most unfortunate."

"Most unfortunate," I echo, easing back a step as the blood at my feet spreads. For the first time in a very long time, I don't want to touch that red mess, don't want to smear my fingers with death.

"I suppose *she's* out there somewhere, hiding from me, helping Juliet find her way."

"I think not." I shake my head. "Her nurse hasn't made contact. Juliet is frightened and alone. If she were receiving aid, I would see it in her eyes. She has no secrets from me."

"You're a fool." He shoves the woman's chair with his foot as he walks past, knocking the corpse to the ground, making that new thing inside me cringe. She is dead. And I am . . . not pleased.

"The Ambassadors have secrets you can't even imagine, and now Juliet knows our secrets as well. Doesn't she?"

I open my eyes wide, feigning innocence as I have so many times before. "I wouldn't think so."

"Oh? You haven't been telling secrets outside of school?"

"Of course not. I've told her nothing."

"You've told her everything." He reaches into my coat pocket, wiping blood on the fabric, pulling out the cell phone tucked away there. "I put a listening device in the back. Two days ago. I heard everything you said in the theater." He smiles, eyes narrowing with pleasure at the fear no doubt dancing in mine. "Technology is its own magic, isn't it?"

"Yes. It is." I nod, and the skeletal remains of my smile clatter to the floor.

He *knows*. He knows I've only pretended to do his work while pursuing my own agenda. He knows I have knowledge far beyond what any lower Mercenary should possess. He knows I've lied and cheated and stolen sacred spells from the hands of their caretakers.

Their *dead* caretakers.

He must know that, as well. There's only one way I could have gotten my hands on the ancient spells. He must know that I am the one who killed the two Mercenary guardians, severed their heads, stole their eyes, and spoke the banishing words so the dark magicians could never bring them back to tell who had dared defy the high ones. It has been nearly two centuries since that particular offense, but time is relative. Flexible. Merciless.

Especially for them.

"You've betrayed your vows, Romeo Montague," he says, leaning against the wall of the crypt, surveying me with amusement. But I know better than to think I have amused him. He's simply savoring my impending pain, contemplating all the wretched ways he will punish me. I have tried to overthrow my gods and now I will suffer as only the gods can make a man suffer.

I shiver as he moves closer, wrapping his hand around the back of my neck. The second his magic-filled flesh touches mine, my skin flares to life. I can feel. Really *feel* for the first time in nearly a millennium. Heat and pressure and the scratch of the clothes I wear and the unbearable softness of his oddly feminine-feeling hand.

Though I hate him as much as I ever have, though I know the pain is coming, I shiver again. With pleasure. To be touched. To be felt. To be real inside living flesh. This is what Juliet and I could have had. An eternity of these moments. Together. It was worth the risk, worth the crushing agony of failure.

His fingernails bite into the cords of my neck, digging, gouging, tearing, until my skin bursts and his fingers squirm beneath, leaving agony in their wake. I fall to my knees at his feet, screaming for mercy, screaming for Juliet.

Again and again and again, her name rips from my lips,

howls through my mind. *Juliet!* I know better than to pray, but still something inside me begs the universe for mercy. Let her have someone on her side, someone to save her from the specter that would take her and from the hell that awaits. Someone to save her from me.

I know what penance the high one will demand, and I know I'll give him whatever he asks, just to have the feeling taken away, to be consigned once more to my familiar prison. I no longer wish to feel. Not this pain, not the soul ache that reminds me of all I threw away when I believed Mercenary lies, when I believed killing Juliet the first time would send her to dance with the angels.

Instead, she has become one. Despite her ferocity, despite the bitterness that's hardened her, she has remained so good, so pure of spirit. I believe I helped in my own way. I haven't tried to turn her, not really. I haven't done my best to bring her over to the darkness.

"You will turn her." He whispers the words I knew were coming, loosening his hold just enough to banish the worst of the agony and ensure I understand my directions. "Her shifted allegiance will bring us great power. You will turn her or this will be forever. You will know nothing but pain. You will become one of the screaming things that haunt the earth, an immortal lesson to the fools who would follow in your footsteps."

"You have no power over me." Defiance boils beneath my words. "I am at the end of my service. I will not turn her, I will not renew my own vows. You cannot—"

"You will renew your vows and do as I say, or I will return you to your own flesh."

That spark of hope leaps inside me again. My own flesh? Is it possible?

"But without the spell, without her love, the ravages time and sin have worked upon the specter will remain." He flashes his too-bright smile. "You will roam the world in that form—rotten and diseased—until your bones turn to dust. And even then, your soul will remain trapped on earth without voice or form, never to reach the mists of forgetting, never to join the ranks of the high ones."

He puts his lips against my ear, whispering his next promise directly into my brain. "I know you've found seven hundred years without physical feeling to be a great misery. How pleasantly do you think a few *million* years such as that will pass? When you are a phantom and no one can hear you scream?"

His fingers bite into my skin once more. Pain and more pain—hot and pitiless—and then the smell comes. The smell of Nancy's death, of her body's waste clinging to her filthy dress, the smell of her blood on the stones near my feet. I scream and gag, empty stomach heaving. "You wanted your senses returned so badly, Montague. Enjoy them. You'll miss this when you are one of the spirits of the damned."

He shoves my face into the blood on the floor. There will be no escape, no good choices, no mercy or pity. Not for me, not for her, not for anyone.

Somewhere deep inside me, the spark of hope dies, howling like a child left alone in the dark.

NINETEEN

The afternoon fades to evening and the storm grows teeth and snarls outside the door, dimming the gray light in the barn. Ben and I climb into the hayloft, make a bed of straw and the dry sides of our jackets, and lie down. And then we hold each other, whispering in the benevolent darkness.

He tells me about his childhood, about all the things he's painted and wants to paint, about the weird odd jobs he's worked to raise money for art supplies. He tells me about his brother and sister-in-law and his niece, who does dinosaur impressions that make everyone laugh. He tells me about his mother, how she loved him and his brother so fiercely, how he cared for her the way a parent cares for a child before she died, how there was never time to study and he fell behind in school.

He tells me how angry he was with his brother for staying away when she was at her worst, and, after his mother died, how his anger kept him living in a cramped apartment with cousins he knew were dangerous, despite his brother's insistence that he and Marianne wanted Ben to live with them.

I am more vague, telling him things I wish for, things I believe in, simple joys and everyday doubts and fears.

And finally, as the night turns colder and the darkness complete, I hug him close and whisper the question I've been turning over in my head for hours. "How far would you go? To save someone? To save yourself?"

"What do you mean?"

"Would you . . . take things into your own hands? If you knew it was the only way to save the person you love?"

He stiffens, the muscles beneath my cheek tightening. "Listen, I know . . . I probably looked scary today, but I swear it won't happen again. I just went crazy when I saw Dylan with his fist in your hair. I lost it, but I don't normally–"

"No, Ben, that's not–"

"The counseling group the court made me go to is over in a couple of weeks, and I don't want to stay in a group with Gemma," he says. "But I'm going to keep seeing another counselor. My brother thinks I should. At first I thought it was a stupid idea, but he's right. I'm still angry. At a lot of people. And I've got to get that under control so I don't do what I did today unless I really, really have to."

"I know. I'm not worried about you." I find his hand in the dark and squeeze. "I'm worried about . . . I'm worried Dylan won't stop until he hurts someone."

"He'll stop," Ben says, with the assurance of someone who doesn't understand the relentlessness of true evil. "We'll tell my brother what happened and you can get a restraining order. I'll get one too. We'll make sure Dylan can't walk within fifty feet of either of us."

"I don't think a restraining order will be enough. He needs to . . . go away. Forever."

"Are you saying what I think you're saying?" he asks, voice careful.

"He's not going to stop until someone is hurt," I say. "Maybe even dead. Trust me, the world will be a safer place without Dylan Stroud."

"Is that why you have a paint knife in your pocket?"

"How did you–"

"Is it?"

I hesitate. "Maybe."

"Mermaid. You are . . ."

"Crazy?"

"The *persona más temerosa*–the fiercest person I've ever met." His hand grips mine tighter. "I get what you're saying, and why you're afraid, but I promise you he's not worth it. Even thinking about something like that . . . It won't make the world better. It'll only make you worse. Believe me."

I shiver but don't pull my cheek from his chest. There's something in his voice, something that reminds me of the way he promised he was good at keeping secrets. "How do you know?"

It's his turn to hesitate. "I've never told anyone."

"I'm not anyone."

"No, you're not," he whispers, the love in his voice tearing me apart and putting me back together at the same time.

"So tell me."

"I . . . My brother . . ." He hugs me and sighs. "Remember I told you about that cigarette burn I got when I was a kid?"

"Yes."

"My stepdad, Ray, did that. One afternoon my mom was working late and I was running through the house. I crashed into the table near his chair. The ashtray was overflowing and when it fell it made a big mess. Ray got so angry, so fast, and he just . . . did it. Without even thinking. Just jabbed it at my arm." He pauses. "I actually think he felt bad after, when I started crying, but . . ."

I don't say anything, just hold him and listen. There's nothing to say that hasn't been said a thousand times before, nothing that can come close to expressing how sorry I am.

"Victor was there and saw him do it. I was only five. Victor was eleven. He pulled me away from Ray, ran to the bathroom, and locked us inside. Ray banged on the door and yelled at us for a while—about how we'd better not tell Mom what happened and how it was my fault and on and on. We sat in there for hours, with my arm under the cold water, trying not to listen."

Ben's muscles bunch ever tighter. "He eventually got drunk and passed out in his chair. Victor peeked out and made sure Ray was asleep. Then he left the bathroom and went into Ray's closet and got his shotgun. He had it loaded and aimed at Ray's head before I understood what he was going to do."

I hold him tighter, wishing I could erase all this pain from his past, give him back the innocence he lost when he wasn't much more than a baby.

"I started crying and ran over and pushed him. I got there just before the gun went off. The bullet shot into the kitchen and destroyed our microwave. No more corn dogs, not for almost a year," he says, a note of finality in his tone that leaves me reluctant to ask what happened next.

How did his family get through that? What did his step-father do to his brother? What did his mother say when she got home? How long were they forced to live with that monster? Had their mother known what a dangerous person she'd set loose in her sons' lives?

But I don't ask any of those questions. This is Ben's story and he'll tell it his way.

"My mom divorced Ray and didn't really date anyone after that. Even though she was a total babe when she was young. I mean, obviously I got these looks from somewhere," he says, and I can tell he's smiling. "But Victor was never the same. It was like . . . even though he didn't shoot Ray, a part of him did. He knew he shouldn't have picked up that gun and he never forgave himself for it." He shrugs. "I think that's why he became a cop. It's some kind of a test or some-thing. To see if he can carry that gun and only use it if he really has to."

We're silent for a long time, listening to the rain pounding on the roof, the wind whipping through the spaces in the wood planks, and the thunder rolling on to destinations farther south. I want to lift my head from his chest and find his mouth with mine, to let him know how much his trust means with a kiss.

But touching Ben anymore is dangerous. Instead, I say the truest thing I can think of. "I love you."

He laughs beneath his breath. "I like that a lot better than 'sorry.'"

"Me too." His hand smoothes my back, up and down, slower and slower until I can tell he's getting close to sleep. "Ben?"

"Hmm?"

"Thanks for telling me. It helped."

"You could never hurt anyone anyway, Mermaid." His lips find my forehead, kissing me softly. "Even if you wanted to."

Maybe he's right. I'm not sure I *can* kill Romeo. I've never been able to damage him without feeling horrified by what I've done, let alone do anything more serious. But even if I could, I shouldn't. Ben is right. Nurse is right. Taking a life is an act of darkness, no matter how foul the person, no matter how many awful things he's done. Even if the Ambassadors are a lie, that is a truth I will cling to.

I'll just have to find some other way to deal with the threat Romeo poses.

"Just promise me you'll be careful," I whisper into Ben's neck. "Promise me you won't be alone with Gemma or Dylan ever again. Promise me you'll stay safe."

Ben is quiet for a long moment before his breath snuffles out through his crooked nose. He's asleep. And he snores. Just a little. I smile, treasuring this new thing I've learned about the boy I love, praying I'll be able to learn more. Learn it all.

Maybe I can work out a bargain with Romeo, persuade him that he has to leave this town—or better yet, the state of California—as soon as the spell is complete. Surely he'll see there's no point in staying with me. I don't love him. I never will.

Then you'll never reclaim a body of your own.

Right. Romeo insists that the spell requires love, and the

specters' words seem to confirm his claim. But maybe he's wrong . . . maybe if I can get a closer look at this spell . . .

I hold tight to Ben, to hope, letting it warm me as the night grows colder and I finally fall asleep in his arms.

The lights come in the middle of the night. Bright lights and loud voices, calling Ben's and Ariel's names. My eyes fly open and I sit up, sending a scattering of hay floating into the air. "We're up here! In the hayloft!" I yell, turning to wake Ben and finding him already sitting up beside me.

"That's my brother's voice," he says.

I hear a woman cry "Thank god" and burst into tears and know Melanie is down there waiting for me as well. This isn't going to be good. At all. I meet Ben's eyes and he takes my hand, squeezing tight for a second, sending me strength I feel seep through my skin. A second later, we're both hurrying toward the ladder. A man's face appears at the top just before we reach it.

The relief in his expression hits me in the gut. This must be Victor, Ben's brother. I had no idea he'd be so worried. I knew Melanie would be out of her mind, but Ben and I have been "missing" for less than a night. "We thought you two . . . we thought—" The man bows his head. I can see his throat working, fighting back tears.

"I'm sorry, Victor," Ben says, going to his brother, putting a hand on his arm. "I swear, I didn't mean to worry you. We got trapped out here and our cell phones weren't working and—"

"I'm just glad you're okay." He climbs the last few steps and pulls Ben into a hug. "I love you, *hermanito*. You know that, right?"

Ben's eyes go wide. "You too, bro."

"Are they okay? Is she really okay?" Melanie's voice sounds from the ground below, so high and strained it drowns out the murmur of men's shouts and the electronic fuzz of radios announcing that we've been found.

"They're fine. Not a mark on them," Victor calls over his shoulder. He pulls away from Ben and reaches a hand in my direction. "I'm Victor, Ben's brother."

"Ariel."

"Marianne says I'm going to love you."

"You will." Ben smiles at me. I smile back, trying not to think about the fact that Victor will have to learn to love someone else if I have my way. At least a different body. But I can't think about that right now. I have to get down there and make sure Melanie knows how sorry I am for worrying her.

"Let's get out of here. It's freezing," Victor says. He starts toward the ladder but stops and turns back to us, lowering his voice to a whisper. "You two have to know something. I hate to tell you, but it's going to be all over the news tomorrow. It's the reason we were so worried."

"What?" Ben asks, fear in his voice. "What happened?"

"Nancy Kjeldgaard was found about six hours ago. In the cemetery on the ridge outside of town. Looked like she'd been held there for a couple days before . . ."

As soon as the word *cemetery* is out of his mouth, I know. Romeo has done something. Something awful.

"Before what?" Ben asks.

"She was murdered."

"Dios mio," Ben says. "Did you . . ."

"Yeah. I was there earlier, but I was worried about you, so they let me help with the search." He clears his throat. "But it was brutal, and some people with experience say it looks like a cult ritual, a ceremonial killing or something. Whoever did it is . . . I don't want either of you leaving the house alone, or even *thinking* about hanging out in deserted places until these sick freaks are caught."

Ben nods. I do too, my head bobbing up and down as I wait my turn to climb down the ladder and struggle to find a reason why. *Why* has Romeo killed an innocent old woman? Soul mates come in all shapes, sizes, and ages, but Nancy wasn't one of our soul mates. I saw her myself, and her aura wasn't glowing.

So why do this? Even Romeo doesn't go out of his way to kidnap people or commit elaborate murders just for the hell of it. He's killed before, but usually impulsively, people who happen to be in the wrong place at the wrong time. I can't imagine why he'd do something like this.

I push the dark worries away as I climb down into a barn full of three other policemen, a man in waders with a flood-light, and my borrowed mother. As soon as I step off the ladder, Melanie rushes me, pulling me into her arms.

"Oh my god, I'm so glad you're okay." She presses a firm kiss to my hair. "You're okay, right? You're–"

"I'm fine, Mom, and I'm so sorry," I say before she can get another word in. "I found Ben and we started talking and by the time we looked outside the car was under and we weren't getting any cell service and it wasn't safe to walk home in the storm because of the lightning and–"

"It's fine. I don't care. I'm just glad you're safe."

"The car's underwater."

"I know, we saw it on the way in, and I thought . . ." She swallows and smiles through the tears that still stand in her eyes. "It doesn't matter what I thought. You're okay." She bites her lip. "Did Victor tell you about Nancy?"

"He did." The tears that rise to my eyes aren't forced. I only met her for a moment, but Ariel's memories of Nancy are of a tirelessly good woman. Nancy was extraordinarily kind; she was a gentle soul who has been stolen by evil. Whether Romeo is the evil responsible I mean to discover as soon as possible.

Ben appears at my side and gives Melanie a shy wave. "Hi, Mrs. Dragland. I'm Ben Luna."

After the slightest pause, Melanie smiles. She isn't sold, but she's obviously trying to keep an open mind where the boy I've confessed to loving is concerned. "Hello, Ben." I watch them and a sick feeling swims through my stomach. Why did I say what I said?

I know why. Because I didn't guess the truth in time, didn't dare to believe. But now, the last thing I want is for Ben to become any more ingrained in Ariel's life. I can't stay in this body. I have to leave, and to keep him safe I need him to leave with me.

The thought makes me shiver as one of the policemen wraps a big blue blanket around my shoulders. What if I find some way to work the spell, but Ben doesn't realize I've left Ariel's body? What if I'm wrong and he doesn't see soul-deep? What if this skin—and a nice girl inside it, who will remember him as her new boyfriend—are enough for him?

And what about Ariel? Will she grieve the loss of Ben if he *does* realize his soul mate has shifted bodies? Will I have made her life worse, when I set out so determined to improve it? What am I doing? How can I—

"Don't worry," Ben whispers as we follow the policemen and Melanie to the barn door. "Everything's going to be okay."

I turn to look at him. How did he—

"It is." He reaches out, takes my hand. "I promise."

I slip my fingers through his, praying he's right.

TWENTY

The flag at the school flutters at half-mast, waving mournfully in the harsh wind of yet another storm.

Nancy Kjeldgaard wasn't a head of state, but she served coffee, hot chocolate, pastries, and sandwiches to three generations of Solvang High School students. She listened to their stories and slipped extra treats onto their trays and offered kind words and encouragement when they were needed most. To the kids slumping into school today on the worst Friday most can remember, she was more important than a president. She was someone who loved them.

From my chair in the office waiting area, I can see the flag and the concrete path beneath, watch people on their way in pause beside it and look up, fear and sorrow mixing on their faces. It's the biggest reaction I've seen out of most of them. It makes me wonder what Solvang High School would be like if there were more people like Nancy here.

But at SHS, most of the adults are as disinterested as the students.

Even Mr. Stark seems more bored than angry to be starting his day with a disciplinary meeting. He sits in the principal's office with Mrs. Felix, awaiting the arrival of the super-intendent, nursing an extra-large coffee and staring blindly out the window. Mrs. Felix answers an endless stream of phone calls, not bothering to stifle her yawns as she assures one parent after another that the campus will be locked down tight during lunch until whoever murdered Nancy Kjeldgaard is caught. But even murder doesn't seem to arouse her interest. Her finely wrinkled face sags with exhaustion, and her brown eyes remain as dull as dirty pennies.

Melanie is the only adult who seems truly awake. She fidgets next to me, thin fingers laced together, her hands resting on one bouncing knee. We're fifteen minutes early. Ben and his brother have yet to show and there's no sign of Dylan or Gemma.

I wonder if Romeo will even bother. If he killed Nancy, there has to be some reason. I know she wasn't a soul mate, but . . .

Another horrible thought drifted through my mind as I lay awake for the few hours left in the night by the time Melanie and I arrived home: What if Romeo found a way to work the spell to reclaim his body alone? What if Nancy was a blood sacrifice for some dark ritual? What if Romeo achieved his goal without me and is now free to roam the earth in his own body? What will I do if my chance has passed me by?

I try not to jog my heels, almost grateful when Gemma arrives, giving me something else to focus on. She breezes into the waiting room in a black turtleneck and black jeans, the diamond chandelier earrings dangling from her ears the only break in her mourning gear. She sighs and claims a seat on the opposite side of the room.

Melanie makes a *humph*ing sound but doesn't dignify Gemma's arrival with a greeting. I don't either. I narrow my eyes, letting her see the fight in me. Last night, on the way back to town, Ben told his brother and Melanie that Gemma almost ran me over. Melanie was livid and insisted we press charges.

Ben and I have a date to give our statements at the police station Saturday morning. I don't think it will result in any real punishment for Gemma, but I want her to know she isn't getting off the hook. Melanie called Gemma's mother this morning and warned her to expect a call from the police about Gemma's "dangerous and insane behavior." Her mother threatened a lawsuit and hung up.

Gemma, however, seems unperturbed. She ignores Melanie's grunt and my glare and stares at the ceiling, her aura blazing crimson, sipping orange juice as if her conscience is blissfully clear. Her gaze doesn't waver until Mike walks in, and then she offers him only the barest nod. He nods back, lifts a nervous hand in my direction, and claims a seat a careful distance from both of us.

I give him a hard look, wondering if he had anything to do with Nancy's death, but the suspicion vanishes before it can fully form. Suddenly the truth is as clear and bright as the fluorescent lights glaring down on the waiting room. Mike isn't the Mercenary working with Romeo; he's a man in love. True love.

My eyes widen as I home in on his chest, on the rosy glow that certainly isn't coming from his black polo shirt. Holy . . . *crap.* There it is. Not quite as bright as it should be, but it's definitely there, the telltale glimmer of a soul mate.

Why didn't I see it before? Why didn't I guess?

Because I haven't seen him in the light. Mike has his break during my English class. I've only seen him after school, in the shadowed wings of the theater. The backstage lights aren't on during rehearsal, and the stage lights aren't bright enough to illuminate someone standing outside the action. Then yesterday, when we were outside, it was dark under the awnings covering the walkway. Still, I should have seen it. I *would have* if I'd been focused.

Every word he'd said yesterday had been a dead giveaway. *I don't know what you've heard. Did you tell Ben? If you tell . . .*

I close my eyes, feeling like a fool. Mike's hand on Gemma's back, the way he stood up for her at rehearsal, their shared laughter as they put away the props, her talking about his "hotness" that night at my house—it makes sense now. Ben said Gemma had another "friend" she was unwilling to name, probably because a relationship with him is forbidden. Mike can't be more than twenty-two and Gemma's eighteen and legally an adult, but he's still a student teacher at this school and she a student. He'll be in a big hairy mess of trouble if they're found out.

Another Romeo and Juliet, I think wryly as I open my eyes. *Damn it.* And now . . .

Well, who knows if I'll be able to bring these two together?

Their love is practically illegal, fraught with complications, and Mike's aura isn't exactly on fire. But then, the consequences if they're caught are a lot more serious for him. He's probably aware of that and—

My cell bleeps in my backpack, pulling me from my thoughts. I reach for my bag, but Melanie stops me with a hand on my arm. "I think they're almost ready for us." She points toward the office, where Mrs. Felix and Mr. Stark have risen from their chairs.

"But the superintendent isn't here," I whisper. "Neither are Ben and his brother or—"

"Wait!" A breathless Romeo appears at the door, dark circles under his eyes, a tattered brown scarf wrapped around his neck. He looks even worse than he did yesterday, more dead than alive, but no one else seems to notice. Melanie shoots him a menacing look and Mike ignores him altogether as Romeo steps inside, spoiling the energy in the room. My stomach pinches, relief and dread twisting my insides until it feels like I'm being turned inside out. I hate him, but I need him. Like it or not, my future lies partly in his hands.

I brace myself for eye contact, but he doesn't look my way. Instead, he goes to Gemma. "We can't do this. We can't lie. Ariel and Ben didn't do anything wrong."

Gemma's eyebrows shoot up and her eyes flicker to me for half a second. Just long enough for me to see the fear inside her. "What are you talking about? She told me she was going to kill you. I heard—"

"You didn't hear anything. You know you didn't."

Gemma points an accusing finger at Romeo's chest. "Don't you dare start changing your story now, Dylan. You're the one—"

"Dylan, Gemma, let's save it for the meeting," Mike says in his teacher's voice. He doesn't sound like a man who's talking to a rival, but I don't miss the hint of jealousy in his eyes when he looks at Dylan.

Romeo ignores them both and turns to me. "I'm so sorry," he says, his expression holding the perfect mix of fear and regret. There isn't a spark of mischief, not a whisper of an evil agenda. He seems *truly* sorry.

God, what is he up to now? Why the sudden change of plans? What can he have to gain from playing nice other than . . .

He still hopes I'll help him with the spell. That *has* to be it. Maybe it isn't too late.

"I'm going to tell Mrs. Felix the truth," he says. "I'm–"

"Okay, we're ready for you." Mr. Stark appears at the principal's office door and stops to scan the waiting room. "Dylan, where's your dad?"

"He couldn't make it." Romeo's gaze doesn't waver from mine. I hold his eyes, even when my blood runs cold. There's something awful in his expression, lurking beneath his yellow skin. What's happened to him since we parted yesterday? Has he seen the specters again too? Or is he haunted by something worse?

Mr. Stark sighs. "Dylan, the note you took home expressly said that you would be expelled if your father didn't–"

"He doesn't care if you expel me, Mr. Stark." He faces Mr. Stark, the picture of a penitent come to plead for forgiveness. "But I'm here because I do care, and I want to do the right thing."

"Yeah, right." Gemma snorts. "You're *insane,* is what you are."

"Gemma, please." Mr. Stark sighs again. "Okay. Fine. Let's just get this over with." He waves his hand and Mike, Gemma, and Romeo move forward. Melanie stands beside me.

"But Mr. Stark, what about Ben and his brother?" I ask, casting a glance back at the door. "Shouldn't we wait?"

"They're not coming," Mr. Stark says. "Mrs. Felix filed the paperwork to expel Ben from school yesterday."

My jaw drops. "What?"

Mr. Stark shrugs. "He's been in trouble before, Ariel, and we have a strict no-tolerance policy for repeat offenders."

"But he wasn't in trouble at school," I say, ignoring Melanie's hand on my arm silently urging me to keep quiet. Defending Ben is instinctive, imperative. "And not at *this* school. Please, Mr. Stark, I–"

"Ariel, it's not my decision. I had nothing to do with it." Mr. Stark backs toward the principal's office, where Romeo, Gemma, and Mike have already found seats. "Anyway, it's decided. Ben's brother came and cleaned out his locker this morning. I think he also picked up a study guide for the GED. Ben can still get a diploma if he passes the exam."

I shake my head. Anger flashes through me, followed closely by a spark of hope.

This will make it easier for me to convince Ben to leave. He isn't going to be able to finish senior year at SHS. There's nothing to keep him in Solvang but his family, and life with his brother hasn't exactly been smooth. He might jump at the chance for a fresh start.

But a fresh start with a girl he doesn't know? Or doesn't think he knows? With no money and not even a high school diploma between us? It's me and Romeo all over again. Ben and I probably won't starve to death or be killed by highwaymen, but our future won't be a bright one. Not at first. Maybe not ever.

In the cold light of day, without Ben's arms around me, the challenge of convincing him that the soul of the girl he loves has shifted into another body seems far more daunting. Not to mention the fact that I've yet to accomplish the shift. What if the spell doesn't work? What if Romeo is right and loving him is the only way? What if the high Mercenary watching him finds a way to stop us before we reclaim our old forms? What if—

My cell trills again. Ben. It has to be him, trying to let me know he won't be coming back to school. I reach for the zipper on my bag.

"Come on, Ariel. Let's go." Melanie tugs at my sleeve. "We'll deal with Ben later. It's time to think about *your* future right now."

I *am* thinking of my future. *Ben* is my future. At least, I hope he will be. I long for a tomorrow with him with a need that's terrifying in its intensity. I want to run from this place. I want to go to him and hold him and promise him that everything will be okay, the way he promised me last night.

Instead, I follow Melanie into the office.

Everything isn't okay. Everything is awful and time is running out.

Gemma and I received a week of after-school detention, while Dylan—as a detention regular—was ordered to report every afternoon for the rest of the year. I lied and said Dylan and I had had a misunderstanding, Gemma refused to say anything at all, and Romeo apologized so many times Mrs. Felix finally asked him to be quiet. No one was expelled or suspended. Not even Dylan, who'd allegedly earned a mandatory suspension for hitting another student. But he's playing Tony in the play, which opens tonight. Mr. Stark told Mrs. Felix the production would have to be canceled if Dylan was banned from campus for a week, and she didn't want to punish everyone who'd been working on the play.

Or deal with phone calls from the parents of angry drama students.

After one last dress rehearsal this afternoon, the show will go on, with Romeo in the lead. Even though he looks like hell, and is acting like a lunatic.

We're only ten minutes into third period and he's already squirming in his seat, picking at the skin around his fingers, tugging at the scarf he's still wearing knotted around his neck, though the air in the classroom is stifling. Mrs. Thurman always keeps it too warm. It's unpleasant on a good day, but today, with the infant pig carcasses we're about to dissect warming in their trays in the back of the room, the heat—and the accompanying stench—is almost unbearable.

The metallic odor of blood mixes with the chemicals used to preserve the animals, turning the air thick and noxious, making everyone a little greener than usual. But nothing like Romeo. He's rotting before my eyes. Dark veins creep away from his hairline in delicate swirls, and his lips are so bloodless they're almost purple. I can't keep from staring at him, from looking around the room to see if anyone else notices that Dylan Stroud is a dead man.

We're dead, Juliet. Dead. I see you as one dead, in the bottom of the tomb. Romeo whispered the words to me as we crossed paths in the hall before first period, and my stomach has been in knots ever since, even after I finally read the text messages from Ben.

The first was from seven-forty-eight this morning: *I've been expelled. My brother's going to send me to live with our great-aunt in L.A. tomorrow after I give my statement at the station. I can't change his mind, but he won't change mine, either. I love you. We'll make everything work. Ben.*

And then, only a few minutes later: *Meet me at the back door to the theater at intermission tonight. I'll find a way to sneak out. I have to see you alone. I don't want to say good-bye (even for just a few months) in front of the dictator.*

The dictator. He's angry with his brother, in the perfect state of mind to run away. If only I could pick up and run with him without worrying about slipping on a different skin. If only we could buy a one-way ticket to anywhere and leave tonight.

"Mrs. Thurman?" Romeo shouts the teacher's name, cutting off her lecture. His arm shoots into the air and stays there, trembling. "May I be excused?"

Mrs. Thurman clasps the cross at her neck for a moment, thrown by the interruption, then waves him toward the door. "All right, Dylan, but hurry back. We've only got forty minutes. We need to get started, and you *will* be graded on team participation."

Romeo races to the door, stumbling over an empty desk in his hurry to leave the class. A few people laugh, but I know there's nothing funny about his sudden flight. He isn't having a bathroom emergency; he's running away from a monster. From the putrid remains of his true self.

The pen in my hand falls to my desk with a distant clack. There it is, in the corner of the room, crouched behind the model of the human skeleton Mrs. Thurman calls Mr. Bones. Romeo's body scuttles from its hiding place, a savage grin on its face, as if it realizes it's playing a joke by hiding one skeleton behind another.

I suck in a breath and grip the edges of my desk, eyes sweeping from one end of the room to the next, desperate for someone to notice the thing, to assure me I'm not alone. But no one seems to see the hissing corpse prowling down the last row of desks, gurgling, choking . . . laughing.

It's laughing. Relishing each slow step that brings it closer to its prey, giddy with the knowledge that I don't have anywhere to run. Down one row and up another, its grin still in place, its yellowed nails clicking on the tile. It passes by again—this time with only two desks between us—and pauses to stick out its black tongue, wagging it back and forth, jabbing it through the hole in what remains of its cheek.

Bile rises in my throat and my hand shoots into the air, but Mrs. Thurman ignores me, continuing with her instructions. Only one person can be excused at a time. I know the rules. I'll have to wait until Romeo gets back. Or run from the room without permission, earning more after-school detention and furthering the general opinion that Ariel is a freak and probably out of her mind.

Not her mind. *My* mind. I'm the one who's losing her mind. This thing can't hurt me, not right here in a room full of people. Can it?

No one else can even see Romeo's corpse. He's been sent for Romeo, and if he follows the pattern that's held so far, he'll be gone soon enough. And I'm tired of running. I'll wait right here, show it that I'm not afraid. I'll face it here in this room full of people or anywhere else it chooses to—

"Yes. Now. Love." The whisper makes me spin in my seat. Even hushed and husky, I know that voice, *my* voice.

Only a few feet behind me—still dressed in my blue wedding dress—stands my old body, reaching for me with her pale hands. Hands that are covered in blood. I suck in a breath and hold it, refusing to cry out, though the hole in her chest is more horrifying than ever, a raw place where skin and flesh have been torn away. I can see the whites of her broken bones and the frantic racing of her heart behind them.

Her heart. I can actually *see* it. Slick muscle tissue that pounds faster and faster in time with my own speeding pulse.

"Close. Better now," she says, one hand pressing against her chest, fingers slipping between her shattered ribs, probing the trapped animal behind. I feel the echo of those fingers inside Ariel's body—curious invaders tracing things inside me that were never meant to be touched—and scream.

A couple other girls scream as well—responding instinctively to the terror in my voice—a few boys laugh, and Mrs. Thurman shouts my name, but I can't think about the reaction I've caused. I only know I have to get out of here, have to run, have to—

"Ariel had a spider on her neck. It was huge. I think it bit her." Gemma suddenly appears beside me and slips her arm around my shoulders, helping me stand and pulling me toward the door. I stumble after her, heart clenching in my chest, throat so tight I can barely breathe.

"Oh no," Mrs. Thurman murmurs as we pass by her desk and keep moving. "Well, did you squash it? Is it still—"

"It crawled away, it's probably still down there on the floor somewhere, looking for fresh meat," Gemma says, making half the heads in the room turn to survey the ground around them.

But my eyes are all for the girl with her heart in her hand and the horror crouching beside her. Romeo's corpse is squatted by my old body's feet like a pet, head cocked, curious to see me leave when she has told me–

"Better now. Close!" She smiles and I fight the urge to scream again as I meet my own brown eyes. Who is in there? It isn't me. She's empty, a husk with a shadow inside. I'm not there; I'm here. I'm Ariel.

No, not Ariel, but not–

"I'll take her straight to the nurse." Gemma pulls me out into the hall, tossing her final words over her shoulder. "Back in fifteen!"

Her expression hardens as she hustles me down the hall, glancing right and left, rushing past the entrances to the other classrooms toward the exit at the south end of building four. I have to hurry to keep up with her, work not to stumble when I turn to check the door to Mrs. Thurman's class, making sure the specters aren't following me.

"Thank you," I finally manage, knowing I have to say something to explain my behavior, to thank Gemma for coming to the rescue. She lied for me and–for whatever reason–I'm grateful. "I don't know what happened, I was just–"

"Shhh, don't talk," she whispers. "Not yet."

My racing heart drops into my stomach, and the place where Gemma's hand still rests on my shoulder begins to burn. I turn to look at her and catch the flash of something familiar behind her eyes, something . . . ancient. "Where are we going?"

"I told you," she says, her voice deeper, different. "I'm taking you to see the Nurse."

TWENTY-ONE

"Twenty minutes until places." Mr. Stark rushes through the backstage area, lifting every prop box, as if he'll find Gemma hiding under one of them, dressed and ready to go on.

But Gemma isn't under the boxes. She isn't at home, she wasn't here for the last dress rehearsal, and she's not here now. Gemma is missing. Her parents are terrified, there's a rumor circulating among the cast that she's been taken by Nancy's murderer, and I'm petrified that the gossip may actually be true.

What to do now? What? *What?* It's impossible to think past the fear swelling inside me, tap-tapping a crazy-making rhythm on my bones.

"Okay, Ariel. Looks like you're going on tonight and to-morrow night," Mr. Stark warns as he passes by where I huddle by the backstage door. "You were great at the last dress this afternoon. You'll be fine. You ready?"

I glance down at my black T-shirt and jeans. I'm in my Sharks costume. "Ready."

No, I'm not ready. And I won't be fine. No one will. Gemma isn't here. For all I know she's dead, and Nurse's soul has been banished to the mist, never to return.

The original Mercenaries are killing the high Ambassadors. They've grown so powerful they no longer require the balance of light and dark to sustain their eternity. It's become so dangerous for the high Ambassadors that they're forced to hide when they venture from the safety of their realm—their lives and the lives of the bodies they borrow demand it.

And so they hide. Often in the last place the Mercenaries think to look.

The rosy glow of a soul mate's heart hides the golden light of an Ambassador aura, offering protection while allowing the Ambassador to look after a soul in need at the same time. Nurse has been inside Gemma from the beginning, sharing the body of the soul mate I was sent to protect, swimming below her conscious mind, spying on me as I work through my final shift.

I bury my face in my hands, going back to this morning, searching every word Nurse spoke for some clue to where she—and Gemma—might be now. . . .

"They killed Nancy last night." Gemma—Nurse—says as soon as we're hidden in the bathroom at the end of the hall, wrinkling our noses against the ammonia mixing with the rainwater dripping into the stalls. We are in the last stall, the one with the steel bar and more room to try *not* to breathe. "They knew I'd come to observe your final mission. I can only assume they thought I was borrowing Nancy's body. To Mercenary eyes, the aura of a high Ambassador is golden. There are humans whose auras are the same, as a result of their good hearts. Nancy was one."

I shake my head, sickened by the knowledge that I had anything to do with that poor woman's death—even indirectly—and sickened to learn that Romeo was telling the truth about the high Ambassadors' auras. What other truths has he told? I want to know, but a part of me fears knowledge as much as I crave it.

What if the things Nurse tells me destroy the last of my hope? For humanity? For myself? For a future with Ben?

She crosses her arms and pins me with a long look. "And now they will know they haven't found me. They will look harder, Romeo and his maker."

His *maker*. So there *is* someone watching him. Someone kidnapping for him, killing for him, trying to make sure he succeeds at any cost. Meanwhile, I've been left to flounder in ignorance. As usual.

"So you've been . . . *there* the entire time?" She nods and I grit my teeth. "Then why did you wait so long?" I ask, not bothering to hide my anger. "Why didn't you—"

"Gemma's soul is still here. Inside this body. I can lull her to sleep and replace her memories with substitutions for a short amount of time, but I couldn't risk interfering with her life until her aura was secure."

"It's been secure for at least a day. Why didn't—"

"It wasn't safe to reveal myself. Even to you."

"You could have found a way for us to be alone," I say.

"You had to see that I needed your help. At least to keep Gemma from running me over yesterday at the barn."

She looks down at the mud-streaked floor. "I apologize for that. I would have stopped her, but her thoughts didn't give me warning. It wasn't a premeditated action, just another destructive impulse she found difficult to control."

I can't stop the breath that huffs from my lips. "Yeah. She's full of them. Some soul mate."

"She is difficult." Nurse shakes her head. "But I have to confess . . . you've been difficult at times as well, Juliet."

My mouth opens and closes twice before I can force out a word. "What?"

"The magic created by your vows is coming to an end. I think it's time for you to leave our service. I can take care of Gemma and Mike. Gemma's love is sealed, and Romeo's sudden change of heart put an end to her destructive relationship with Dylan. From this point, it will be a small matter to rise within her and say the things Mike needs to hear to secure his commitment, to put them both beyond Mercenary reach."

"What? But–"

"You haven't performed as we'd hoped," she says, only the barest hint of sadness in her tone. "It shouldn't have taken this long."

"What shouldn't have taken this long?" I snap. "And why would it be better for me to go? I've done a good job. I've done everything I promised I would do, even when I hated it. Even when I hated *you* for turning me into this *thing* that I am."

"Yes. Hate." She sighs and crosses her arms, leaning against the scratched gray door to the stall. "That's your problem."

"Oh, it is?" I bite the inside of my lip, pretty sure I haven't been full of *this* much hate for quite a while.

"It is."

"Here's what I think," I say, struggling to keep my voice even. "I think *lies* are your problem. I think you're a liar. Romeo told me what you are, he—"

She laughs, an acidic sound that reminds me more of Gemma than Nurse. "And we all know Romeo has never told a lie."

"Not about that. You *are* what he said you are. Aren't you? You and the Mercenaries were—"

"Yes, I am what I am. And the Mercenaries are what they are, and long ago we were brothers and sisters in hope and magic," she says, as if this weren't a revelation. "I would have told you those truths when you were ready. If you'd shown true dedication to your work."

I sputter for a moment, choking on my indignation. "I have worked tirelessly for over thirty shifts, I've—"

"Exactly. You should have found your way so much sooner."

"What way?" I fight the urge to grab her shoulders and shake her until she stops speaking in riddles.

"The heart of our magic is love, *real* love, not good works performed with bitterness and rage as their motivation."

I laugh my own nasty laugh. "So this is because I didn't give you service with a smile? Is that it? So everything I've done has been for nothing?"

"No, not for nothing. Your good works have sustained us— just as Romeo told you—and helped heal the world, but your freedom would have given so much more," she says. "To our cause, to the world, to yourself."

"My freedom. How could I be free when you've—"

"By finding your way to the peace and happiness you've longed for."

"Don't you think I want that?" I ask, anger flooding out of me.

"Not enough." She puts a hand on my shoulder. "That girl you saw in the classroom shouldn't be here. She's a soul specter, created by fear and regret and hate. They come at the end for the Mercenaries' converts, to haunt them with the evidence of their sins and finally escort them to the mist for all eternity. The appearance of Romeo's corpse isn't a surprise, but yours . . ."

"But Romeo said the specters were creations of the universe, sent because we've disturbed the natural order, unbalanced some cosmic equation."

"He forgets that there are universes of our creation," she says. "Where balance or imbalance is of our own making. But neither the universe within nor the universe without tolerates imbalance. He's right about that."

I shiver. Another truth sprung from the mouth of the boy I hate. *Hate.* Is that why the specter urged me to love? Is there still a chance I can change my fate? "Can anything be done? If I try to forgive him, to . . . love him?"

"Perhaps . . . but love and forgiveness have never been your strengths, Juliet." She smooths a bit of hair from my face, as if that soft touch can take the sting from her words. "I don't know what the future holds for you. I've only seen this happen once. The young man embraced his specter and vanished. Afterward, we searched the mist, but his soul was beyond our reach. If you touch the specter, or let her touch you . . . . *When* she touches you, there will be nothing anyone can do."

I back away, suddenly suspicious of her confidence. "Romeo said we could reclaim those bodies. With a spell."

"You could." One eyebrow lifts. "But would you want to live in that damaged body until the end of time? With Romeo forever by your side? That is what that particular magic entails."

I shake my head, sickened by how close I came to tying myself to the man I hate. *Hate*. There it is again. I do hate. Nurse is right. But I also love. I do. I've cared for the people I've helped through the ages, and now . . .

Ben's face drifts through my mind. His kind eyes, his lips whispering against my skin, promising everything will be all right. My eyes slide closed and pain shoots through my body, squeezing everything inside me in a vice of longing and regret. Ben is the antithesis of hate, but Ben is . . . impossible.

"What about Ben?" I ask, though a part of me already knows the answer. "I love him."

"You do."

I open my eyes and find the hint of a smile on her lips.

"Is it as wonderful as you remembered?"

"It's better. *He's* better." I search her face. "But how could this happen? I thought soul mates were rare. I thought each soul had one perfect match and—"

"Love is not an isolated incident, Juliet. Love is everywhere. It always has been. You just have to choose to see the light in the darkness, the sun shining through the rain."

The rain that has been falling without ceasing, that creeps in through the roof and drips onto the tile all around us. My jaw clenches. Sometimes there is no sun. Sometimes there is no light.

"Ariel is coming back." I keep my eyes on Nurse, some

stupid thing inside of me still searching for a reason to hold on. "She'll be coming back into this body."

"She will. And she'll be transformed by the love you've given her. It's a good thing you've done, and if I could reward you for that and all the rest, I most certainly would. There are so many gifts I wish I could give you."

I suck in a breath and hold it, afraid I'll scream if I let it out. This is it, then. There is no hope. I've been deemed unworthy of Nurse's gifts, and Ben will be Ariel's. And she will be transformed by love and they will be happy. I try to be happy for them, to see that goodness as the spark in the darkness, but there is no room in my heart for anything but pain.

Maybe Nurse is right. Maybe I'm not good enough to be an Ambassador. Haven't I always suspected? Haven't I always known?

My heart beats faster. "Can't I keep trying? I haven't failed completely, I've done my–"

"You've been a loving servant, but we won't ask you to renew your vows. It would be unfair to you."

"Fair." I laugh, but it comes out sounding more like a sob. When has life or death ever been fair? "So . . . where will I go? Back to the mist? Forever?"

"I'm sorry," Nurse whispers. "But you could still find your way. Don't lose your faith."

Too late. It's already lost. If I ever had it. The only thing I have faith in is Ben.

"I need to make sure Ben's okay. How do I make sure he's safe before I go?"

"I told you the day you became one of us. Hold love highest in your heart and all good things will follow."

I fight to keep my frustration in check. "Can you get more specific? Please?"

"That isn't our way."

"Why?"

"We believe the only real truth is a truth discovered. Not told. But I will give you this. To help." She reaches for me, twining her fingers through mine. The second our palms connect, images flash behind my eyes. It's like the magic of those first few moments in a new body, when the particulars of a life come pouring in to fill up the empty places in my mind. But this time it's *my* life I see.

Or rather, my death. Through Nurse's eyes.

A trembling girl with blue lips, eyes rolling back in her head, half mad with thirst and the terror of being locked in the dark. The friar has his hands on her, pulling her out of the tomb. Nurse wants to go to her, but she can't. It would be suicide. She can only watch. And wait for the chance she hopes will come.

The girl is screaming, knocking away the flask of water at her lips. She's seen him, the boy lying so still on the floor. The friar tells her that her husband took his own life so that he might join her in the afterlife.

"Why didn't you call out?" the friar asks. "Why didn't you let him know you lived?"

The girl is mad with grief, weeping despite the fact that her body can produce no tears. Three days in the tomb. Three days with no water. It's no wonder she lost the strength to scream, but she finds new strength now. She reaches for the dagger in the boy's belt and drives it into her own heart.

Nurse presses her hands to her mouth, stifling her cry. The friar watches, a smile on his face, pleased with his deception, even more pleased when the boy rises and kneels by the girl's dying body.

"Juliet!" His hands cup her pale cheeks. "I didn't think she— I-I've changed my mind. Bring her back. Bring her back!"

The girl reaches for his face, running trembling fingers over his lips. Then she reaches for the knife. But she's too weak to pull it from her chest. Her hands fall away. The boy clutches her body to him, weeping, but the friar pulls him away as the girl grows still on the floor.

Nurse creeps from the darkness. She's nearly too late. The girl will be dead soon. There isn't time to tell the old stories, and she wouldn't even if she could. She's lived for thousands of years, sworn hundreds of souls into the service of the light. It's always better if they don't know some things, if they come to the real truths on their own.

The girl repeats the vows, and Nurse watches her go to the mists of forgetting, wondering how long it will take for her to find her way to freedom, to understand the gift she's been given.

My fingers slip from hers, severing our connection. Somewhere deep inside me, where all the knotted pieces of my past tangle together, I find the thread she's put in my hand. It feels familiar, true, despite the fact that I've spent every conscious day since my death denying what I did.

Romeo didn't kill me after all. *I killed myself,* just as the story said. I did this to myself. I'm not a victim; I'm a fool and as much of a liar as Nurse ever was.

"Why?" I stumble away, until the backs of my knees hit the toilet. I collapse onto the seat, shaking too hard to bother trying to stand. "Why didn't I remember?"

"You didn't want to remember," Nurse says. "But now you do. Use this gift, and find your way."

A gift. It doesn't feel like a gift. It feels like a curse, one last parting bit of misery. One more burden to carry. Speaking of burdens . . .

"What can I do for Gemma and Mike? To make sure they're safe before . . ."

"Gemma's relationship with Dylan did some damage, but Mike is closer to a commitment than you think. He and Gemma have similar demons, scars on their hearts that can only be mended by love. Gemma plans to tell Mike that she loves him tonight. That may be all it takes. Mike's aura could burn red by morning."

"And if it does . . . then Romeo and I . . ."

"You will remain in Ariel's body until the soul specter claims you. Maybe a day, maybe two. And as for Romeo . . ." She shrugs. "His fate is in his hands. If he chooses to renew his vows, he'll remain a Mercenary."

"Then let me renew my vows too. I can still fight him. I can keep going. I can—"

She stops me with a hand in the air. "It has been decided." It's the second time I've heard those words today. They don't sit any better this time around, but I don't say a word as she turns to slip the latch on the door. There's no point arguing. My fate is written in her impassive face. "If we don't speak again, remember I will always hold you in my heart."

And then she leaves. And I stay in the bathroom until the bell rings. Ariel's going to get an F on the dissection project, but at this point I can't bring myself to care. There are too many bigger things at stake. Like lives.

"Five minutes!" Mr. Stark calls out, snapping me back to the dreadful present.

He's making another breathless sweep through backstage, but stops to jab a finger in my direction. "Get ready, Ariel. You're going on. Break a leg."

I wait until he's passed by before reaching for the backstage door. Outside, a sickly orange light illuminates the concrete path leading around the building. Still no Gemma. Beyond, the night is dark and quiet. The rain has finally stopped—something everyone in town is celebrating—but the air seems more ominous for the stillness. The world is holding its breath, waiting to see if good or evil will win back the night.

"She's not coming," Romeo whispers from behind me.

I face him and nearly gag as I get a whiff of his stench. He reeks of death and disease, to the point that the rest of the cast has finally begun to notice. Everyone has given him a wide berth since he arrived, the few boys in the production hurrying to change into their costumes and leave him alone in the men's dressing room.

"My maker knows the truth," Romeo says, leaning closer. I press my hand to my mouth and back away, until my shoulders hit the brick wall. "He knows Gemma's not alone in that body. He lost her when she left campus after lunch, but he'll hunt her down and end it. Tonight."

Oh god. If only Gemma were answering her phone, if there were some way to warn her before it's too late. "Who is he? Where's he hiding? You have to—"

"Jason's dead," he says. "My maker killed him so he could have a body close to me." Romeo smiles. "I don't know why I never thought of that, killing for convenience. Suppose I'm not as diabolical as everyone believed."

Jason. I'm not surprised. Seems there's a good reason he made my skin crawl.

"It's easier for the high ones to hide when the body's freshly dead," Romeo says. "I know you can't see our auras, but they're usually black. Black as sin, as inescapable as a shadow." He reaches a hand toward me but stops when I flinch. "Yours was always golden. Until now."

Golden. Like Nancy's. "Did he do it? Did he kill Nancy?"

Romeo smiles. "Of course he killed her. And he will kill Gemma and that boy you love and you and me and the blood will never stop flowing," he says, the sadness in his voice scaring me more than his delight ever has. Panic swims inside me.

How to stop this? How to stop the Mercenaries when they feed on the very violence that seems the only thing that can end them? Murder isn't the answer. I believe that now. But what is? What?

"They don't seem to care as much about love anymore." Romeo sighs and swipes his curled hair away from his forehead. "Not even enough to destroy it."

"Places, people!" Mr. Stark flashes the backstage lights three times, the sign that we should find our spots in the wings. I try to move past Romeo, but he steps in front of me, blocking my path.

"It's too late. We can't work the spell."

"I wouldn't. Even if we could."

He nods, slowly, thoughtfully. "I loved you," he whispers. "I did. And I was sorry. I remember that I was, that I wanted to get up off the floor and tell you that—"

"I know what I did." I suddenly want him to know the truth, to understand that I'm not the same fool I've been for the past seven hundred years. "I know it's my fault, that I did this to myself."

He shakes his head, fingers the scarf he's insisted on wearing though it isn't a part of his costume. "No. It was mine. I deceived you. I can remember the guilt. I can't feel it anymore, but I remember." His eyes are distant, his expression blunted by pain and fear. For the first time I feel pity for the monster.

"What did they promise you?" I ask, wanting to know before it's over.

"They promised me your happiness." He smiles, a vague, confused smile. "Eternal happiness and joy, more than I could ever give you. But as soon as I saw your face, I knew you'd never have it. Even if the Ambassadors hadn't claimed you. I could see the truth in your eyes. You hated me too much to ever be happy."

No. That isn't true. Something's wrong with what he's said. Something small but important.

I close my eyes, letting the memory of my last few moments of life drift through me, rubbing it between by fingers, trying to name the exact nature of the feelings that pulsed beneath my skin. Despair, pain, sorrow, and, yes, hate. There was hate there, but not for Romeo, not *only* for him . . .

The realization strikes like a beam of light, making me blink. It *isn't* Romeo I've hated for all these years—at least not entirely. It's . . . myself.

I hated myself for giving everything to a boy who didn't realize the gift he'd been given. I hated myself for loving him. I hated myself for dying for him—so much so that I tricked myself into believing a lie for my entire afterlife. I hated myself for continuing to give him power, for spending so many useless years hating him when I should have spent that energy loving others, loving myself.

"Places," Mr. Stark hisses from a few feet away.

"I was sorry. If I could feel, I'm sure I still would be." And then Romeo turns and walks away, but I can't seem to move.

I should have been loving myself. *Myself.* Can that really

be the answer? Could that even be what my soul specter was trying to tell me? Something so simple and stupid-sounding and—

"Come on, Ariel, don't freak out on me now," Mr. Stark says, urging me toward the edge of the wings. I go, shuffling like a zombie, lost in the tick-tick-tick of the pieces falling into place inside me.

Is it stupid? Is it really?

I've lived inside so many people, and I've never deemed one of them unworthy of love. I've tried to show them that they are valuable and their lives worth living. I've urged them to forgive themselves and the people who've wronged them, to choose a loving future over a bitter past. I've even done it with Ariel—wanted her to see that she's beautiful and worthy of respect, felt pity for her that she can't see the truth.

And all this time *I've* been just as lost. I've never granted the girl I was forgiveness. Forgiveness for being naïve, for the mistakes she made. I've never given her the compassion she deserves. Given *myself* the compassion I deserve.

I've failed at many things, but Nurse is wrong, I haven't failed at love. Loving Romeo, loving the people I served, loving Ben—none of them were mistakes. It doesn't matter if they loved me back or were grateful or if they even knew my real name. I've loved them and it was good. *I* am good. I am worthy of adding my own name to my list, of letting go of the regret and shame that have poisoned me for so long.

So I do. I let it go, and know peace. It's like a door has been opened inside me, revealing endless, bright, airy rooms I've never walked in before.

I hear Mr. Stark making the welcome announcement, listen to him dedicate this performance to Nancy, and urge everyone to keep her and her family in their thoughts. And then the opening music surges inside the theater, lifting me up along with it. This is it. *This* is the freedom Nurse talked about. I know it, the way I've known every other truth in my life. The way I know I love Ben and it is perfect and wonderful for however long it lasts, the way I know mistakes don't have to be forever and love can be as powerful as evil.

When I step out onto the stage, there's no fear left inside me. Only excitement. Anticipation. For the fight, for the future, for the chance to look into Ben's eyes and tell him that I love him even more than I did last night. I love him more because—for the first time in seven hundred years—I love myself.

"The Sharks are gonna have their way tonight. . . ." I sing each song with more enthusiasm than I've sung anything in my life, not caring that I can barely hold a tune with both hands. The audience doesn't seem to care either, and I wish Melanie were here tonight instead of tomorrow. But still, there are over two hundred people filling the seats—teachers, students, parents, friends—and they are with us. With *me.* I can feel it in their applause as the Sharks rush on and off the stage.

Even hearing Romeo sing about love in his divine, soul-twisting voice can't dampen my enjoyment. I am alive for the moment. There is no fear or worry, only this strange assurance deep inside that everything *really is* going to be all right. I can't wait to tell Ben. I can't wait to kiss him until he is as breathless and believing as I am.

One scene flows into the next in front of sets that would make any production proud, and then we're nearly finished with the first act. The fight-scene music trills through the theater, ominous, but beautiful, skin-tingling. I join the other Sharks onstage, creeping through the spaces in the flats, slinking from one pool of light to another. Then the Jets are there and the fistfight begins. Left fist, right fist, careful not to touch, careful not to hurt. It's all part of the dance, perfectly contained violence boxed in by choreography, clean and safe.

And then Romeo is there and the knives come out. The music rises, pounding faster and faster as we jab forward and back, hitting the marks we've learned in rehearsal.

Shuffle to the right—swipe. Shuffle to the left—jab.

Swipe, jab, swipe, jab, and the music pulses louder, faster, louder, and he comes for me with his blade to end the first act, to send the audience out to the soggy lobby for the lemonade and popcorn the seniors are selling to raise money for the graduation dance.

The one Ariel might have gone to with Ben if he weren't being sent away. The one she might have gone to with Gemma—just to say she'd gone—if they'd still been friends. But now she won't go, and she might not even be alive to mourn the lost chance.

I see it a second too late—the lights reflecting off a blade too shiny to be plastic or retractable. A blade made of steel and sharpened to such a fine point that it slides into my stomach like I'm made of butter. Soft, warm things inside me burst, giving way without a fight as Romeo shoves the knife deeper and deeper, using his hand on my shoulder to urge my torso forward as he guides my body to the ground.

My head hits the stage floor with a sound that echoes in my mind. Above, the lights glare bright gold like the glow from an Ambassador-enchanted mirror, illuminating Romeo's curls. He is a dark angel sent from heaven to hear my confession, leaning close while the rest of the actors dance away, sticking to the steps that will take them into the wings, seemingly unaware that the knife—and the blood spilling onto the stage— is real.

"This is better," Romeo whispers in my ear. "Better to die than to be turned or stolen away to the mist." His voice catches and something damp falls on my neck. "You can rest now, sweet Juliet, and perhaps that heaven we haven't dared believe in will be there for you after all."

And then he's gone, running off the stage as the music fades and the police siren sound effect blares through the theater, warning the Sharks and Jets that their rumble has been discovered. The audience bursts into applause that crashes over my face, making me flinch and tremble.

It seems Romeo has grown a conscience.

And it is just as deadly as the rest of him.

TWENTY-TWO

The lights go down, and for a moment I am blind in the dark. Trapped. Dying. In the dark. Just like the first time.

But I refuse to give up. I'm surrounded by people, and the lights are about to come on again. Mr. Stark will see what has happened and call an ambulance. As long as I make sure Romeo doesn't get his hands on me again, I can make it through this. *Ariel* can make it through this.

Moving slowly, carefully, I roll onto my side and then climb onto all fours and begin crawling toward the help that waits in the wings. My Ambassador-given gifts are fading, but I'm still healing faster than a mortal girl. I can feel the torn pieces inside of me doing their best to mend. If I can get to a hospital, if I get help holding life inside this body, then maybe–

A burst of sound cuts through the air and someone in the audience screams. Then another person, and another, fear spreading like a fire through the auditorium. Despite the darkness still blanketing the stage, I think they've seen me, the bleeding girl dragging herself across the boards, leaving a gruesome, shining trail in her wake.

But then I hear the sound again and know what it is. Gunfire. Coming from the other side of the stage. Someone is firing into the audience.

With a soft groan, I turn to look over my shoulder. Romeo stands downstage at the end of the apron, gun aimed just high enough not to hit the people running from the auditorium. He isn't shooting to kill; he's shooting to ensure that chaos rules, to make sure no one comes to my rescue. Perhaps so that I can die tragically–*poetically*–by his hand, as I believed I had for so long.

But he will shoot me if he sees me. He wants me dead. I crawl faster, praying he won't turn to look my way. Behind the curtain I hear the dancers who've just left the stage shouting for everyone to run. That "Dylan has a gun!" and "We're going to die!" and "Hurry, the back door!"

The back door. Ben. Intermission. It's time. He's there, waiting for me.

He'll figure out that something bad has happened quickly enough. And then he'll come searching for me, to make sure I've gotten out, and Romeo will be waiting with his gun. Ben won't have a chance. If he sets foot in this theater he's a dead man.

Biting my lip to keep from crying out, I force myself to my

feet and stagger toward the stage door, clutching at the knife that burns in my core, sending flames to lick my spine. My heart thuds dully in my chest, my ears, my brain, struggling for survival. What remains of my healing gifts aside, I'll be dead within the hour if I don't get help. I'm losing too much blood, and something feels . . . wrong. Romeo has hit something important.

Important. I have to get to Ben. I have to keep him safe.

I push through the curtains and aim myself at the exit. Everyone else has already fled. The backstage is deserted and the door closed. No. Open. *Opening.*

Ben's face appears in the space between door and building, backlit by that sickly orange. He sees me and I feel his relief, followed closely by his fear. It's too dark to see the blood, the knife, but he can tell that I'm not walking the way I should.

"Ariel? What happened, what—"

"Run. Dylan has a gun," I rasp as I reach for him—taking the support he offers, urging him back out the door. He doesn't ask any more questions, just puts his arm around my waist and helps me out into the night.

I know the second he sees the knife, feel the tremor work through his body, tearing at things inside him. "Oh god." It isn't a curse, it's a prayer, a plea to save something he's afraid is already lost. "He did this to you."

I don't bother to answer. I'm channeling all my energy into moving my feet down the concrete path. He already knows the truth.

"I shouldn't have left you alone. I'm going to kill him," he says, choking on the words. "I'm going to cut him apart with—"

"Don't. Please." I find the hand he's placed on my hip and squeeze, shocked at how warm he feels. He's burning up.

No, I'm freezing. Cold. Dying. The thought makes my next breath catch. I don't want to die and leave Ben, especially not bearing the same curse I've suffered for far too long.

"It's not your fault. There's nothing you could have done." I stumble as we veer off the path, through the sodden grass, toward the line of cars parked along the road. The parking lot wasn't big enough to handle the number of people who came to the show. People who are now running for their lives, streaming out into the night, jumping into cars where they assume they'll be safe.

I have to make sure Ben is safe.

"Forget about Dylan. Just leave this place. If I don't make it to the—"

"You're going to make it. I love you," he says, a hitch in his voice.

"I love you too," I whisper. It's getting harder and harder to breathe, but at least the pain is fading, drifting away from my body, an iceberg floating out to sea.

"Please don't die, Ariel. Please." He wraps his arm tighter around me, until his hand brushes against where the blood has soaked through my shirt, gluing the fabric to my skin. He flinches, then turns and slides his arm under my knees, sweeping me into the air. The sudden shift makes the knife move inside me. I groan and my head falls back, eyes filling with dark sky.

"Put your hands over it and push down," Ben says. "Apply as much pressure as you can. I'm going to put you in the backseat and drive like hell to the hospital. I'll get you there faster than an ambulance could get here and back." Ben's voice is strained and breathless, giving testimony to just how fast he's moving as he rushes down the row of cars. He's running for my life, and pauses only a split second as we pass a group of sobbing people to order someone to "call the emergency room at Cottage Hospital. Tell them I'm bringing in a girl who's been stabbed in the stomach."

"Oh my god, is she okay?" someone asks.

"She's been shot?" The girl's voice shatters in the cold air. "He shot her?"

"No, she's been *stabbed*. In the stomach. Call Cottage Hospital and tell them we'll be there in five minutes." He throws the words over his shoulder, more focused on getting me to the Corolla than stopping to explain things to a bunch of traumatized kids.

Still, his instructions penetrate the fog for someone.

"Five minutes. Got it." It takes me a moment, but I recognize the voice. Ben—in his attempt to get me the care I need as fast as possible—has made a horrible mistake.

I look over his shoulder, meeting the reptilian gaze of the Mercenary inhabiting Jason Kim's body. Our eyes lock for a moment and then the man I once knew as Friar Lawrence is gone, moving off into the night. Ben leans down, guiding me into the backseat of the car. I turn to him, a warning on my lips, but the sky presses even closer, smothering the words I would speak. I try to lift my hand, to make some sign that he has to watch out, but my hands are too cold, too heavy.

Freezing. Heavy. Dying.

And Ben doesn't know to watch out for Jason, doesn't know about the monsters.

I should have told him the truth, no matter how crazy it

would have sounded. At least then I . . . At least then . . . Maybe he would have . . .

Dimly, I'm aware of Ben screaming for me to be tough, to fight back. And then the car is running and we're moving fast. Faster. Faster. The world fades out, then back in again, consciousness slipping through my fingers, life slipping from my—

Something slams into the side of the car and we're suddenly off the road, spinning in a circle, the smell of wet grass and exhaust filling the car. Ben cries out as we stop turning and begin sliding—down, down, down—careening down a hill so steep I can feel the car wheels rising off the ground, tempted to follow gravity's urging and go tumbling. Ben screams again. I would too, but there's nothing left in my mouth. No words, no screams, no breath. Ariel is dying. I'm dying. Ben will be all alone, without anyone to protect him.

The car has barely slid to a stop when faces appear at the window. Two of them—one a pale, evil moon rising in the passenger's window, the other a sad, miserable mess with part of his head missing. Romeo's curls are gone on one side, blown away, revealing skin and bone and slick, smooth pink that I don't want to think about. He's been shot. By himself or by Jason—I suppose it doesn't matter which.

What matters is that Romeo is here now, and he's grabbing Ben's door, pulling him out of the car.

"No," I whisper, finding the strength to lift my hand and reach for him, though it does neither of us any good. I see Romeo's fist draw back and hear the sick thud of bone hitting flesh and know the end is near.

Jason opens the door at my feet and crawls into the backseat, leaning over me, wearing the same evil smile he wore when he was the friar, when he watched me bleed on the floor of the tomb. I want to claw the smug, foul sneer from his face, want to drive my thumbs into his eyes and steal his victory away. I don't want him to watch me die, to watch Romeo beat Ben to death, but I don't have the strength to turn my head away, let alone do any damage. Even when he reaches for the handle of the knife and jerks it from my stomach, triggering a fresh wave of agony that bubbles inside me, I can't do more than twitch reflexively before lying still once more.

"There, there." Jason's hands push my hair from my face, gentle in the way of a spider wrapping a fly in silk. There is no comfort in his hands, only terror, torture. If it weren't for Ben, I would be grateful for the cold closing in all around me. Better to drift off to the forever sleep than go out screaming for mercy.

"I have a present for you, Juliet," he says, voice soft, but loud enough to be heard over the sounds of the beating outside. Romeo's fists continue to fly. I can hear them hitting their target, hear the groans and sharp cries as Ben learns what supernatural strength can do. I feel every sound slam inside me. Ben's pain is worse than my own. Far worse. I would rather suffer than hear him suffer, this boy I love, this good soul who will never get the chance to be a man. "I think it's time you experience dark magic firsthand."

His hands turn to stone around my neck, fingers digging into my skin, making me cry out and my eyes squeeze shut. He can strangle me to death, but I won't give him the satisfaction of watching the light go out of these eyes, I won't . . . won't . . . not a second time . . .

Power squirms inside me. I can feel it flood in through his fingertips, ooze into my veins, race—hot and horrible—into every cell, a ruthless invader that won't stop until every weak thing is burned away. Heat scalds my bones, cold fire freezes my core. My back arches and a scream bursts from my lips—a sound so raw it tears my insides as it fights its way out.

I am dying, but I'm also being born, melted and re-formed.

He pulls his hands away and I suck in a breath, gasping, shocked to feel my lungs expand without difficulty, to feel the necessary things inside me shift without pain. My hand comes to my stomach. My T-shirt is still hot and sticky with blood, but the skin beneath is smooth and unmarked. He's healed me, saved my life.

I bolt upright, eyes finding Jason, who has already made his way out of the car. He holds a hand out to me. I ignore it. His healing isn't a gift, it's a bargaining tool, a manipulative measure, some new way to torture me that I don't understand just yet. But I know better than to think this is over, or to believe for a second that he won't just as quickly take my life as give it.

I scramble out of the car, darting past Jason and the truck that drove Ben off the road, searching for the only person I want to see. The car has been knocked down into a pasture, but it stopped before reaching the bottom of the hill, where the collected rainwater forms a lake. If it had hit the water, Ben and I could have drowned.

But maybe that would have been better. At the moment, I don't know. All I know is that when I finally find Ben—a dozen yards away, illuminated by the car's headlights, his back against a tree where Romeo has propped him up, his body limp and his face a bloody mess—my body fills with an agony worse than any weapon could ever cause.

"Ben!" I run to him, shoving past Romeo, who stands swaying on his feet. I don't spare him a glance, don't worry when I kneel next to Ben, turning my back on him. He won't stab me again—obviously that wasn't on his superior's agenda or I wouldn't be whole right now. But even if he does, I don't care.

Let him do his worst. Nothing can be more horrible than hearing Ben's soft moan as I hold his broken face in my hands, watching his lids flutter as he tries to look at me but fails. His eyes are so swollen it looks like someone has slipped golf balls under his skin. His cheeks, chin, and forehead are split open and bleeding, and he's lost several of his front teeth. His nose is broken and maybe his right cheekbone. Maybe both cheek-bones. Even if he lives, he'll never be the same. He will always be damaged and scarred and—

Scarred. Some faraway part of my brain senses the smooth skin on my right arm, feels the slight breeze stirring the soft blond hairs that have grown on my neck and face. Jason hasn't simply healed me, he's *healed* me, reversed years-old damage, something Ambassador magic has never been able to do.

And if he could do it for me . . .

Gently, I lean Ben's head back against the tree and turn. Jason is already there, a few feet behind me, waiting for me to work things through with a smile on his face. Romeo stands woodenly beside him, staring blindly at some spot high in the tree, his lips moving without forming words, as if he's in a trance. I begin to wonder how much is left of that brain I can see shining in the harsh yellow of the headlights.

"What do you want? I'll do whatever you want," I whisper through the tears that stream down my face. "Just . . . heal him."

Jason shakes his head, feigning regret. "I wish I could, but my powers only work on those touched by my magic. Ambassadors or Mercenaries. We're all from the same source, you know."

"I know." I suck in a breath. My nose is running along with my eyes. If it could, I know the rest of me would weep as well. I can see where this is going, see the inevitable conclusion to our talk.

"So . . ." He lets the word trail off with a shrug. "In order for me to help Ben . . ."

I don't say a word. It's impossible. I'll never do what he asks. Never.

"Come now, Juliet. Life doesn't always have to be such a tragedy," Jason says, laughing softly. "You've been granted an amazing opportunity. A second chance at true love that you shouldn't let go to waste." He tosses the knife he pulled from my stomach in the air, letting it spin once, twice, before catching the hilt in his hand. "I promise, it's much more fun to play when you're on the winning side. Just cut this boy a little here, a little there, enough to prove your lethal intent. Then you'll take your vows to us, and she . . ." He turns to look over his shoulder, gesturing vaguely into the darkness before turning back around. "Well, she's out there. I can feel her."

I stare into the night, remembering Nurse's shared memory of waiting in the darkness, watching, hoping. Is she out there hoping now? Why didn't she show up at the theater and stop this before it started?

"She likes to wait until we're gone," Jason says. "But she'll come take care of this boy. She'll administer the vows and transform him into a vessel of light."

I sob, unable to keep the sound from bursting from my lips.

I can see it now, this new life he describes, a second eternity stretching out before me, but this time it will be Ben I fight. Ben on the other side of the divide, bright and beautiful and unreachable. Ben, who will only know that I hurt him, betrayed him, that I didn't love him the way I swore I did. This monster will never allow me to tell him the truth.

Maybe I won't even want to. Maybe by the time I see Ben again, however many years from this moment, in whatever corpse I'm inhabiting, I will have become so twisted by the darkness that I won't remember what it feels like to love. I'll be like Romeo, wicked and hollow, the love I feel for Ben dead inside me.

Life is precious—*his* life especially—but there are worse things to lose.

I turn back to Ben, brush his hair away from his ruined face, a part of me wishing he was conscious so I could say good-bye, the other part glad that he's beyond feeling pain. I lean my lips down to his ear, and the Ben smell of him drifts into my nose, making my heart break all over again. "I love you."

"I assume that means your answer is no." I turn to see that Jason has moved closer. His smile is lower on his face, his knife higher in the air. "You know what that means."

I know. It means he'll kill us both. Slowly. Torturously. See how long we'll last before we break, *if* we break. If or when. I don't know which it will be, but I know I'll hold tight to the love I feel for Ben, to the light in my darkness.

I don't answer Jason's question, just stare into his empty eyes, wondering which are more vacant—Romeo's because he has so little brain, or this monster's because he has no soul.

None at all, not even the ghost of a memory of what it is like to love, to be mortal and gloriously, horribly vulnerable.

I suppose that's why he doesn't expect it.

I don't expect it either, but when it happens I'm not surprised. Romeo is as wrong as he's ever been—as he's *always* been—but I heard the truth in the words he whispered onstage. He truly thought he was helping me by shoving that knife in my gut, just as he thinks he's helping me when he lifts the gun tucked into the front of his pants and fires it twice.

Once into the center of Ben's forehead. Once into the center of mine.

TWENTY-THREE

There is a moment of unbelievable pressure as the bullet pushes through bone, and then I'm floating, falling backward in slow motion, eyes sliding closed. Dimly, I'm aware that I've fallen on top of Ben. His knee is pressed into my back, the softness of his belly cradles my head, and I'm glad. It's good to touch him, to know he's close, though he lies so terribly still. But even the fear that he's already dead doesn't upset me the way it should. The moment is surreal, something happening onstage that I watch from a distance.

There is no pain, only the feeling of drifting inside my body and a strange, determined detachment.

I can imagine what I should be feeling as I listen to Jason

scream at Romeo and then the air goes quiet–quiet like the tomb, quiet like the mist, quiet like the end of the world.

I can remember the panic that should prick at my skin as the headlights illuminating the night fade to black and it begins to rain, cool drops that sting my face and slip between my parted lips. And then the sounds come, a soft sigh in the night, a hushed whisper to *"Come, now,"* and I know I should be afraid. My old body is coming. I can hear her in the distance, feel her on the wind, but I can't move, can't run. I should be afraid, but I'm not.

I haven't betrayed Ben. He hasn't betrayed me. We haven't betrayed the promises we made or the things we believe. It is . . . good. And whatever comes next will come next.

And then I feel her hands on my face, hear her voice calling to me, and fear creeps into my borrowed heart. "Juliet! Juliet, please. Hear me. Open your eyes."

My lids slide up, obeying her command. I don't want to, but I can't seem to help myself, can't keep from struggling to focus, from pulling Gemma's–Nurse's–shadow from the surrounding night. There is no moon; there are no stars, no more headlights. It's almost impossible to see. If she hadn't spoken, if I couldn't smell the hint of her expensive perfume, I wouldn't know whose fingers feather along my neck.

"I've frightened that thing away. It's not too late," she whispers, voice bright as she finds my pulse. "You're still alive and you're ready. I can take you with me."

I try to shake my head, to ask her what she means, to tell her I don't want to go, that I want to stay with Ben until . . . until . . .

But I can't move. I can only blink, disturbed, confused.

"You've found it. Your peace." She sighs. "Now I can offer

you sanctuary and power. You will be one of us, safe in our realms, only coming to earth when you feel moved by the light to fight against them. When you feel ready."

Her hand runs down my neck, over my shoulder, down to my hand. She takes it in hers and squeezes. "I'm so glad I found you in time."

In time? She hasn't found me in time. Ben is dead. *Dead.* Gone forever, and the world is a darker place for it. And what about Ariel? She has a bullet in her brain. No matter how detached I feel, some part of me knows that this body is dying.

"Where . . ." I swallow, wincing. The pain is beginning to find me, crawling over my flesh, a thousand tiny insect feet bearing misery. "Where . . ."

"I had to leave the school. I needed someplace safe, so I sent Gemma to Mike's apartment before the play, instead of after," she says, not a hint of regret in her voice. "And then they starting talking, and I didn't want to interrupt them. I could tell they were so close to finding their faith in each other. And I was right!" She actually claps her hands together in excitement. "Gemma and Mike are both burning bright. We can go. Both of us. Back to the light."

"What about . . . Ben?" I ask, fighting the tears that rise in my eyes. I don't have the time to cry, or the strength. "Ben and . . ."

"Gemma and Mike were the soul mates you were sent for. What happened with you and Ben was . . ." She squeezes my hand again, a gesture I can tell is meant to be comforting, but isn't. "Well, it was beautiful, for both of you, but it wasn't meant to be. It's time for you to leave this body, and Ben and Ariel aren't soul mates. In the end, they wouldn't have fueled our cause the way Gemma and Mike will."

So that's it. Ariel and Ben are secondary concerns because they aren't suitable food for the light. Romeo was right. The Ambassadors might be a more refined breed of vampire, but that's all they are. Vampires, masquerading as a worthwhile cause, as champions of goodness and defenders of true love.

They don't know nearly as much about love as they assume. Love doesn't want people to stay ignorant and frightened. Love doesn't value obedience over all else. Love doesn't judge and find some lives—or loves—more valuable than others. Love doesn't use people and throw them away. Love stays, and makes you stronger, even when the person you love is gone.

"Don't cry, dear. You will be one of us now," she says, misunderstanding the reason for the sob that escapes my lips. "Come, we must hurry. Gemma won't stay buried much longer, and the specter could return at any—"

"No."

"No?" She shakes her head, a stirring of shadows in the night. I catch another whiff of Gemma's perfume and then another, lighter smell. Rosemary and roses and dust from familiar roads. The wind blows harder, pushing the clouds away from the crescent moon.

"I don't want to be one of you." I turn my face toward the sweet wind, knowing *she* is coming. Ready to take her hand. Nurse said touching my old body would take me where the Ambassadors and Mercenaries can't find me. It sounds like a place I'd like to be.

"Juliet, please, this isn't the time for—"

"Go away," I say, at the same moment the whisper threads its way through the darkness. *"Come. Come."* I can see her now, a silhouette gliding across the damp grass, her long hair blowing in the wind. It catches the moonlight and flashes in the dark, curled fingers urging me to find my way.

I pull my hand from Nurse's and hold it out toward her. I can't go to my other self, but I know she'll come for me.

"What if I grant you and Ben another chance? Would your answer still be the same?"

My hand trembles, dips lower in the air. Is such a thing possible?

"If you renew your vows, I can send you back to the moment you entered Ariel's body, just before you met Ben," she says. "You'll be able to keep him safe in another reality, while doing more good work for the Ambassador cause."

"Another reality?"

"There are hundreds of realms where events play out differently than they have here. It is the greatest secret of Ambassador magic, so great that not even the Mercenaries know we possess it. But we have power over time and space that they do not."

"So . . . I could really go back? And he'd be alive?"

"He would. And you can keep him safe. All you have to do is make sure he doesn't fall in love."

The thought gives me pause. The connection between us was so immediate, so undeniable. I would fall in love with Ben again in a hundred versions of reality. I can't help but think it will be the same for him. And if so, Nurse's offer doesn't necessarily ensure that he won't die again.

"You can bring Gemma and Mike together again, help Ariel find the peace she so desperately needs, and it will be as if this mistake never happened," she says. "At least in one version of the world."

As if this mistake never happened. Ben and I were not a

mistake. Love is never a mistake. The fact that she can speak those words proves she was never the person I thought she was. I don't trust her, and I won't let her steal Ben from me. I'd rather go to hell than be her puppet for another day. "No."

"No?"

"No."

"But you could do good work for the cause," she says. "Ariel needs you. I see darkness in her future without Ambassador intervention."

"I see death in her future," I whisper, knowing it's true, knowing that there are worse things that could happen.

Nurse's eyes grow cold. "Yes. So do I. In this reality, at least. And perhaps that's best."

"You . . . are . . . a monster." I barely have the strength to force out the words. The end is nearly here. I can feel it.

"I am a god. There's a difference." If I could laugh, I would. Instead, I turn my face to the whisper on the wind. "Gemma will rise soon. I cannot hold her. This is your last chance. If you do this, you will never be one of us again," Nurse says, voice tight. "Never. There are no second chances for people like you, Juliet."

People like me. People who question? People who disobey? Disagree? Discuss? Distrust? People who make mistakes? People who love so hard it hurts and heals and then hurts all over again?

I don't ask her what she means. I don't care anymore. I only know that I am grateful when she pulls in a sharp breath and the real Gemma cries out my name. "Ariel? Oh my god. Oh my god! Is that Ben? Who did this? Oh my god!"

"Help," I whisper, hoping she knows what to do.

"Oh god. You're alive. Hold on. My phone's dead, but I

can call nine-one-one from the car," she says, smoothing a trembling hand over my hair. "Hang on. Don't you dare die. I love you, and I'm so sorry. I promise I'll make everything better if you'll just live." She sobs, a sound of such grief I know that her profession of love is true, and I wonder if maybe I've been seeing Gemma through warped glass as well. If maybe she isn't as awful as I wanted to believe, as I needed to believe to make it okay for me to love the boy I assumed was hers.

"I'll be right back." I hear her footsteps hurry through the squishing grass and then, a few moments later, the voice of the specter comes again.

"Come. Now," she says, and I smile. Because I'm ready. And I'm not afraid.

I can see the change in her as she crosses the last few feet between us. Her dress is no longer torn, the hole in her chest has been replaced by smooth skin, and a scrap of lace is tucked in her collar. As she kneels by my side, a feeling of certainty and peace rises inside me and I know that Nurse and Romeo are wrong. I don't know where this journey after death will take me, but it won't be to the mist or to hell or anyplace dark or unnatural. She is pleased with me, smiling, her brown eyes steady and calm, though still not quite right. She needs something to make her whole, something only I can give.

And so I do. I slide my hand into hers, even as my other hand reaches up, finding Ben's face. "I love you," I whisper, wanting those to be the last words I ever speak.

And they are.

TWENTY-FOUR

Death is a long, quiet sleep in a cool room. Cool and damp, with the scent of old stone and murder lingering in the air.

The thought makes me stir, helps me discover that I still have a body. One with which to feel the press of unforgiving marble, smell the oils they rubbed into Tybalt's skin before interring him in the family tomb, in his own sarcophagus, only a few feet from where I now sleep.

Where I am *buried.*

My eyes fly open to more utter blackness. Open or closed, the sights are always the same in the tomb. *The tomb.* I am trapped inside it. Again. Trapped. Trapped. *Trapped.* I shake my head, whimpering as my skull rolls against more hard stone. No, this isn't real. This can't be happening. It's a dream, a nightmare, a hallucination.

My heart slams inside my chest even as my hands reach out, pounding against the roof of my prison, striking hard enough to make me cry out in pain as my knuckles hit and come away bruised. The sound leaps from my throat, strong and easy, helping slow my racing pulse.

I swallow. My throat doesn't ache as it did at the end. I'm not thirsty; my mind doesn't swim with confusion and fear. I shift again, feeling the clean linen of my skirts rub against my legs.

My thoughts hum inside my brain like dozens of angry bees. I'm back in my body—I can feel the rightness of being in my own skin with everything in me—but where am I? *Where?* Surely I can't have gone back in time. Nurse said she had such power, but I refused her offer. This has to be a mistake, a trick of madness.

Or a curse.

My breath comes faster. What if Nurse made this happen? What if this is the Ambassadors' punishment for not joining them in their realm? Or what if Romeo was right and the universe has chosen this cruel method of elimination rather than the mist? Or what if we've all been wrong and there *is* such a thing as hell, and it is the place that terrified me above all others? What if I've been sent here to die, once and for all? Or worse, to be trapped here for all eternity?

"Help! Help me!" I scream, voice echoing in the tight stone.

"Hello?" The answer is faint, distant, but the voice is most certainly male. There is someone outside, someone who's heard my cry.

I bite my lip, regretting my decision to call out. What if it's the friar? What if I *have* traveled back in time, or perhaps to some alternate reality, and am now about to be pulled from the tomb a second time? What if Romeo is out there, playing dead on the floor? What will I do?

I *won't* fall on that knife. That's for certain. But what should I do instead? Should I run? Try to find someone to help me? To keep me safe from the boy I willingly married and from a seemingly kind and gentle man of the cloth? If this truly is the past, my parents will kill me for marrying without their consent. Or force me to live with the man I chose to avoid shame and ruin. At this point I don't know which would be worse.

Ben. Ben. Ben. I squeeze my eyes shut and cling to his name, to his face, to the smell of his skin and the feel of his arms warm and safe around me. I will never forget him, never forsake him. If I am married to someone else, I will . . .

I will run away. I will find a way to survive on my own. I'm not the same frightened girl I once was. I am strong enough to find my way, strong enough to escape whatever evil waits for me on the outside.

"Hello? Who's there?" The voice comes again, closer. This time I find the strength to answer.

"I'm in here! It's Juliet Capulet! I'm alive!"

"Jesus . . . dear god." His words are muffled by stone, but so close now I know his voice is familiar. Very familiar. But not Romeo's voice, not the friar's. "Hold on, I'll get you out."

I brace myself as the stone above my head scrapes and shifts, slowly, slowly, inch by inch, shove by shove, until there is a space wide enough for a person to slip through. I blink against the sudden invasion of the light, so blinded by my time in the darkness that I can't make out the face attached to the hands that reach down and lift me out.

But I know those hands. I know the smell that swirls around me as he pulls me close, helping me stand with the strength of his body. I know that gentle voice telling me, "It's okay. You don't have to be scared."

My heart lunges into my throat. I *know* where I've heard those words before. In the car. That first night, when Ben and I met. Ben. It has to be! Still, a part of me is terrified to believe until I've seen him, until I've looked into his eyes.

"Ben?" I ask, hands smoothing up his chest, finding his face with my fingers. I feel him flinch in surprise but relax quickly beneath my touch. Full lips, smooth cheeks with just the hint of stubble, and that perfectly crooked nose. It's Ben! I know it, even before my eyes sting into focus, homing in on his face. I smile and a sound half laugh, half sob leaps from my throat. "You're alive!"

His brow furrows, and his nod is the barest tilt of his chin. "More importantly, *you* are. When I found the note, I was sure he'd gone mad. I couldn't fathom such a thing but . . . here you are."

"And here you are." He is. He really is. His hair is longer, covered by the hood of the green wool coat he wears, but it's Ben. Sweet, perfect, impossible, undeniable Ben. I drink in the beauty of him, knowing I will never take the light in his eyes for granted, never let the heart inside him doubt how treasured he is.

"Ben." I sigh his name, a promise, a prayer, an offer of thanksgiving to whatever force has brought us back to each other. God, magic, love, hope—it can use any name it wants. All I know is that I am grateful. So very grateful for "Ben."

"My mother calls me Ben," he says, voice soft, confused. As confused as the eyes staring into mine, as confused as the shake of his head a moment ago. "Did Romeo tell you?"

My heart skips a beat. "Romeo?" How does Ben know Romeo's name? Why doesn't he seem to know me? And why . . . why is he speaking in Medieval Italian? The language is so familiar that I didn't notice at first, didn't realize—

"I can't imagine Romeo discussing anyone but himself in such depth, but I . . . ." He swallows and relaxes his arms as if he will push me away. I cling to him, forcing him to stay. I can't be away from him. I just can't. "I'm sorry. I know he . . . and you . . ."

"He means nothing to me."

Ben's eyebrows arch. "Truly?"

"Truly, truly, truly."

"Then I suppose this will be easier for you to hear than I'd thought," he says, making me brace myself for the worst. "He's left Verona. He's run away with Rosaline."

I blink. "Rosaline?"

"Yes, she . . . Apparently she's not so resolutely chaste as we all assumed. She's with child. Romeo's child. They were married at her home this morning." His words seem to remind him how close we are. Propriety demands he step away. This time, I let him. It's obvious he has no memory of our past . . . our future . . . our life in another future's reality. Whatever it was. He doesn't know me; he doesn't love me. In fact, he seems to think I'm out of my mind.

"Do you understand me?" he asks, speaking slowly. "He and Rosaline are married. They've gone to Mantua to live with her aunt and uncle. They have a sizeable estate there, and after his exile, Romeo thought—"

"Good," I say. "I'm happy for them."

Now it's his turn to blink. "You are?"

"Yes. I am." Romeo left me for another woman. It's far preferable to what happened the first time I lived this moment, and spares me the trial of finding some way out of our marriage. Hopefully, this is really the end of it. Hopefully, I'll never have to see his face again, so long as the prince rules Verona and Romeo remains a criminal of the state.

"But in his letter . . ." Ben seems uncomfortable. I smile, hoping to make whatever he has to say easier for him. I only succeed in driving him another cautious step away. "Romeo said that you'd been married in secret. Friar Lawrence's chambers burned last night—and the poor friar along with them—so there is no record of the union, but Romeo seemed to think you would insist it had taken place. He said you'd taken poison to fake your death and allowed yourself to be buried in—"

"How do you know Romeo?"

"He's my first cousin," he says, allowing the change of subject the way Ben always does. Underneath those new clothes and eloquent words, he's still Ben, the same boy I fell in love with hundreds of years in some other future. "I'm Benvolio Montague."

Benvolio. I've heard his name before, when Romeo and I first . . .

Romeo. Did he realize that Ben looked exactly like his cousin? That they were the same person, somehow occupying two different places in time? If he did, I never saw any sign of it, not a single flash of recognition. But then, maybe this is a different past, a separate time, one of those places Nurse talked about where new beginnings and endings are possible. And somehow I've come here on my own, with the specter's help.

Suddenly her urging to love, her assurance that things would be better, make a miraculous kind of sense.

Ben is definitely miraculous. And he's here. And that's all that really matters.

"I was at your parents' party." He blushes, looking more and more like his old self as embarrassment colors his cheeks. "Without an invitation, of course, but . . ."

"I don't remember seeing you there." I take a step closer. He allows it.

"I was in costume."

"I was a fool." I take another step, until I stand so close we will touch again if I lean forward.

He smiles down at me. "What do you mean?"

"Do you believe in love at first sight?"

His smile fades, but when I lay my hands on his chest he doesn't pull away. "No. I don't."

"Me either," I say. "I think we'll need at least three days."

"Three days?"

"To fall in love."

His smile—his real smile, the crooked one that lights him up from the inside out—breaks across his face. He throws back his head and laughs. When he finishes, his arms are around me again and a familiar gleam is in his eyes. "You're very sure of yourself."

"No, I'm sure of you." I curl my hands into his coat. "Of us."

"I warn you," he says, his head tipping down, down, until our breaths mingle in the space between us. "I'm nothing like my cousin."

"Thank all that is good."

Soft laughter puffs against my lips, making it nearly

impossible not to press my mouth to his. But I can't. Not yet. But soon. He is Ben, he is my love, and it won't take long for him to remember what we are. I know that deep in my clean, uncluttered heart, where there is no room for doubt.

"But I *am* a Montague." He brushes my hair from my face, letting reddish-brown strands curl around his finger before dropping them back into place.

"You are."

"Our families would never approve." I loop my arms around his neck. "It would make courtship difficult to say the least." I press up onto my toes. "We would face opposition from every–" I find his lips with mine, deciding that three more days–even three more minutes–is too long to wait.

He hesitates only a moment before pulling me close, arms tightening around me, mouth meeting mine the same way it did before. Purely, sweetly, wickedly, perfectly. He sighs against my lips, a sound of such relief it echoes through my skin, making me smile and our teeth bump together. I know exactly how he feels. How it feels to come home, to find sanctuary, to be handed that missing piece that makes life not something to be endured, but something to be celebrated.

"I was wrong," I whisper, my eyes still closed, relishing the memory of his lips. "I don't think it will take three days."

"No. Not nearly."

I open my eyes to find him smiling down at me–wonder and confusion mixing in his features. I smile back at him, helping wonder win the battle.

"Perhaps your parents will be so glad to see you alive that they'll forget this ridiculous feud once and for all," he says. "Perhaps they'll be so grateful for my hand in saving you they'll invite me to stay for dinner."

"Perhaps. I'll talk to my mother, see if I can bring her around to looking at things our way," I say. "But if not, we shall simply have to run away together."

"I've heard it's the fashionable thing to do if you're a Montague," he says, his grin fading. "Did you really . . . marry him?"

I meet his eyes, unflinching. "Does it matter?"

The question makes him pause for a long, thoughtful moment before slowly shaking his head. "No. It doesn't. I don't mind not being the first, as long as—"

"You're the last," I finish.

"Exactly." His cocks his head, surveying me fondly down the bridge of that same crooked nose. "You . . . are very strong. And a very unusual girl."

"You have no idea." I smile. "I've got quite a story to tell you, someday soon."

"But not today?"

"No. Not today. Today, we have better things to do than tell stories." I take his hand and pull him back to me, stealing another kiss, smiling against his lips as he kisses me back.

And kisses me again.

And then some more.

And I know he is mine. For now, for the rest of our lives, no matter what comes next.

CODA

Romeo

I crouch in the shadows in the corner of the abandoned train station, watching the morning light creep into the birds' nests near the ceiling, clutching the blanket I've stolen from one of the crackheads who called the condemned building home. There were five of them, one a Mercenary of some sort, judging from the blackness hovering in his aura. They ran screaming when I crawled through the door, my skeletal hands scratching against the bird-shit-covered boards, rotted flesh dripping a trail of horror behind me.

Even the Mercenary ran. He knew what I was, saw what I've become, and feared that the curse I've acquired might be catching.

Cursed, damned, cast out to suffer for eternity.

It's all true, and I've suffered greatly in the weeks since Juliet passed. My senses have been returned to me so that I might know I smell like a plague pit and look like a monster. So that I might feel the pain of the entire world slam into my chest, echo in my brain with every step I take. I am truly a thing of darkness now, a being so wretched I can do nothing but hide in humanity's corners, fighting to stay warm as the wind whistles through my bones.

The only thing that keeps me from taking what is left of my sorry life, from laying my head on the train tracks outside and letting the steel beast sever me in two, are the dark lord's words.

How pleasantly do you think a few million years such as that will pass? When you are an invisible nothing and no one can hear you scream?

The greatest liars always tell the truth when they can. Everything else he said was true. I have been cast out of the Mercenaries and returned to my old body, a body ravaged by the atrocities I've committed.

What if the rest is true as well? What if my soul will remain even after this body is gone? Even *this* has to be preferable to *that*. *Something* preferable to *nothing*, to the torture of a voice without an ear, to existence without confirmation.

Even a scream as people run away is something. Something . . .

Hoarse sobs break the silence, a wounded animal keening at the sun streaming across the wall. I have cried more in the past weeks than in my entire life and afterlife combined. It's the worst part of this body—the way the emotional pain leaks from my face, shakes my heart like a wolf with teeth sunk deep.

My soul is a raw thing newly reborn in a rush of blood. The ghosts that haunted me when I was a Mercenary rub against my insides, crowding me with pain. Remorse. Regret. Hate. Fear. Love . . .

I loved her all along. I didn't realize how much until she was gone, until I was returned to my body and crept back to the place where she died and touched her lifeless hand, cried over her wide, sightless eyes. Juliet. My Juliet. Her soul is gone forever. I can feel the difference in the universe, the absence that is a world with one less spot of light. I tried to save her. I hope, in some fashion, I did. I hope she's at peace in the mist . . . or wherever it is good people go.

I hope that boy she loved is there with her. I didn't weep for him, but I felt sadness for what he lost. For the first time in hundreds of years I wished I'd had some other choice, that I could have spared them both.

But there was nothing else I could have done. I couldn't overpower the dark lord, and their love wouldn't have survived his torture. The best I could do was put them beyond his reach, offer myself in their place.

Maybe someday I'll regret my decision, when these weeks of agony stretch into years and decades and centuries and finally I am nothing but dust and even the luxury of tears is denied me.

Perhaps, perhaps, perhaps . . .

Best to cry while I still have eyes.

My sobs bruise the silence, stirring the birds from their nests. They leap into the air, wings snapping like sheets hung to dry in the wind, so loud I hunch lower in my blanket, letting it cover my ears. There are hundreds of them, so many the floor is mounded with waste, humming with flies.

This hole isn't fit for anything human to live in. . . . It is perfect for me.

"There you are. I've been looking for you." The voice comes from the door, a melody of chipper notes that sting at what is left of my skin. It's a woman, a beautiful redhead with flesh so pale the blue of her veins show through at her temples and beneath her dark brown eyes.

"That's quite a trail you left." She smiles at me, the bow of her lips curling with hard determination.

So she's come to gloat. I'd thought the Ambassadors above such petty pleasures, but she's definitely one of them. One of the golden ones, maybe even Juliet's Nurse. Her aura is certainly bright enough, so bright it outshines the morning sun cutting through the broken windows, makes me squint and turn away as she crosses the room and squats down by my side.

"Now then, Romeo. How are you finding your retirement?"

I turn to her, slitting my eyes, letting a hiss escape my mouth.

Instead of running for her life, she laughs, a soft chuckle that assures me I am a very small, very foolish monster indeed. "As good as all that?" She nods. "I thought that might be the case. That's why I've come. To offer you a way out."

A way out. I freeze, my raw soul shivering inside me. I haven't allowed the possibility to enter what's left of my mind. There is no way out. This is the way I will end. This is the inescapable pit at the end of the last road. This is all there is.

But what if . . . what if . . .

"The Mercenaries have been stealing our converts for centuries," the woman says, reaching out, tugging down the edge of my blanket until my head pops free. "Some of my friends disagree, but I don't see why we shouldn't do the same. Such a complete reversal of allegiance generates a great deal of power. We need that now, when so many of our high ones have been lost."

Not lost, murdered. Slaughtered by the Mercenaries who fight dirty, who kill for what they want, who will not stop until their fires are the only light burning at the end of the world.

"Is that something you would consider?" she asks. "Becoming one of us?"

I know relatively little about the inner workings of the Ambassadors, but I know the Mercenaries. And I know they will win. The Ambassadors are weak, their hands tied by the goodness required of their magic. Becoming an Ambassador would be suicide.

I smile and nod like a puppy. Yes, I will shift my allegiance. Yes, I will serve the Ambassadors. Yes, I will trade this misery for mindless years in the mist and long days in bodies that can feel. Yes, I will serve for however many hundreds of years they require, and then I will be free. To die as she died. It is more than I could have hoped for, if I'd dared let that feathered thing take roost in this cage.

"Excellent." She holds my chin in her hand, as if I'm not a vile creature, as if I am something precious she has plucked from the water just before the current carried it away. "But you must prove yourself true, Romeo. You must prove your commitment to us above all else. If you do so, I will come to you and administer the vows of a peacekeeper, one of our most valuable servants. If not, the magic I'll lend you will run dry and you will find yourself back here in this body, without a single hope in the world."

My head bobs again, brushing against her hand, smearing my death on her clean fingers. I will be true; I will be faithful. I will serve as no Ambassador has ever served because no Ambassador has ever known the horror of being what I have been.

"Good. Here is what you must do." She leans in close, whispering into my ear, telling me impossible things, spinning an improbable scenario, tying it all up with a promise to come for me at the end when I have saved a life and perhaps even the world.

I. Romeo. *I* will save the world. Or at least, one version of the world.

A strange sound rasps in my throat. It takes a moment to realize it's laughter. When I realize, I laugh again, just to see if she will pull away from me, to see if she will recognize what a broken thing I am.

But she only pats my back, tilts her face closer to mine. "You will do as I say? You will fight for me? Love for me?"

I smile. "When I am finished the girl will believe she is the sun, the moon, the stars in the sky. She will think my name and ache with how wondrous it is to love. To be loved. To hold such a treasure in her hand."

She laughs. "Good. Ariel will require all of your extraordinary charm, and then some."

Ariel. But she's dead. I killed the body that hosted Juliet's soul, put a bullet in her brain.

The woman stands, watching my face, somehow reading my fear in the scraps of skin that cling to my cheeks and chin. "I know what you did. That is why only you can undo it. Our choices create many realities. I can send you back, give you the chance to make another choice, to create a different reality, and a new place for Ariel in the world."

I let the blanket slip from my shoulders. "I'm ready. Send me now."

"Patience," she says, even as she presses her hands together, summoning a light so bright it burns my eyes. "I must send you back to the body you wore when you killed her, to a moment when Dylan Stroud's fate split in two very different directions."

"Very well. He will suit my purpose." Dylan is handsome, reckless, damaged—all the things young girls love before they grow wise enough to realize it isn't smart to play with fire. But Ariel is young. She will be drawn to him, seduced by the flames. I smile at the thought of her big blue eyes, her silver hair.

This might not be such a chore after all.

"Remember, you must make her believe in love," she warns, moving her hands farther apart, building the knot of power she holds there until the air hums with potential energy, with magic. "It doesn't matter what you feel or don't feel, but you must make her love you. Banish the darkness inside her, set her on her true path."

I wave one skeletal hand in the air. "Consider it done."

The redhead's mouth curves again, but this time there is something predatory in her smile. "Then go and do well, Romeo. Make the most of your one and only chance." Her hands fall to her sides and the golden ball flies at me, striking me straight in the face, making the world explode in a shower of sparks. I am on fire, dropped into a pit of flames, a torturous molten world where there is no air to breathe, no mercy to be found. I burn and burn for what seems like hours, blinded by agony, nerves sizzling.

And then, just as suddenly, it's over. I'm in another body, on a dark road, driving through a cool spring evening.

I suck in a breath, pulling air into my lungs. It streams in through the open windows, carrying night smells—evergreen and freshly cut grass, rosemary growing wild on the hills and the faint hint of cow manure from a nearby field. It's . . . glorious. I pull in another breath, holding it until my lungs ache, then finally let it out with a satisfied sigh. Beside me, in the passenger's seat, someone makes a sound closer to a growl.

I'm not alone. I turn my head, catching Ariel Dragland's impossibly big blue eyes. She huddles in the seat next to me, glaring at me with thinly veiled hatred, her arms crossed, those long, spidery fingers of hers rubbing at the collar of her shirt. I feel Dylan's memories of her swim inside me, a strange new sensation after so many years living in the cold, empty bodies of the dead.

He'd thought the shirt made her prettier, made it less of a chore to fulfill the bet he'd made and seduce the school freak. He'd nearly succeeded, nearly won almost five hundred dollars. If Jason hadn't texted him, if Ariel hadn't seen . . .

But she had seen. And she'd been enraged, the mad fury in her eyes burning bright enough to scare even a young villain like Stroud. Ariel might really be as crazy as everyone said. She's certainly angry. And faster than one would think.

I barely have time to flinch before she's reached for the wheel, tugging hard.

I curse beneath my breath, understanding the Ambassador's smile when I waved off her warning as the car begins to spin, hurtling toward the ravine where Dylan died and I first entered his body. I've been sent back in time to woo a girl who hates the body I've entered. For good reasons.

Even if we survive this crash, I am doomed. She will never love me.

No, she'll never love Dylan. You are a different monster, one with soft words and gentle hands.

Sometimes gentle, sometimes not. I reach for the wheel,

ripping it—none too gently—from Ariel's grasp, turning the car, offering just enough resistance to slow our spin. We hit the guardrail and bounce back onto the road, the tail end of the car skidding across the center lane before coming to a stop on the deserted highway.

For a moment, the silence is broken only by our swiftly drawn breath, the narrowness of our escape stealing all our words.

Ariel is the first to recover. "I hate you. I will destroy you, Dylan Stroud. Just you wait and see!" And then she is out the door, running down the highway back toward Los Olivos, silver hair shimmering in the moonlight.

I glance into the rearview mirror, watching her run, an unexpected smile on my face. She is glorious in her hate. The Mercenary I was can't help but admire her. Too bad the Ambassador I've become has to put out that particular fire, smother it with the sweet press of true love's kiss.

"True love's kiss. True. Love's. Kiss!" I belt out the song and reach to turn on the radio as I spin the wheel, pulling around, heading after the girl who has no clue she's going to love me.

ACKNOWLEDGMENTS

Many thanks to Michelle Poploff, Rebecca Short, and the entire production team at Delacorte Press for excellence and awesomeness. Thanks to the Ithaca College theater department for all the background on the Bard, and to the Bard himself, of course. Thanks also to my critique partners, Stacia Kane and Julie Linker; to the Debutantes of 2009; to Maria Montes, my Spanish expert; and to my amazing readers. Special thanks to Riley and Logan, for being the best boys a mom could hope for, and to my husband, Mike, my soul mate, my best friend, my love. Thanks for always knowing when to say "Everything will be okay," and for making me believe it.

NOW READ ABOUT
THE ULTIMATE BAD BOY
IN *ROMEO REDEEMED*,
THE SEQUEL TO
JULIET IMMORTAL!

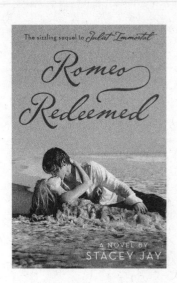

Cursed to live out eternity in his rotted corpse, Romeo, known for his ruthless, cutthroat ways, is given the chance to redeem himself by traveling back in time to save the life of Ariel Dragland and getting her to fall in love with him.

Ariel doesn't know it, but she holds the fate of the world in her hands. She's at the center of a power struggle between the Mercenaries, who fight to destroy love, and the Ambassadors, who try to keep it alive. If Romeo can win Ariel's heart and make her believe in true love, she will turn from her darker side once and for all. She'll no longer be a threat to the Ambassadors or to the world—and Romeo will be guaranteed protection from the wrath of the Mercenaries.

The seduction begins as a lie—Romeo is only out to save himself. But little by little, he finds that the lie has become truth: he's in love with Ariel, just as she is with him. So Romeo vows to protect her from harm and do whatever it takes to win her heart and soul. When Ariel begins to suspect that Romeo's love is a deception, however, she becomes vulnerable to Mercenary manipulation, and her inner darkness may tear them apart.